Devil's Demise

Lee Cockburn

Clink Street

London | New York

ISBN: 978-1-909477-26-1
Ebook: 978-1-909477-27-8

Chapter 1: Evil Awaits

Sweat trickles down the side of his face as he crouches in the shadows of the oak tree at the side of the house, wanting, waiting, his breath visible in the cold night air as he thinks about the night ahead. He had watched her for weeks: her soft but striking features, her slim toned figure and her locks of golden brown hair that reach half way down her back. He bites his lip with uncontrolled desire, so hard that it bleeds; he licks his lips and smiles at the taste of blood, remembering the pleasure it had brought him in the past. He looks up as he hears footsteps coming towards him; his breath quickens, his heart racing as his mind fills with anticipation for her. He leans forwards to look, jolting back as a blood curdling snarl echoes through the still night air; just through the fence he looks down and there facing him is a large Doberman, teeth bared and staring straight at him. Its muzzle curled up with aggression, saliva slowly falling from its open mouth, and eyes focusing with a hunter's instinct upon him.

A whistle cuts through the night and the dog turns back just for a second, giving him enough time to move nearer to the house and drop down behind a bunker up against the house.

An older man walks up and tethers his dog. "What is it, girl?

Leave it be, come on," he says as he tugs on the lead, but the dog keeps on pulling desperately towards the fence, growling and snarling, sensing the danger from the hidden terror.

The dog becomes more and more excited, staring straight towards the shadow where the evil presence is still hiding; the man holding the lead stumbles as the dog lurches powerfully forward, pulling him straight down onto his face, the lead slipping from his grasp. The dog races round the railings to the open gate heading straight for the lurking stranger who holds his breath, grinding his teeth, waiting to solve this little problem; he feels no fear, just excited anticipation. A shrill painful whine pierces the night air as the knife grinds downwards, slicing the dog's chest wide open and rendering the poor animal defenceless, leaving it mortally wounded on the ground, whining for her master to come to her. Come he does; holding his already bloodied face from the fall, the dog's master races toward the cries of his faithful pet. He turns the corner of the house, dark shadows making it harder to focus, his heart pounding as he sees the blood pouring from his faithful dog; the blood glistens under the moonlight, his sadness turning to terror. The hair on the back of his neck begins to bristle, standing straight up; a shiver courses through his body as he stands frozen to the spot.

An overwhelming sense of terror fills the air as the old man looks up into the stony lifeless expression of a demonic face: black passionless pools for eyes, a grin so monstrous he knows his life will end that night. He seems to float out from the shadows; gripping the older man's throat, he tilts his head sideways, staring emotionless at the helpless struggle of the old man. It thrills him to watch the life of another slowly drain away before him. The man's legs quiver as he gives in to the monster. This is a first for him; to kill a man is an unexpected pleasure, an unplanned delight, a thrill before the main event. He is strong, tall and motivated by pure evil, with hatred and dissatisfaction dwelling within him. He looks down as the dog gurgles its last breath, laboured and painful. A smile comes across his face as he wipes the dog's blood from his face and from the knife. He leans back against the wall, his heart still fluttering with the thrill of murder, his blood lust fuelled by the start of the evening.

¤¤¤

Susan gathers up her things from her office; she is running late because her meeting has overrun. She is the director of a very successful lingerie company, a very powerful woman in the business world, but also a contagiously likeable person. All those who know her seem to either look up to her, want her or want to be her, as she is impressively beautiful and very sexy - although she doesn't think it herself. She chats cheerfully with her colleagues about her lazy night ahead, comfy clothes and a glass of wine, blissfully unaware of the darkness that awaits. They head out of the office block saying their goodbyes, the night air cold and crisp as she pulls her coat tightly around her. She walks the short distance to her Audi A4; nothing overly fancy, as she doesn't like to flaunt her success. She drives through the night, following the same old familiar route as she taps her fingers on the steering wheel, singing along with the music playing on the stereo.

At last he sees her car come into the street, his patience faltering as his wait has made him cold and impatient. He has watched her for a long time and she is usually home much earlier than this; she will regret making him wait, he will make sure of that. He focuses on the car, tension growing with the excitement of taking her beauty forever.

Susan pulls the car into the driveway, turns off the engine and gathers her things; she is still humming the song from the journey home as she steps out of the car. Her heels crackle on the ground as she turns slowly toward the front door. She stops on the steps, searching her bag for the house keys, her long silky hair hanging down over her face as she looks up, noticing the street is quieter than normal; empty, in fact. She looks at her watch and it's 11.20 pm. Where did the evening go tonight? she thinks to herself. She had no idea that the meeting would have taken so long. The moonlight is shining on the door as she looks around her, the shadows seem darker where the moon can't reach. The wind blows lightly, making the branches of the old tree rustle together, giving the night an eerie feel; she feels a little uneasy, but can see no reason for it. She feels a presence, something nasty, something cold and unpleasant in the air. She turns towards the door, putting the key in the lock and opening it, letting herself in, shaking off the unwelcome fear as her just being silly. She closes the door behind her, bolts it securely and closes over the curtain, shutting out the cold night air. She shudders as if someone has just walked over her grave, an uneasiness still clinging to her tightly.

Her cat Baxter comes running up to her. He is a big blue eyed tabby cat with smooth shiny fur; he rubs round her legs, hoping she will feed him. She bends down and strokes him, instantly relaxing and forgetting the presence she had felt out on the steps just moments before. She makes her way through to the kitchen and pours a glass of wine for herself and fixes a bowl of food for Baxter. She takes the wine through to the lounge, puts her feet up and switches on the TV. The late night news comes on, the usual stories: the war in Iraq, murder and the general unpleasant behaviour between human beings taking over the main stories, nothing happy to report as usual. She flicks through the channels and starts to watch the end of a movie - Pretty Woman, a pleasant change from the news. She has seen it many times before but enjoys the fairytale ending, an ending she hopes one day she will be lucky enough to enjoy for herself.

Outside he still waits, biding his time, savouring the terror that awaits the beautiful woman in the house. He rubs his face with his enormous hands, pulling his face downwards as he struggles to control the urges deep inside him.

Susan's head lurches abruptly forward as she wakes up with a start; the film has ended and she has fallen asleep on the couch. A cold air is now present in the living room. She rises up from her chair unnerved by the change in temperature; she hesitates before heading into the kitchen at the back of the house, her hesitation unexplained, a feeling, a sense. She straightens up and stops herself from allowing her thoughts to frighten her even more than they are already. She switches on the hall light and makes her way to the kitchen. The door to the rear of the house was closed, but when she reaches to check it, she notices that the lock is unlocked; undamaged, but unlocked? Searching her mind, she remembers putting the rubbish out that morning, but is positive she had locked the door behind her when she came back in. Again she shrugs off any wrongdoing and puts it down to her haste to leave with her busy schedule ahead that morning. She locks the door, double checking it this time, and puts the chain over. She makes her way tentatively up the staircase. Several water colours by Monet decorate the walls leading to the upper landing; the last picture at the top of the stairs, a wonderful landscape stretching over hills, crystal waters and sun filled skies, is slightly out of line. Susan stops to straighten the frame, a pause that he is aware of; he is not normally clumsy, always very careful. He wonders if she will try and flee, realising that something is not right, an evil lurking in the shadows. He moves forward staring out from the darkness; she is motionless at the top of the stair. She turns and hesitates as if she is about to go back down the stairs, but stops and he hears her muttering to herself, convincing herself that she is acting crazy. He pulls back into the shadows as she walks in his direction, resuming his position in the darkness.

Susan enters her bedroom, her space, her haven, and she relaxes almost instantly. Her room is grand and spacious with a sprawling bed with soft comfortable bedclothes and pillows, expensive and tasteful. Her furnishings coordinate, creating a warm and safe place to escape from the world. Soft sensual lighting creates a pleasant ambience. She starts to undress, removing her work clothes: a black pinstriped skirt and matching jacket, a white blouse, fitted to her neat, toned figure, her underwear, a set, white lace, perfect against her tanned skin. He watches through a gap in the doorway, heart pounding at what he is looking at; an unexplainable stirring moves within him, not a normal desire, not that of lust, but one of hateful fear, repulsion and resentment towards her. A need to stamp out her success, her beauty and the unhealthy things he feels as he watches her.

She climbs into bed pulling the covers over her; she's wearing a nightdress, not a flattering one, one that will protect her from the cold of the night. She wishes now that she had someone special in her life to share these lonely nights with, someone that would take away the fear, the ridiculous fear that she is trying to clear from her mind. She is drifting off to sleep when her thoughts turn to Baxter; where is he? "Baxter, Baxter," she calls out, "Where are you, you stupid cat?" Eating again no doubt, she thinks as she lays her head back down to sleep.

Baxter comes to the top of the stairs a short time later after hearing his name being called - a typical cat, only coming when it suits him. As he turns casually towards Susan's room, he stops dead and his hackles go straight up; a gentle hiss comes from him as he arches his back, his senses sharp, acutely aware of the predator close by and watching him. He recoils in terror, knowing the danger this thing in front of him poses, and quickly scurries away.

Susan finally falls asleep. Baxter comes back up the stair, returning in hope that he can join her in the room. Slowly, a dark figure stirs from the shadows, staring straight down at the animal, dark eyes meeting blue. The cat lowers itself closer to the ground, instantly fearful of the deadly stare from the cold eyes. Baxter crawls back, not daring to take his eyes from the beast before him; once at the top of the stairs he turns and sprints silently down, instinct telling him to hide this time, to preserve himself from certain death.

The intruder walks slowly into Susan's room, standing at the doorway, examining his prey, tilting his head in a puppet-like fashion; demonic eyes staring, salivating at her vulnerability, lunacy and uncontrolled madness oozing from him. A savagery inside him demands to be set free. Susan opens her eyes, sensing his stare upon her, terror rushing through her veins; a blood curdling scream escapes from her mouth as he grabs her foot, pulling her towards him. She kicks out at him with her free leg, narrowly missing his face, but this only makes him more excited, a frightened little creature desperately struggling against its master's strength. He grabs her face, pulling it within an inch of his face, his breath rotten and tinged with death.

Tears flow over his fingers as she realises her earlier apprehension and fear were signs of danger, signs she had brushed off with her sensible mind; the human belief not to be frightened of what couldn't or shouldn't be real, animal instincts trained to be kept deep within no longer recognised as danger, but these instincts should never be ignored. He is real, very real and kneeling right before her, the strength of a madman coursing through his fingertips. He throws her backwards, hitting her head violently against the wall, leaving her feeling dazed as he crawls slowly towards her, his eyes fixed on hers, a vicious looking blade in hand, pointing it right at her face; his movements controlled and sadistic, the knife missing her eye by millimetres as he taunts her. She curls back trying to push herself through the wall to escape her hideous tormentor. He slashes her arm, a deep cut - almost to the bone - opens up as she tries to grip his hair, her futile attempt to fend him off easily brushed aside. He smirks at her struggle and kneels down on her thigh, a searing pain rushing through her as his weight pushes her down into the bed. He places his huge hand round her throat, gripping tightly as he thrusts his fingers deep into her; her eyes widen in agony, gulping at the violation, the degradation and pain he inflicts on her. The hunting knife lies alone beside his leg, confidence of his superior power to crush any attempt of escape apparent, as he controls her simply with a single hand. He loosens his grip; she pleads with him, struggling to speak with the pain from his brutal hand still gripping sadistically into her face, "Please don't hurt me, I'll not tell anyone," she gasps.

He pulls his face menacingly towards hers and speaks to her in a low growl. "I know you won't!"

He pulls down his jeans, exposing his erect penis, and leans forward and pins her to the bed by the back of her head, his grip so tight he pulls her hair out at the roots; she is moaning and struggling against him, another futile attempt to stop him as he forces himself into her, his thrusts so violent that she can feel herself tearing at the sustained assault. She can barely catch her breath with the force with which she is being pinned to the bed. He doesn't care that she can barely breathe as he climaxes inside her. He grabs her arms and wrenches her round to face him; he grips her hair even tighter and pushes himself into her mouth, his thrusts desperate, determined to come again, his desire uncontrolled. His grip is so violent, as he forces her face onto his penis over and over. He fucks her mouth with no concern for her at all. Her head spins with the lack of oxygen and she gags, choking on his cock being forced down her throat. He looks down at her as his rage intensifies at not being able to climax again yet.

"Come on you fucking useless bitch, suck that cock and do it right, you lazy fucking tramp."

He punches her face and threatens to poke out her eye with his thumb as he presses down hard on her eyelid. She can feel her eye being pushed back into her head, so she grabs his penis and sucks in a desperate attempt to save her sight. She has no desire to please him, just an overwhelming desire to live. She feels his grip releasing and he moans out in pleasure as he comes in her mouth. Susan visibly boaks as she tries to spit; he shoves her backwards on the bed and begins punching her, hitting her face until she can barely see, the punches ferocious and cruel. He wants to disfigure her, make her ugly, take away the beauty that gives her so much power over weak men. He is angry that he felt good for a moment when he came; he is livid at the fact that the slut in front of him has weakened him, made him feel. He goes mad, standing up on the bed to kick her; her ribs, her legs, her arms. He stamps down on her, all over her, until she is unrecognisable, black and blue from head to toe; he cuts her with the knife, taunting her, deliberately avoiding killing her as he still has plans for her. Susan floats out of consciousness and lies there motionless, at last her body at peace from his persistent abuse. He looks at the pathetic creature before him and his cock is rock hard again with his night's work. He turns her over onto her back and rips her legs apart, forcing his thighs between hers; he bends over and tastes her pussy, smiling at the sweet taste of her, but he has no desire to pleasure her, he just leans over her and forces his large rock-hard penis into her. Vaginally raping her this time, as deep as he can go, he fucks her as hard as he physically can, her limp body rocking uncontrollably with his thrusts, her head twisting on the headboard as he forces himself inside her over and over again. She is now bleeding profusely from the savage abuse created by his loveless act of pure hatred towards her. Her eyes re-open as he clenches his teeth with effort, his whole body weight forcing himself into her, onto her, the pain searing through her like a knife cutting her, every violent push tears her, hurts her beyond anything she could ever have imagined, the violation unbelievable for any normal person to comprehend. He looks down at her and lies on top of her, full weight, his face right in front of hers. She can smell him, stale sweat, foul breath, dirty teeth, a sneer that is truly terrifying. He bites her face hard, and she screams, tears soaking her face, as he continues to ram himself inside her, her stomach aching in pain, as the size of his penis in her slight frame fills her unnaturally. He growls as his teeth grind together at his climax so intense; he grimaces at her and all she can do is lie there helplessly underneath him, unable to do anything. He pulls her face forcefully towards him and kisses her, open mouth, his tongue forcing into her and down into her throat, his cock still buried in her as he does so. She winces, repulsed at his every act; she wishes that she could die and end this cruel torment. He throws her head back down and climbs off her, looking at her like shit on his shoe. He shoves his cock back in his pants, blood smearing all over his already soiled underwear.

Susan struggles and manages to roll onto her front, pain coursing through her body; she reaches up to her face, but what she feels is not familiar, it is swollen and deformed, unrecognisable; she can't see properly because her eyes are swollen shut. She tries to pull herself away from him, trying to crawl, but her body just won't work. His assault on her has been so violent, so damaging that her injuries are too bad to overcome. She can only slump down and lie there, her spirit finally broken and all her fight gone.

Stripped bare, Susan lies face down on the bed, blood soaking through the sheets; hours of torment bleeding from her every vein, the beauty beaten from her face, clumps of her beautiful hair lying beside her, blood spatters up the walls from the sustained beating. Sexually violated in every way, forced over and over to perform depraved acts with him, eventually giving in to his strength in hope he would spare her life. Panting, her breath is rapid and shallow, her pulse weak as if life is slipping away from her. He sits up at the side of the bed, feet on the floor, and calmly speaks to her; she jumps, as she thought he had already left.

"You made me do that, you tease people, you slut, you deserve everything you got, bitch, and more." Her eyes are awash with tears, mucus smeared over her face, her hands now bound behind her back with cable ties, a task he had carried out when she lay unconscious. A helpless lamb now waiting to be slaughtered, unable to defend itself; her hands are numb with lack of circulation. She feels his hand grip her hair for the last time, wrenching her head back, exposing her slender neck. He licks her, his rough tongue tracing up the taut muscle exposed by his cruel grip. He bites out a small chunk of flesh from her; a soft moan is all that can be heard from his victim, now so weak her senses are dull from his constant abuse. He throws her mutilated face hard against the pillow, like a cat that has finished playing with a mouse. The fun is over, no more pleasure to be had; he pulls up the fierce looking blade and casually plunges it into her already scarred and bleeding back. The evidence of his depravity gouged into her, he rips the knife back out and stands up, staring at his work, his face like stone; an emotionless statue frozen in her room, signs of his trespass left for all to see. He smiles at her, teeth rotten and stained with her blood, and he spits out the small piece of flesh from her neck as one final act of depravity as he turns to leave the room. "Now where the fuck is that shit of a cat?" he hisses.

Like a shadow in the night he skulks through gardens and empty streets, being careful not to be seen by anyone; a careful mind does not risk anything that will tie him to the scene of his private party. He is aware of the CCTV coverage of the area; his weeks of checking which houses have private cameras has provided him with a safe route in and out of the area and back to his lair undetected. The long walk is worth every minute, an untraceable journey that provides no evidence, no path or leads for the filth to follow. He has never been in trouble in his life and, with British law being so liberal, he knows DNA is only taken from those that have been caught and convicted of certain crimes, leaving countless crimes unsolved because not everyone is on the database, just in case precious human rights are infringed.

He climbs the back wall of his garden and enters through the rear door of his house; no one must know he has been out tonight. He is triumphant at the night's spoils; he enjoyed every minute, the power he feels still coursing through his veins. *She's not that powerful now, is she! Weakened by my physical strength, no words or money could have prevented the inevitable.* As he enters the house he taps the metal drum at the kitchen door and mutters, "This is just the beginning." The beginning of a long campaign of revenge and violence against all of those women who haven't afforded him the respect he believes he is entitled to.

Chapter 2: Detective Sergeant Taylor Nicks - Detective Constable Marcus Black

One am on Saturday morning, Taylor trailed her hand over the silky contours of her lover's shoulder, running her fingertips through the long shiny auburn hair, breathing in the heady scent of her musky perfume. Planting soft kisses on her forehead; Taylor teased her awake for another kiss. Kay's head turned and a smile emerged from beneath the duvet, her hand reached for Taylor's head, pulling her softly to her, their mouths touching, lips slightly parted as their kiss developed into passion, their tongues meeting, a soft caress, teasing, then devouring, taking one into the other with a floating sense of desire burning from within. Taylor's long fingers gently stroked Kay's breast, before gripping her nipple firmly with her finger and thumb; a slight moan of pleasure as Kay stroked Taylor's back, holding her head as it went lower, her mouth covering her breast, licking, sucking, gripping the now taut nipples, stiff with anticipation. Her mouth searched the firmness of Kay's stomach, her lips softly brushing against her, tasting her flesh as she followed the delicate lines, the natural path to her intimate pleasure. Kay arched her back in delight as the soft experienced mouth explored her, Taylor aware of what she was doing to her, of what Kay was feeling, a little different from her normal sexual partners. Kay's soft mound was visible just before her, with a fine strip of dark hair leading to the glistening haven. Kay moaned loudly as the wait was over; she writhed backward at the tingling sensation of Taylor's first touch, which was too consuming to control. Her tongue teased her softly at first, creating a plateau of pleasure, an orgasm that teetered on the edge. Taylor's fingers delved deep inside, deepening the pleasure, preventing an uncontrollable and premature orgasm. Her fingers moved with Kay, pushing deep into her, rocking with the motion of her hips, one hand gripping her smooth and curvaceous buttocks, Taylor's mouth creating wave after wave of dreamy ecstasy. The first orgasm was powerful and spiralled throughout her feverish body, the next a desperate and frantic affair with the final pleasure unfathomable, a euphoric sensation and long awaited fulfilment; pure unadulterated satisfaction.

Kay relaxed her taut frame and sank back onto the bed, panting from the effort expelled in the raunchy exchange of flesh and sweat, their kisses now calm and complete, Taylor no longer hungry for Kay's pleasure. Kay pulled her to her and helped her unwind, relieving Taylor, pleasuring her in her own naive and inexperienced way. Kay cuddled into Taylor, laying her head on her olive skin, her perfectly formed breast just before her; she kissed her softly with her arm loosely round her waist as she drifted off to sleep, her body spent with contented exhaustion, head still spinning with her dreamy first experience of a woman's pleasure.

Taylor Nicks was a 34 year old Detective Sergeant in the Major Crime Unit. She had been there for the past four years, based at Fettes Police Head Quarters in Scotland's capital. She was part of a large team dealing with all of the extraordinary serious crimes in Edinburgh and the Borders, those which needed a dedicated team to fulfil the requirements that every unique and notable crime demanded. Taylor was tall, athletic, slim and very beautiful, a powerful woman in a man's world. She had striking features, brown eyes, with long, dark, wavy, shoulder-length hair and she was a popular presence for both men and women, a fantasy for some and a reality for others. She was smart, forthright and humorous. A very confident and astute woman, Taylor was perceptive and quick-witted. A capable woman in her field, she was keen and inventive, believing no problem was too difficult to solve; she was a hard worker who would never give up, always fighting for the rights of the innocent.

Her personal life, on the other hand, was not so controlled: no regulations, no rules; she was flighty, careless with love and until now incapable of commitment, a free spirit who had broken many hearts on her directionless journey through her hectic love life. Her work was her safety net when her feet needed to be planted firmly back on the ground.

Her partner, Detective Constable Marcus Black, was 29 years old; he was a tall handsome man, with an athletically muscular frame, a firm jaw and well-groomed designer stubble. Tanned with short gelled dark hair and a smooth deep voice, Marcus was witty, intelligent and a very popular member of the team. He had a pleasant and honest personality, with a persuasive manner when dealing with people; a genuinely kind man, always polite and respectful to all of those who deserved it. He regularly worked side by side with Taylor, an accomplished duo, rank never being an issue between them; an efficient pairing with a proficient and experienced background, both suitably qualified in their field. He had a long term partner, Maria, and a young son David, and he loved both deeply. He was the opposite of Taylor, a faithful and loving man who lived for his family, but enjoyed the thrill of work.

Detective Inspector Martin Findlay, on the other hand, was a rotund chap; a little dishevelled, his clothes stretching to fit his ever-growing figure. His hand was never too far away from the common household doughnut. He relied heavily upon his far more experienced team surrounding him, one of the boys' club promoted beyond his ability. An aggressive man when challenged by his subordinates, a weakness in his personality and failure to lead effectively. An old school cop, one who thought women should never have been introduced to the force - and gays, well that was another story altogether. He preyed on other people's success, reaping the rewards it brought, taking ownership of the team's hard work. He was also married, but regularly suggested he was unhappy and was only with her because it was too expensive to leave her. He had had affairs in the past, but his appearance these days now limited his chance of much success. He letched over any women in the office, rubbing close at any opportunity and making sleazy unwanted comments when he could get away with it. He found Taylor attractive - a waste of a good woman, he had been heard to say to his peers of similar backgrounds - and thought gays shouldn't be allowed in the force.

Chapter 3: Survivor

Susan opened her eyes; the room was still dark. She took a shallow breath and a gripping pain rippled through her lungs, so sharp it made it painful to breathe, her deep internal wounds rupturing afresh as she moved. Her hair was matted with dried blood that clung to her scalp like glue. She slowly looked around the room, terrified in case he was still there, watching her lying on the bed, enjoying her taking her last breath. She listened for a few moments, motionless, making sure she was alone, then tentatively she rolled over, reaching backwards with her tied hands to her bedside table; she had put her phone there before she went to bed. "Please, please, please, be there." Her fingers fumbled across the surface, groping for the familiar shape; she recoiled in agony as the countless wounds pulled apart as she moved. Blood oozed from the freshly opened tears and brutal stab wounds all over her, the bed now soaked through with her blood. She pulled herself gradually to the edge of the bed, fresh tears running down her face. The pain intensified as she leant backwards over the edge; the phone just out of reach. She yelled, "GOD DAMN YOU, just a few more inches, please!" She flopped from the bed, thudding full weight onto the floor.

She paused for a second, gasping for breath, phone in hand, disbelief that her nightmare might soon be over. The bruising tumble had reengaged all of her pain receptors; face first with her tied hands behind her, she had been unable to break the fall. With her bound fingers shaking uncontrollably, she used her touch memory and eventually managed to dial 999. Her heart leapt as she heard the voice of safety faintly at the end of the phone.

"What service do you require?"

Voice quivering, she replied, "Police."

"Could you speak up please?"

"POLICE, POLICE! I NEED HELP, HELP ME! Please, I'm dying."

The phone was behind her and she worried that her words would not be heard by the operator.

"Just relax, we'll get to you, what is your address?" the call taker continued, but there was no reply, just the sound of weak breathing barely audible from the end of the line.

"Just you stay with us, don't you put the phone down, hold on, hold on, we'll get someone to you right now, you'll be alright!"

A loud crash was heard from down the stairs. The front door crumbled beneath the door ram, as her rescuers burst in, shouting, "POLICE, POLICE." Officers spilled into the house, systematically searching each room, calling out to her as they made their way towards where she was lying. Susan was unconscious on the floor beside the bed where she had fallen, barely visible from the doorway as she was collapsed behind it. The young copper first on the scene entered into her room and just stood in the doorway mouth gaping wide open as he switched on the light; he couldn't believe what he was seeing. Blood and hair covered the bed, walls and furniture. It was like a scene from an abattoir. He snapped out of it sharply as he saw a foot protruding from the end of the bed, bloodstained and petite. He rushed to Susan's side and called for assistance. The medical teams accompanying the officers came rushing into the room as soon as the area was deemed safe. They quickly knelt down beside Susan, checking her vital signs, wondering if it was possible to survive injuries like those before their eyes. The young cop, still staring down at this poor soul, beaten beyond belief, was frozen to the spot with the macabre sight before him. The Sergeant came into the room and took his shoulder gently, guiding him outside, making sure that only those required were permitted to be there.

The room was now a major crime scene. Every piece of evidence inside it would be vital to the capture of the merciless person responsible for such depraved behaviour.

The paramedic shouted out loudly, "SHE'S ALIVE. God knows how, but she is." The medics did all that was necessary to sustain Susan's now fragile life, taking all the essential measures to prevent it slipping away from her during the short journey to the hospital.

The Sergeant arranged for a fast police escort; every second counted as Susan had lost so much blood. She lay on the trolley bed, barely breathing, a helpless soul, her life hanging in the hands of caring professionals who desperately wanted to save her and desperately wanted her to survive this nightmare.

On the way to hospital, the paramedic in the rear of the ambulance had to commence CPR when Susan's heart arrested; her body finally giving up on her. He called through to the driver to update him on what was going on. His partner informed him he was going as fast as it was safe to do so and offered to stop and help his colleague but was told to keep driving as the medic in the rear continued CPR.

"We can't save her without blood, she needs blood, every time I compress her chest the blood is just pumping out of her from everywhere."

The police officer accompanying them felt helpless; she was there in case the victim came round and divulged anything of evidential value. She offered whatever help she could to the medic, who told her to give the inflations with the bag, to allow him to continue with uninterrupted compressions.

The ambulance screeched to a halt in the bay at the emergency department; the crash team already there waiting and prepared to take over. They rolled Susan out from the rear of the ambulance and started working on her before the trolley had even hit the ground. She was rushed into the emergency room where the specialist team and lifesaving equipment awaited them. The team worked frantically to save her; blood, fluids, surgery, hundreds of stitches, sweat and 100% commitment from all involved went into saving her life.

They were not going to let her die; she had fought so hard to live until now and they were not going to let her down if they could help it. The police officer standing in the corner of the room willed her to live; tears glistened in her eyes as she watched in bewilderment, feeling herself engulfed with sadness at the terrible thought that they may lose her after all she had been through. She clasped her hands together and whispered to herself as she looked up to the ceiling; she had never prayed in her life, but this lady needed all the help she could get.

Hours passed with relapse after relapse and many life-saving surgical procedures undertaken to stop Susan bleeding. Her spleen was removed; she had eleven broken bones, no sight in one eye, a fractured skull, hundreds of stitches and she had lost over half of her blood. Her lung was punctured and her heart muscle superficially incised as the final plunge of the knife had crunched through her defenceless ribs; a blow that had been meant to kill her but had failed to reach its intended target. One of the surgeons stopped on the way out of the emergency room and spoke with the officer still patiently waiting there.

"It's a miracle, an absolute miracle! But she's still here, and I think she's got a good chance to make it now, fingers crossed."

□□□

Taylor moaned as the phone rang out loudly beside her in the night; it was dark and she had barely been asleep for two hours due to her enthusiastic visitor.

"Get in as soon as you can. You won't believe this one!" She looked at Kay, longing to share her wonders one more time before she had to leave. Instead she told her that duty called and she had to leave. She laid the spare key on the bedside table beside Kay, and kissed her full on the lips. Flutters raced through her body as the kiss deepened but Taylor pulled herself away; the temptation was deep filled with the reality of what might happen if she stayed longer, the excitement almost clouding her sense of duty and responsibility.

Taylor showered quickly, sad that the scent covering her body had to be washed away, the evidence of the night swirling down the drain. Thoughts gripped her insides; she was moved by what she had felt tonight, stronger emotions than she normally felt or allowed. She got dressed into a stylish professional three piece suit that fitted to her like a glove, her blouse cut low enough to please, but not enough to be unprofessional. Her boots were heeled, lengthening her already long legs, giving her presence and even more appeal. She shook her dark hair out and as it cascaded down her shoulders it shone brilliantly in the light. She sprayed herself with a sweet unisex eau de toilette, the scent a pleasure to both men and women. She stood in the doorway pleasingly picturesque, a handsome woman, captivating beauty oozing from her. Kay looked at her from where she lay and could not believe how the woman looking at her had made her feel. Taylor smiled at her and said, "See you at work, I'll be discreet, I promise." She blew a kiss in Kay's direction. The door slammed behind her, her departure apparent, loud and inconsiderate.

Marcus had received a similar call; he had been asleep for several hours and greeted the news somewhat more enthusiastically than Taylor. He quickly showered and dressed with no time to shave, leaving him looking slightly dishevelled, but ruggedly handsome. Maria turned over in bed and held her hand out to him. He leant over to her, kissed her tenderly on the lips and stroked her hair. She spoke to him. "Be safe, I love you."

He smiled at her and whispered, "I love you too." He left the room and paused at his son's room; he went in and kissed David softly on the head, smiling down at him with the warmth which his child brought him; a love that shone deep within him. He then left the house quietly, always mindful of those he loved the most.

Chapter 4: Discovery

The police resources gathered at the location of the incident, with the Scenes Examination Branch already in the house, combing every inch of it for vital evidence. The POLSA (police search advisor) leading the search team was standing outside, waiting to enter the house once the forensic examination was complete. The search officers, who had been called out in the middle of the night, were instructed by the POLSA to carry out an initial search of the garden and any outbuildings adjacent to the house, prior to entering the house itself. They formed a line, shoulder to shoulder, and walked through the grounds slowly and systematically; it was still dark and they worked under strong beamed specialist dragon lamps. They searched thoroughly for any minute trace of the suspect and anything left by him of evidential value.

As they turned slowly round the side of the house, the first officer stopped dead in her tracks. She smacked the cop beside her in the ribs. He winced and started moaning at her but then stopped too. He could not believe his eyes either. They were looking for a possible weapon or any discarded clothing, not for this, not for a dog that had been brutally slain and a man, presumably the owner, lying dead by its side.

"What the fuck?"

"Who the fuck would do this kind of shit? SERG, SERG, COME LOOK AT THIS, you're not gonna like it!" he yelled out into the night, with a hint of disbelief in his voice.

The Sergeant turned and came round the corner; his jaw dropped as he took in what lay before him, he rasped his fingers over his stubbly jaw looked to the sky and shook his head at the scene. He had been in the force fifteen years and things like this didn't happen in Edinburgh. This was more like something out of CSI on the television. He immediately got on his radio and contacted the Senior Investigating Officer, informing him of the disturbing further developments. Numerous cordons were placed round the outer perimeter of the garden, tents were erected to protect the corpse of the man and the body of the dog, preventing the prying eyes of the innocent public as they walked by going about their business in the morning. The man and dog would remain in situ, to allow forensic tests to be carried out on their bodies and the ground around and beneath them.

Marcus and Taylor arrived at the scene and suited up, putting on white overalls, latex gloves, over shoes and masks - the full works, preventing themselves leaving their own DNA at the scene of the crime. They talked at length with the SIO at the scene and listened as the gruesome details of what lay upstairs were revealed to them. Taylor strode up the stairs, Marcus close behind her, both eager and repulsed to see Susan's bedroom. Taylor stopped at the door and spoke with one of the scene examiners who was still present, swabbing every sample left behind, fully examining the room, making sure every tiny droplet was photographed and swabbed and its location documented. He informed Taylor that the culprit had boldly and arrogantly left his mark all over the room; blood, sweat, semen, hair and saliva on the floor, the walls and the bed covered with his perverted seed. These were signs of a depraved man with a sense of invincibility, taunting them with his conceited disdainful behaviour. A beast that had brazenly left his mark everywhere, with no fear and a belief he couldn't be caught, his whole DNA profile left at the scene with no attempt to hide it or remove it from those who would soon be hunting him.

Taylor stood with Marcus just inside the doorway, both frozen still, statuesque, mouths open in disbelief staring at the bed. Taylor turned to Marcus and exclaimed, "Whoever did this is a totally foul and sinister person, an absolute demon. Just think of what that poor woman went through. It looks like he spent hours here."

Marcus replied, "He's bold as brass. He's left so many biological samples behind him, it seems that he truly believes that we're that stupid we won't be able to catch him."

Taylor stared back at the blood on the wall and stated, "We'll catch him all right. He'll have missed something somewhere that will help us nail him - they always do, fucking cocky bastard. He's not getting away with this kind of shit in our city, no way. He makes me physically sick, fucking treacherous coward!"

Marcus walked further into the room. He crouched down at one of the numbered pieces of evidence. It looked like a bit of flesh on the ground. He looked at Taylor and said, "What a beast, this is one cruel and vicious son of a bitch."

The scene examiner turned and told them, "That's a piece of her neck. It's covered in saliva, which I'm guessing is his."

"I take it there is no way that it could have been stitched back on to the victim?" Taylor exclaimed.

"No, it's been lying there too long and it's no longer viable, I'm sure if they could have they would have done, although they may not have seen it! They worked on her for a long time I believe, I think that was the least of their worries. I heard they lost her a few times before being able to stabilise her. She's apparently a complete mess." Taylor's eyes were welling up a little with the thought of what the victim was forced to endure over a lengthy period.

Marcus walked the room, careful not to disturb anything; he looked at the bed frame and spotted a tooth embedded in it.

"Bloody hell, look at this! That tooth is jammed right into the wood there. Some force would be needed to do that. God, that poor woman, she must have been terrified and in agony."

"This guy is not going to be happy that Susan's still with us you know! That's his first mistake."

Taylor spoke with the SIO, voicing her concern for the victim in the future, explaining to him that if the suspect found out that she was still alive, which he would, then she wouldn't be safe.

"She wasn't supposed to live. He's made a fatal error; she's seen him and can identify him, heard him and that wasn't supposed to happen. He's arrogant but not that stupid."

The SIO agreed with Taylor. "What can we do though? Are we able to hide the fact that she is still alive from him? Could we print some false information and trust those in the know to keep their big mouths shut?"

The SIO replied, "I doubt it. There's always someone out to make some cash, blabbing to the press, spilling their guts for a back hander."

"Are we able to protect her though? Will they part with their precious cash to look after that poor soul - properly I mean? Not the usual half-hearted shit where they make false promises. I mean really protect her, the full bhuna!"

"I'll get on to it, there's already a cop at the hospital. I'll see if armed officers are an option, but I know what the answer's gonna be - namby pamby chicken shits, frightened of the day they've never seen. Politics gone mad, eh?"

Taylor questioned the SIO, "I take it there are no witnesses?"

"Yes, but I think they're the dead ones in the garden," he replied in a defeated tone.

"What about CCTV - buses, taxis, <u>ANPR</u>?"

"Nothing so far. He's like an invisible phantom."

Taylor asked, "How did the dog get on?"

The SIO replied, "They lost the scent three streets away. There must have been a thoroughfare of people walking there after he passed; concrete is not easy for the dogs to track on, if others have been there."

"He's a clever boy, or so he thinks."

"He'll do it again, you know!"

"I know and we've got next to nothing," Taylor replied bluntly.

Taylor and Marcus left the crime scene and headed back to the office; stunned silence filled the car as they drove through the affluent areas of Edinburgh, areas where those wealthy enough to live there expected to be safe in their own homes. The properties had large gardens filled with old trees, perfectly cut grass, rockeries, expensive decking and high walls, walls which ensured privacy. For the predator, such premises were perfect: walls to hide behind, privacy to watch the victims with minimal interruption, a perfect place to wait before callously taking their innocent lives.

Chapter 5:
Unforeseen News Flash

He turned over restlessly in his filthy, sweat-stained bed sheets, the stench of unclean flesh filling the room. His brow was sweaty as he turned to look at the clock. It shone brightly in his darkened room, 11.45 am boldly showing in red digital lettering. *Too early to get up,* he thought, as he was not working today. He decided to take the time to enjoy his thoughts, recapping on every vile detail of the night before; he looked at his fingers, still stained with Susan's blood and other fluids invisible to the eye. He swithered whether to watch a DVD from his vast collection of sadistic porn, which he regularly imported from Amsterdam, or to just put the TV on. His mind was made up by the six foot journey to the closest porn DVD, which was lying on the floor, buried in old fast food cartons, dirty stale washing and months of grime, and he elected to watch TV. With the remote he flicked through the channels to find BBC News 24, hoping his little escapade last night would rightfully be headline news.

Reaching under the bed for his cigarettes he froze, his ears fully alert to the words he was hearing from the screen as he turned his head to see the headlines.

"A WOMAN ESCAPES WITH HER LIFE, AFTER HORROR

ATTACK IN HER OWN HOME." The story went on to state that a man and his dog were slain within the grounds of the property, possibly having disturbed the suspect whilst waiting for his planned victim. The story went on to list Susan Hamilton's injuries, stating that several of them had been life-threatening in their own right. The news reader added that the knife used in what was believed to have been the intended final and fatal blow had only just superficially cut into the victim's heart muscle, narrowly failing to rupture any of the chambers within, but that if hit would have guaranteed her certain death.

He lay there totally shocked, just staring at the ceiling; his breath rasped into his lungs before his fury escaped in a loud wail. It went on and on until there was no longer any air to carry on. He stood up, his tall frame spoilt by his soft belly hanging over his sagging unclean underpants. His arms were extremely hairy, but still noticeably strong from his years of manual labour; his chest still showed the remnants of what was once a very muscular and well-built man. He punched the door, his fist creating a hole right through to the hallway. He didn't even flinch as his knuckles started to swell and bleed, the pain almost giving his anger some sort of outlet to escape. He could not believe after all his good work last night that the fucking bitch had survived; she was so small, insignificant and defenceless and he had totally underestimated her, and her will to live.

John Brennan was a 48 year old recently divorced man. He had worked as a scaffolder for 20 years and had recently taken a job in the City Centre, City and View, the Capital Cities' CCTV hub, which covered all the known troublesome areas of Edinburgh and the busy city centre night spots. He worked there four days on and four days off, leaving him plenty of time to devote to his new project. He was unimaginably punctual and managed to fulfil the requirements of his job, knowing that was how he could manage to appear normal. He could fly beneath the radar and remain unnoticed by the ever present and prying eyes of the police. He was also very aware of the areas not covered by the police's vital source of evidence, the city's CCTV. He knew where big brother could not see him and he intended to make full use of this privileged knowledge.

John pulled out his laptop angrily and started surfing the web for his next important lady. He thought to himself, *isn't free-*

dom of information a fantastic tool for people like me? This was an unguarded window into the private lives of so many people, with lots of helpful information about all of these wonderfully successful women. His deep rooted bitterness, hatred and anger towards the fairer sex radiated from him, his need to erase his recent mis-judgement at the front of his mind. He had spent a lot of time with the last one and didn't feel that he could wait too long to get his next fix, his rage spurring him on and his desire visible.

Last night had made him feel so powerful, totally in control; he didn't have to listen or agree to anything she said, didn't have to do anything she wanted, just stamp his authority all over her, which he had done, over and over with such venom. She had had to listen to him, she had to do what he told her to do. He was much stronger than her, totally superior to her through strength alone, and he made sure she knew it by his merciless relentless savagery. He showed no sympathy, no remorse for the sadis-tic way he acted out his fantasies upon her. He used her like a sex slave and had deliberately prolonged the torture before he butchered her. He looked skyward, at the thought she had seen him. "She fucking saw me, that fucking dirty bitch can fucking identify me, ffuuucccccckkk." His voice bellowed out from within his house, easily audible out in the street but he didn't care.

Chapter 6: Groundwork

Taylor and Marcus headed out to take a statement from Mrs Forrest, the wife of the deceased found in the garden of 15 Grainger Loan, Edinburgh. They were aware that the incident was so recent that getting the information they needed would be difficult, as the pain of her loss would still be clouding her senses, and her emotions would be raw. Marcus sipped at his coffee, as Taylor drove; they were both really tired as sleep was way down the list of their priorities. They worked countless hours to enable the continuity of their enquiries, hours required for everybody to get positive results.

They pulled up at the house and as they walked up the driveway a slight looking, well dressed older woman opened the door in front of them. She knew that they were coming, as Taylor had arranged the visit earlier in the day, to prevent her being needlessly alarmed. Mrs Forrest welcomed them in to her home, a single-storied bungalow two streets away from Susan's house. She led them through to the sitting room where a dog basket lay noticeably empty in the corner of the room. The room was smartly furnished, everything was neatly in its place, with beautiful ornaments in the cabinets, well polished and obviously well cared for. There were two single chairs, very upright and high off the ground. They were close by one another. The sofa looked rather redundant, unused and in perfect condition compared to the two chairs, their position sad to look at now, with one never to be filled again.

Mrs Forrest offered her guests a seat on the sofa before sitting down on one of the single chairs. She lowered her head and looked at the empty chair at her side, his chair, her beloved loyal friend and loving husband's chair. She raised a hankie to her eyes as tears began to roll down her flushed cheeks. She spoke in a quaking voice. "He never came back. He was always on time. He was only out for his usual walk, same time every night just before bed."

Marcus asked, "What time was it he left the house?"

"About 10.30 pm, he just gives Angel, that was our dog's name, a stretch of her legs before we usually go to bed. He follows the same route every night. It's quiet around here, there's never any trouble! I phoned the police an hour after he didn't return and they sent someone round a while later, not immediately though, because I told them there would be some sort of logical explanation and I suppose I made it seem that he was in no immediate danger, well I didn't have any reason to. If only I'd known!"

Marcus spoke softly to Mrs Forrest; his tone was comforting and reassuring, and he tried to let her know she wasn't alone.

Taylor on the other hand cut in asking about the dog. "Would your dog try to protect both of you if any of you were in any sort of danger?"

"She was a kind dog, strong and loyal. We never really had a situation where she would have to protect us, but she might do," Mrs Forrest said. "Why do you ask?"

"I think your husband and your dog may have disturbed our suspect while he was waiting for Susan!"

"Oh that poor girl, I watched the television you know, what she went through. My Arthur was lucky in a strange sort of way, compared to her demise anyway, at least his death appeared to have been quick, but still very cruel and merciless." Her head shook back and forward, her hands visibly shaking, and tears welled in her eyes with a stray tear visible on her cheek.

"Did your husband ever recall seeing anyone any of the nights before this incident took place, anything that was different, anything he might have mentioned to you when he came home after his walk?"

"No, not that I remember dear. Oh yes, yes, there was something one night. A few weeks back, he said he saw a tall man that looked a bit out of place. This was in the next street from Susan's. He mentioned that he had felt uncomfortable when he had passed him."

"Can you be more precise, a date perhaps?" Taylor probed.

"No, no, I'm so sorry, every day seems to merge into the next these days."

"Did he say anything else about this man. Did he see him more than once?"

"No, other than he was tall and not from around here, and that he felt uncomfortable as he walked by him. No, nothing else, I'm sorry."

Marcus asked if there was anything else they could do for her at this time, call someone, get some help from the social services or other agency, but she had said no - it was time that she needed, time to grieve for her losses.

The two detectives walked to their car. Marcus was moved by the loss felt by this woman, whose husband of forty years had been taken from her forever, without reason or mercy. Taylor too showed emotion, but hers was displayed more in anger and disgust at this vile man's utter disregard for human life, and the deeply sad loss he had placed upon this woman and her family. She curled her hands into fists and rapped them off the bonnet of her car making a dent. She winced at her stupidity and the pain that now throbbed from her hands.

Simultaneously the search officers were scouring the house at 15 Grainger Loan, Edinburgh. Every inch of the property had to be covered on their hands and knees; a fingertip search made of every room, the garden and the streets outside, as they attempted to reveal every movement of the beast that had savaged Susan. Small hairs were found and two fingernails in the recess of the upper hallway where they believed he had waited for her: a sign of impatience or nerves - which? It was unknown. The officers were in one of the rooms downstairs when they heard a faint cry like that of a small child. "What the fuck was that!" one of them exclaimed.

It was coming from the linen cupboard at the back of the

room, the door of which was closed.

"Whatever it is, it's coming from that cupboard."

"Oh really? Well I'm not looking in it. That gave me the fucking creeps that did."

"You're such a fucking sap, Stevie! I'll look then shall I?"

One of the other officers strode to the door where the noise had been heard, just as the noise came again and this time much louder.

"Whooaaa!" The cop tried to make a joke out of the noise, trying not to show that he was very uncomfortable but he was noticeably uneasy as he opened the door. He slowly pulled it towards him, trying to peek inside, whilst protecting himself from what might be within. Just as he opened it a little further, a cat came leaping out from the top shelf, wailing loudly as it nearly knocked him off of his feet. It ran frantically from the room and out of sight to hide somewhere else in the house, untrusting of any strangers after what had happened. The others in the room laughed heartily at his misfortune, a regular occurrence for the team when anyone happened to come across any bad luck. Laughter and hilarity were an essential tonic in sad times for the police. Not because they didn't care but to hide the fact that they did and they were affected by things like this.

"You realise we're gonna have to find that furry wee shit again!"

"The lady apparently owned a cat and that was it and we've just fucking let it go."

"Well at least that creep never found it, I can't imagine he would have given it a wee drop milk and a pat."

"He would probably have made a hat out of it or something."

"I suppose I'll have to tell the SIO that we'll have to search the house again."

"Yup, you let it go ya big fanny!"

ㅁㅁㅁ

Kay walked into the incident room, her hands filled with papers, her cheeks flushed with colour as she saw Taylor sitting behind her desk in animated conversation with Marcus. Taylor looked up and spotted Kay at the far side of the room just outside the Inspector's office; she felt a pleasurable warmth flow through her, very unexpected from just a glance. Kay disappeared into the office. Taylor could only imagine her boss's thoughts as Kay leant over to place the papers onto his desk, his leery gaze as he caught a glimpse of her breasts from between the gap of her blouse. Kay was a truly striking and very pretty woman with sleek features, high cheekbones, full lips and an athletic poise. What Taylor was feeling was a hint of jealousy; she wanted to be alone with Kay in the office, not have to share her with many, and especially not that fat prick. Marcus looked at Taylor, and noticed her attention to him had wavered and her thoughts had drifted elsewhere. He followed her line of sight, her gaze focused on Kay as she left the office and then into the incident room.

He looked at Taylor, his eyebrow raised, and asked, "Why are you so interested in her? She's very straight and just come out of a long term relationship with Tom!"

"I know, but even you've got to admit it, she's lovely, stunning?"

"Very beautiful indeed, but not for me, I have my own treasures at home, you should try it, sometimes one person can fulfil all of your needs you know!"

"Oh really!" Taylor got up from her chair and said that she'd be back in a minute, and left the room; she felt he was on to her and wasn't ready to reveal the truth and didn't want her eyes to give it away.

She moved quickly to the exit and disappeared from sight. Climbing the stairs three at once, she was just in time to see Kay three floors up and called out to her.

"Kay, hold on a minute, wait there!"

Kay stopped and Taylor reached her in the empty corridor and grabbed her playfully round the waist. She pulled her towards her, kissing her boldly where they stood, a deep lust-filled kiss, passionate and full on.

Kay momentarily responded to the sensation of unadulterated desire, willing Taylor to continue, but she stopped, realising where they were, and pulled away, whispering, "Discreet? If this is discreet I'd hate to see what the opposite would be!"

Taylor stepped back, her neck flushed with their feverish kiss. "I want you, you're so god damn sexy. When I saw you go into that sleaze ball's office, I may have even been a little jealous, and I couldn't wait another second to hold you and kiss you. God I want you Kay," and she motioned to kiss her again.

Kay let Taylor's lips touch hers, slightly opening her mouth, and then pulled back and asked, "What do you want from me Taylor? The other night was wonderful, an eye opener, but what am I to you, another conquest? I'm not someone you can pick up and put down when it suits you, I'm not going to be that type of lady for you, lovely though you are!"

Taylor, being her usual casual self, hesitated with her answer, which was enough to let Kay know where she stood and she turned and walked away; the silent answer she expected. She turned into an office, which Taylor knew would not be empty and to follow her would be futile right now. Taylor slumped against the wall, a crushing feeling now deep in her heart, an unexpected feeling of loss.

"What an asshole I am. She is so right. What was she to me,? What is she to me? I don't even know myself."

Taylor walked back down the steps and into the office. Marcus looked up at her and couldn't help but notice that her neck was red and a hint of disappointment was visible in her eyes.

"What's up with you? You look like something's got into you?"

Taylor just looked at him, a hard stare without uttering a word. She was taken aback with how much that little rendezvous in the corridor had made her feel. For once she cared and she had been just a little too blasé for her own good.

"Shit," she muttered to herself, Marcus turned to her again.

"Do you want to get a bite to eat? I'm starving."

"You're always starving, you should be the size of a house, you lucky pig," Taylor replied, obviously still in a grump.

"Come on, moody. There's nothing a good old BLT won't sort out."

Taylor reached for her jacket and Marcus smiled as he grabbed his coat and almost skipped alongside her, just to annoy her a little more.

Inspector Findlay popped his unwanted head out of his office; Taylor's stomach sunk with anticipation of the inevitable instructions that were to follow, likely more enquiries, more endless tasks that all seemed to lead nowhere.

"DNA results are in. Surprise, surprise - no match found with anyone on the database, but there certainly wasn't a shortage of it, he certainly wasn't shy; oh, and they've found the cat. I now want you to look through all of the outstanding missing persons, I don't think for a minute this was this bastard's first victim."

Taylor nodded as they headed off for lunch. She moaned to Marcus, "That freak better not put a foot wrong; anyone who does anything these days is having their DNA taken. He better not even sneeze in the wrong direction or we'll have him, the arrogant bastard."

Chapter 7: Why

Early one September morning, about a year before, Louise Brennan, the ex-wife of John Brennan, walked happily to her house; she was enjoying the autumn sun on her face. She was free at last from years of torment at the hands of her brutal husband, she never thought she'd ever see that day. She now walked with a permanent limp caused by one of her husband's assaults; he had stamped down on her thigh as she lay at the bottom of the stairs, snapping her femur in two places, causing one leg to be shorter than the other after the repair. Her face had numerous old scars, each telling its own silent story, her bones deformed in many places with enlarged areas where they had calcified on their repair. None of the assaults was ever reported to the police due to her fear of even more violent reprisals.

The house they had owned had been sold months ago; John had received his share of the money and more. Louise had tied up all of the loose ends and intended heading off to France to live in peace and start afresh. She had a year's lease for a quaint holding there, all paid for in advance, with the keys waiting for her under the mat on her arrival.

Her mother had died two months ago leaving her a small fortune, none of which she had to give to John because the divorce had been finalised the month before. John was raging about this, but he was always raging about every tiny little thing. *Good riddance,* she thought to herself as she turned the key in the lock. She stepped inside and everything was just as she had left it, the furniture all to be left as part of the lease. She toyed with whether to spend her last night in a hotel or not but thought it would be easier just to stay where she now called home.

They hadn't been able to have children, another thing John had blamed her for, never considering for a moment that the problem could have been on his side. Louise longed for children but became glad in a way that they didn't have any because of John's temper; what would he have been like with the children? She could barely contain her shudder as she thought about that.

She walked through to the kitchen, the paperwork for the house and the information regarding the final arrangements still lying on the counter where she had left them. Everything was signed over and all that was left to do was leave the keys and the letting agent would collect them as she had already given over all of the other sets of keys. She was fearful of the massive step she was about to take but the further she was away from John the better; she had no relatives, as she was an only child and both her parents were now dead. She didn't care if the rest of her life might be spent alone; she only cared that she would not have to feel fear and pain anymore. She wouldn't have the anticipation of being raped whenever he wanted her. Being safe and her freedom was all that mattered.

John had pestered her to go back to him for a short while after she had left him but strangely he had stopped as if he had accepted that she was never coming back. He had signed the divorce papers and taken his share of the money. Little did Louise know that his mind was already planning a sinister final solution of his own to their sorry excuse for a marriage.

She opened the door to the living room and froze on the spot, her breath shallow and fast; there in front of her he stood, his eyes twinkling with a strange sense of triumph. He spoke in a calm voice. "You didn't think I was going to let you go, did you? I've waited patiently for you to sort everything out for me, for you to erase yourself from society so as I don't have to cover my tracks. As far as everyone is concerned, the few that may know you, you've already left."

Tears rolled down her face as she dropped to her knees, her voice at a whisper. "Why, why won't you just leave me be, let me go John, please let me go John, I'm begging you."

"Never! You're mine, and I decide when you leave me! In fact you'll be leaving soon, for good," he smirked and walked over to her.

She looked up at him, his eyes cold and unfeeling as they met hers; she gently held on to his trouser leg, her fingers weak and her touch soft, her fingertips pleading to John's softer side that he once had shown her many, many years ago.

"I told you that I'd never let you leave me, and I meant it." He reached down to her and pulled her up to her feet; she was much smaller than him, half his weight and of frail appearance. He placed his hands around her throat and she whimpered meekly like a defenceless lamb waiting to be slaughtered.

"Don't John, I'm sorry for leaving you, everything's my fault."

His thumbs pushed slowly into her throat, to savour the moment; her hands gripped his wrists, a futile attempt to stop him, his piercing eyes fixed on hers as he slowly choked the life from her. He pushed harder and harder. Louise lost consciousness and then he violently snapped her neck with his bare hands. He held her up, his strength easily holding her weight before dropping her to the ground; her limp lifeless body lay there. At last her prolonged and tormented battle against him was finally lost. Escape had been so close but yet so far.

He brought through a large case and savagely stuffed his beloved wife into it. There was no care for her as he jammed her limbs in, bending and twisting bone and cartilage to make her fit. There was now no obvious trace that anything had ever happened in that room.

Chapter 8: Next

He moved the barrel in the kitchen; it was quite heavy, as his wife's decaying body lay folded double within it. Her head was pressed against her ankles, sadistically folded over like a rag doll. The barrel was sealed shut as John had welded it after he placed her there, months before, a grotesque resting place for a kind and loyal woman that he had shared such a large part of his life with. There was an old, manky, stale stained table cloth covering the wooden circle, which lay on top of the barrel which he now used as a table top, sometimes eating his food off it, thinking of her inside. It gave him pleasure when he thought of how he had shown her that he was the boss and that she could never leave him now - *stupid bitch.*

He pulled on a semi clean pair of pants, his work uniform, a half ironed shirt which had only been worn once and his clip-on tie. He looked in the mirror, and combed his hair, a sly smile sneaking onto his face as what he saw in the mirror was a completely different impression than others would see. He saw somebody that commanded respect, a powerful man, someone that women should obey. He thought that women should be more like they were in the fifties: subservient to men, look-

37

ing pretty for when men needed relief, tea on the table on time and conjugal rights as and when they chose. There was no law against raping your wife, that wasn't classed as a crime. He had always taken full advantage of this with his wife, even though the law had changed many, many years ago. He had beaten her regularly for the tiniest thing - burnt food, being late home from the shops, not being quick enough with his beer - the list was endless, his savagery growing as the years went by. He kicked the barrel hard as he left for work, thinking how that bitch had dared leave him, he was her master and she disrespected him; but he showed her who was in charge, that she shouldn't have left him, and he would show the rest of them.

He climbed into his Ford Escort, not an old car - he had used some of his wife's divorce money to buy it. Inside was like a tip, just like his house. He had no respect for anything and he was a slovenly creature. He carefully put on his seatbelt, not because he was a law abiding citizen, but because he didn't want to draw any unnecessary attention from the police, as even the slightest misdemeanour could bring him to their attention, and he didn't want that. He was bold enough to leave his DNA everywhere as he believed he was invincible, and couldn't risk having to give it over. He drove down his street, dull grey three-storey blocks on either side, some graffiti on the walls; pictures displaying sexual deviancy always caught his eye and made him smile to think that there were others that shared his own thoughts. He drove down through the meadows, a large expanse of green belt, where the student population relaxed on hot days and played a multitude of sports throughout the year, in between their studying and partying. Two slim female joggers ran past his car as he stopped at the traffic lights and he did not hide his gaze as his head turned in an owl-like fashion to follow their svelte bodies for as long as they were in view. They wore crop tops and lycra shorts, their taut flesh on display, unaware of the evil watching from the vehicle that they had just passed. He was tempted to turn round and have another eyeful of those girls, but better judgement prevented him. As with the seatbelt, a complaint against him would lead to life behind bars for the atrocities he had committed. He was beginning to regret leaving his identity practically gift-wrapped for those who hunted him. He shook his head and focused on getting to his work, where he had to hide who he really was and act like normal old John.

He pulled into the staff car parking area beneath the building; the swelling beneath his trousers had only just subsided and he could go about his business as normal without any unnecessary attention. His heart was still racing with the unhealthy thoughts still present in his mind regarding the girls in the park; he wanted them, but not in a way that a normal person wants something. He wanted to do unspeakable things to them, to hurt them, to make them beg before him for the very breath that they breathed.

"Hi John," a warm and friendly voice came from behind him, almost making him jump.

"Oh hi there, I was away in a wee world of my own there."

"Good days off?"

"Yep, just the same old same old. You know how it is eh? Boring old Edinburgh."

The woman who had spoken to him was quite new to the department and always full of the joys, every day, never up, nor down, always friendly to him and very polite. She was in her forties, confident and relatively pretty for her age. Her name was Rachel Davies and he actually liked her, because she was genuinely a non-judgemental type of person, and he never felt anything false about her. He never felt judged by her and in his mind she was safe.

She said to John, "Do you want to walk me in?"

John hesitated, almost stunned that he was being asked to walk with her.

"I won't bite," she said, and John got out of his car and locked it behind him, almost fumbling with his keys. He quickly gained control of himself and walked into the building with her, sharing a little small talk, but nothing more as he would not reveal anything of himself to anyone, least not to a woman. He couldn't afford to let anyone get close, although he did really like her.

Once inside Rachel headed for the stairs and John went to the lift. She mentioned that the stairs were better for his health, with a smile, but John just carried on towards the lift. They exchanged pleasant goodbyes and the lift door closed. Inside there were two women and another man. The women were both dressed in skirts and blouses, one very modest and conservative, the other wearing her clothes in a slightly more revealing fashion; not trashy, but worth looking at. John stood behind them, his eyes wandering all over them. Every curve, their calves, necks and buttocks; every inch was being measured and their details stored in his mind for future thoughts. The younger woman turned round and caught him looking her up and down; she was the one wearing her blouse tightly fitted and a skirt which revealed her well-shaped legs. John dropped his eyes quickly and regretted allowing his mind to linger longer on what he wanted to do to them. The woman turned and adjusted her clothes, an obvious physical reaction to being leered at. She had felt his eyes boring into her from behind, an unhealthy feeling of being watched. He had sent shivers down her spine and they weren't pleasant. She felt very uncomfortable. The lift door pinged and both of them got out, along with the man who paled into insignificance to John; he only had eyes for the ladies. The women walked down the corridor and John just caught a glimpse of them talking to each other, he shuddered slightly, hoping he hadn't stepped over the line. He didn't want to have to sort anything out this close to home.

The younger woman said to the other, "He gives me the creeps that guy! I just caught him looking at my legs."

The other woman gave her a friendly shove and said, "No wonder he was looking at you. Look at you, ya hussy." They laughed it off and headed to their respective offices, not realising just what type of man had taken a shine to them.

John walked into his office and sat at his work station, the numerous screens shining brightly in front of him; already he could see people interacting, arguing, loving, hating one another. He loved his job because he fed off other people's misery and this place was a perfect place to prey on women. He always used the screen enhancement function to zoom in on any female's body that caught his eye, obviously only when the others were on a break though.

His colleague Peter Smith came into the room and said hello to John, who returned the greeting. Peter asked if there was anything interesting happening. "No, not yet, I've checked all of the cameras, everyone is blissfully happy," he replied with a hint of cynicism. There were computers within the work area for the staff's use, and John couldn't wait to get using one; he was impatient to find his next special lady.

Eventless hours passed and Peter eventually got up to take his break; this gave John forty five minutes of privacy to get hunting. He checked out numerous sites which named and described successful business people, their places of work and other rather boring details about their companies and the ins and outs of what went on in their day-to-day running. None of this information held any interest for John, he just wanted to look at the pictures of the executives, not them all of course, only the women, the attractive women! The women that made him feel inadequate as they stared out of the screen right at him, in his mind, looking down at him, laughing at him, belittling him.

His rage was burning deep within him. "How dare they, how fucking dare they." He stared straight at the screen, straight at a full sized picture of a striking blonde woman, in her forties, slim, blue eyes and full lips. Anna Watt, director of her own company; she had an accountancy firm in the New Town in Edinburgh, a self-made millionaire, unmarried and currently unattached - *well, until I come to visit her of course,* John thought.

John visibly jumped up as Peter arrived back from his break; he deleted Anna's photo immediately, certain he was quick enough to stop Peter seeing him.

"Your turn. Don't have any of that pie - it's minging. God knows what they've put in it. Anything interesting on the net?"

"Naw, same old shit mate. Have a look for yourself but I'll have to sign out, you know all the regulations an' that, eh!"

"Catch you in a bit then," Peter said as John left the room.

John went to the gents', the façade of normality wearing thin on him; he hated the mundane chore of normal life, he thought he was better than that. *Why the hell should I have to work day in day out for practically nothing?* A flashing image of Anna's face now invaded his mind and he could feel his stomach tightening, his vile mind already decided - *that arrogant rich cow is my next customer.* A hideous smile spread over his face and a strange comfort came over him, the stress and anticipation dissipating through him as he could now focus on what mattered to him, what now consumed him: getting rich and showing these women who was in charge.

John walked back to his work station and said to Peter, "I don't feel well mate, I'm going to head off home, I'll call back in when I'm better."

Peter looked up and said, "I told you not to have the pie. You do look like shit though. I'll get on the blower an' tell the boss to get you covered for a while then."

"Thanks Pete."

Chapter 9: Addiction

Back during Halloween a year ago, the work had a night out at a pub in the centre of Leith, a refurbished boat recently changed to a chic bar and night club. It was furnished with modern but comfortable fittings. Lit with a warm ambience, it was busy with a mixed crowd and the drinks were flowing. John was talking to the lads from his department at the end of the table while the women were gossiping down at the other end. They were dressed to impress and there was a little flesh on show for those who wanted to look. The confident younger lads were strutting their stuff, making any excuse to walk past the ladies, exchanging the usual flirtatious and suggestive banter, a tactic John found degrading and demeaning. He thought it was like begging for their attention and only if the girl decided he was worthy would she encourage further chat and maybe more. John shuddered inside at the power women held just for a guy to get a bit of pussy. Men were so god damn gullible when it came to getting their leg over. John surveyed the pub; there were women barely dressed in his opinion, flaunting themselves and begging for it. *No wonder things happen to them,* he thought, almost visibly grinding his teeth. He felt uncomfortable, mixed feelings between arousal, jealousy and resentment, *fucking bitches*; his temper was starting to boil and he found himself feeling unable to remain calm and maintain his façade of normality.

Since killing his wife, John could not stop thinking about the arousal and the ultimate power he had felt as he took the most precious gift from his traitor of a wife, her life! He craved that fix again, that power. He wanted to feel his blood surge through his veins once again, pulse racing; feel that stiffness of his cock again as the desperation of another woman to survive thrilled him like never before. He wanted these women in the pub, all of them, he wanted to destroy their beauty one by one, teach them a lesson by taking their confidence away from them. "Sluts, flaunting themselves like that," he muttered, *they'll get what they deserve one day.* His body was now tensing up and he began to feel a little conspicuous and tried to relax himself a little, as he knew he didn't want to raise any suspicions of what he truly was.

"Hey John, do you want another pint?" asked Dave.

"No." John suddenly snapped out of his thoughts. He turned politely and said, "I'm off, I don't feel too well and don't want to get trashed tonight, I'm off home, I'll catch you all at work next week eh. Cheers." And he was off, just like that.

He was relieved to be out of the claustrophobic atmosphere. He walked a short distance along by the river and climbed into his car where he sat for a while never. He hadn't intended to drive home, but he'd only had three pints and he was a big man and reckoned he might just be under the limit, and he certainly didn't feel pissed. He started the car and began to head home. He did not intend to indulge in anything more that night, but something stirred within him and he decided to change direction and drive along the sea front onto Salamander Street towards the area where prostitutes openly walked the streets touting for tricks. He had never used a prostitute before as he believed he should never have to pay for sex; the fact that a woman got some sex from him should be enough for them. His thoughts turned foul and he decided he was going to find the youngest prettiest little whore and teach her that she hadn't made the best choice this evening; selecting him for a trick would put her career choice seriously into question and maybe even her life.

He smiled a treacherous smile as his eyes narrowed and he drove with more conviction and purpose.

He pulled onto Seafield Road and there were several women underdressed for the weather, long thigh length boots, basks and the shortest skirts imaginable. John was already hard from his previous thoughts and his desire was becoming overwhelming. He drove slowly past the women and watched, leered at and examined their faces and bodies, memorising every detail for when he made his final choice. He drove by several times and looked to see which of the whores had a pimp in tow and which did not. He didn't want any male attention tonight, just the ladies; he didn't want a fair fight, he wanted to instil terror and dominate and control.

He parked up in a street, just off Salamander Street, where he knew there was no CCTV coverage and a safe route out to other streets that avoided the gaze of the lens, areas not covered by the watchful eye of the city's cameras. The night dragged on as the women were picked up and dropped off; not long for each customer, just enough to get their rocks off. *What a waste of money,* John thought to himself, *I certainly won't be as quick and I certainly won't be paying.* The night drew on and his patience was finally rewarded. There was a pretty young Polish looking girl heading towards him. The pimps were nowhere to be seen.

She spotted him sitting in his car, something that didn't surprise her. Lots of men sat and stared, waiting for them to approach. Her thoughts clouded with the awful things that were expected of them. Men seemed to think if they paid for sex that these girls weren't worthy of any respect, care or freedom from being forced to carry out depraved acts, which they would never dream of asking their partners to perform. She was really tired, but could see that there was still money to be made and the more she got, the less likely she was to receive a beating from her pimp. If her earnings were up on the night before, she could sneak a little more for herself and pay him enough to keep him off her back, or stop him demanding favours for himself and he wasn't a kind and caring man. *Hey, what harm can it do,* she thought. There was big business on party nights, men drunk and filled with desire, desire that the women that waited in their homes would be less than willing to fulfil. There were also men who didn't have women in their lives, who don't score very often, coming down for a genuine need to be with a woman, to get some company and a little sexual pleasure before heading for home alone.

Layla was a slim pretty young lady, trim waist, ample breasts and long legs that led to the shortest skirt imaginable, barely covering her panties. She had an unwanted heroin habit, one that was forced upon her by her pimp; this made it possible to control her, because once addicted, he could provide the only thing that she would eventually want and need. She was bright and came to this country with ambition and desire, but couldn't get a job and was preyed upon by her pimp, masking himself as someone who cared, providing her with accommodation and food, which turned quickly into her owing money and being trapped into a spiral of despair and slavery.

She leant into the window of John's car but before she could even speak he gripped her throat so tight that she could not make a sound. He pushed her harder and she lost consciousness and dropped to the pavement like a stone, banging her chin as she fell. He shoved her ruthlessly with the door of his car to get it open and quickly bundled her into the rear seat, her chin now stained with blood oozing from the fresh gash on it. He climbed back into the car and was about to switch on the engine when a cop car moved slowly into the street, which was a regular occurrence in that area to try and keep the situation there under some sort of control. John froze, not wanting to be seen sitting in his car in this area; he slumped down and flattened himself to the front seats, hiding his large torso from sight, and hoped the cops in the car hadn't seen him prior to ducking down, that the patrol car would just pass on by. Layla began to moan in the rear seat and tried to rub her throat and touch the blood on her chin; she let out a scream as she realised it was blood. John could see she was about to sit up in the back of the car and give them away, so he reached through the gap of the seats and viciously gripped her hair, pinning her head. She screamed even louder and he hissed instructions to her, but she ignored him and carried on screaming. The police car was now right alongside their car and the two officers were talking to each other. One appeared to have spotted something up ahead. A man had stopped his car beside a lady of the night just a bit further up the road. The police car sped off in that direction. John heard its engine revving as it pulled away. He sat up and was now able to savagely punch Layla straight in the face repeatedly, mercilessly until she lost consciousness once again. He muttered to himself, "You'll regret that, you nearly had me caught, you stupid little tramp."

John carefully put his seat belt on and followed his planned route away from the area, avoiding the police vehicle parked up further along the road, now booking the kerb crawler. He smiled, but also shuddered at just how close he had come there to being caught. He travelled along the coast and then across the country to a wooded area in the middle of nowhere, not even a farm house within several miles. He was now on a single track road and he hadn't seen any other traffic on his travels whatsoever. *Perfect,* he thought, *privacy for my next performance.* He stopped the car and violently jerked and yanked at Layla as he carelessly and cruelly pulled her from the rear seat by her feet, and ripped off what clothing she had on, masturbating frantically until he ejaculated all over her; he couldn't help himself, his arousal driving there was getting in the way of his rational thoughts.

She started to come to and saw him above her; the realisation of the predicament she was in hit her chest almost painfully and she drew in a sharp and noticeable breath and started to crawl backwards as quickly as she could, pain pulsing through her face and her head clouded with the previous assault, she realised how much danger she was now in. He adjusted himself, sorting his fly, and moved towards her, noticing that she had awoken and was going to try to get away; she turned and pushed herself up and started to run from him. She had no clothes or shoes on but she was now in full flight, sprinting into the darkness, not worried about her bare feet and the pain stabbing into them as each footstep landed on undergrowth sharp and damaging; anything to get as far away from him. She could hear him following her and her heart sank further as the light from his torch lit up the area behind her, taking away the cover of darkness. John bellowed out to her and his words echoed through the night, "YOU'RE GOING NOWHERE, I'VE NOT EVEN STARTED WITH YOU YET, BITCH."

Layla sprinted even faster, wishing for the first time in her life that her brutish pimp would appear from the trees to save her and stop this maniac from hurting her. This was not to be, and she could now feel the ground cutting into her and branches whipping into her face, slashing her skin and slowing her down. The torch light was getting further behind as her youth and speed put distance between them. She took the chance and dropped down to her knees in a patch of long grass and nettles. They burnt her skin as she crouched there, trying to hold her breath and keep quiet; rasping desperate breaths still heaved from her lungs which were starved of vital oxygen from her frantic flight. She could hear her tormentor heading in her direction. He too was panting from the chase and had now started to walk as he had lost sight of his prey and his paunch was slowing him down. Her heart was pounding so hard, that she feared it could be heard out with her body, her knees and hands trembling uncontrollably with fear and pain. Her skin was slashed to ribbons from the blind run she had just taken, no concern for her physical well-being, all effort going in to saving herself from her pursuer. She felt the night had taken a sinister turn and she didn't think his intention was just purely sexual; she now believed he would kill her, and terror engulfed her and tears rolled down her cheeks at the desperate predicament she was in.

John looked into the trees, but could only see dark shadows. He shone the torch further into the trees and long grass and there was no movement. He held his breath and listened in an attempt to hear her, hoping she would give herself away. Layla could now see him standing at the edge of the trees, shining the torch all around him. She could see his contorted face, and she could now see just how big a man he was, over six foot and strong, although out of breath too, from their chase. She herself was only five foot four inches and of slight build, just the way the customers liked her, but no match for the hunter before her.

John whispered in her direction, sending a chill down her spine.

Shit, shit, shit! Does he know I'm here? Can he see me? What should I do? Run!

John spoke with a sly taunting tone. "I can see you, you vile little whore, I can smell your unwashed body, come to me and I'll show you a little mercy, DON'T MAKE ME CHASE YOU LADY, YOU WONT LIKE ME IF YOU MAKE ME ANY ANGRIER."

She was just about to run, thinking he had seen her, when he turned the other way and focused on a noise in the other direction. He took several large strides away from her and she lost sight of him as he disappeared into the trees. She clutched her knees and rested her face on them; she'd frozen to the spot, all she could hear was the slight breeze rustling in the grass just beside her. It was cold and she had no warm clothes, she started to shiver and could not stop herself. She tried to warm herself by wrapping her arms round her, close to her. Adjusting her position just a little in the long grass, she curled up motionless in an attempt to survive the cold and the predator that was hunting her.

Layla opened her eyes after resting them for what she thought was only seconds. The grass beside her was still rustling in what she thought was the breeze, but the breeze had subsided and suddenly a face appeared right by her side, suspending her breath in terror. All she could see were his gritted teeth in the light of his torch as he lunged towards her with no words, just savage blows to her face and body. He pinned her down and raped her viciously where she lay. She whimpered and begged him to take what he wanted but to spare her life, but he stared at her blankly as he turned her over and violated her once again, holding her face down in the grass and mud. She could barely breathe as he forced himself painfully into her anus over and over. He was out of control and hit her repeatedly with his fists like an ape; he bit her back, tearing away pieces of her flesh. Her screams were loud but unheard by others. He had beaten her so savagely that he was beginning to get tired, and he eventually chose to end the torment by holding her head with all of his weight into the dirt and pushing her as hard as he could until her face was pinned to the ground, sealed to the earth, preventing any air getting to her lungs; her eyes bulged in desperation and eventually her body, defiled, deformed and battered gave in and went limp. His heart was racing with the thrill of what he had just done, no remorse, just a powerful sense of triumph; his conquest lay still, unable to seduce another.

His eyes were dead of all emotion as he grabbed her foot and dragged her through the woods, her body light and fragile; but he did not care as her skin was once again torn by the trees he passed. He stopped at the car and pondered on what to do with the body. *Should I just bury her here?* Then he remembered she had a small bag with her. He leant into the car and checked it, and as he suspected there was a phone inside. "Fuck," he exclaimed out loud, a traceable source, a beacon to where they were and what they'd just been up to. "Damn you, fucking bitch."

He dismantled the phone, and placed it back in her bag. He drove several more miles back to a bridge that he had seen as he drove there earlier. Below the bridge there was a fast flowing river, deep and dangerous. He wiped the phone as best as he could and threw all of the pieces he had dismantled into the river. He then carried on miles further up the road and stopped at the edge of another copse of trees. He gathered up Layla's limp and bleeding body and her things and started to walk, his torch giving the only light. Once he was a fair distance from his car he dug a shallow grave using a small folding spade that he carried in case his car got stuck in the snow. Perfect for what he was about to do: get rid of tonight's conquest. *Nobody comes here, the animals will have her devoured before she is found,* he hoped. *Who cares anyway? They can't trace me, dumb fucks.* He thought of the police trying to trace him, when he was right there under their noses.

Chapter 10: Back to Basics

Present day. "Marcus honey, come back to bed. You're never at home these days!" Maria called from the bedroom. Little David was safely tucked up at his Grandmother's house, leaving the chance for a little peace and privacy. Marcus stepped out of the shower, torn between what he should be doing and what he wanted to do. He dried himself and wondered what Taylor would say if he was late. *Hmmm!* She would ask why, then smile and completely understand as she had numerous pre convictions for similar reasons, her lateness also due to untamed intimate pleasures.

Marcus entered the bedroom to see his wife lying partially covered by the silk sheets, a tasteful but seductive set of underwear revealing enough to arouse any man. Marcus smiled at her, his heart pounding with desire as he gazed down at her with his mind no longer in the grip of indecision; he moved towards her, his arousal very obvious to see. Maria reached up to him gripping his hair and pulling him onto her, Marcus kissed her with full and focused passion, an intimacy between them that had kept their relationship on fire for many years. He moved to pleasure her in an unselfish way, but Maria just whispered in his ear and gripped his head. "Just fuck me Marcus, I want you inside me now, I want you, I want you." She kissed him feverishly and he pulled her panties to the side and smoothly and powerfully entered her, her moan making his face flush and his stomach twist with the pleasure he was feeling; his penis went deep into her, his mouth devouring hers, his rhythmic thrusts making her head roll backwards, her hips lifting up to let him grip her pert bottom, allowing his pelvis to rub her over and over, her orgasm overwhelming, her breathing quivering as he continued to enter her. He wanted more. She wanted more.

Marcus turned her on her side and re-entered her from behind, his hands caressing her silky swollen pleasure from the front, his kisses powerful and demanding, Maria turned her head round to allow their mouths to meet, Marcus finally giving in to his physical need and letting go, his hands and thrusts continuing until Maria tensed her body, trapping him in the grip of her orgasm; he took hold of her, kisses still manic and desperate although not with the animal desire previously felt. Maria freed herself from him and turned to face him, her face and neck flushed with the pleasure of their intimate hot sex. She held his face and kissed him, her tongue savouring his kiss, his meeting hers and the tenderness overwhelming.

"I love you, Marcus Black."

"I love you too, Mrs Black."

"You do realise that I'm going to be really, really late, young lady and I won't know what to say."

Maria smiled at him and whispered to him, "You're not going anywhere."

She pushed him over onto his back and used her mouth to arouse him again. She straddled him and demanded more, her body taking him into her, his hands slipping over and over her silky mound, again and again she came hard, her body tensed and needy; Marcus looked at her in disbelief, not unpleasant disbelief as she eventually sighed and slumped against him.

"I've really missed you."

Marcus held her tight and said, "Not half," and laughed with her, their bodies joined together in their twisted sheets, bodies glistening with beads of sweat and faces flushed with the glow of pent up desire and exhaustion.

After another shower Marcus finally left the house and headed to work. He rang his boss. She answered, "Yes, DS Nicks."

Marcus fibbed as he said, "I'm sorry I'm late, I was caught up."

"In the sheets," Taylor cut in. "It's about time you lived a normal life like me, flying by the seat of your pants and telling lies about being stuck in traffic, cause that's what you were going to say, wasn't it?"

Marcus remained silent with a big warm smile spreading over his face; he couldn't have wished for a better boss, and hot too.

Taylor informed him, "I'm up at the enquiry office looking into the outstanding missing people files. You could meet me there. That will stop Findlay getting in about your mince. See you soon, you naughty boy."

The enquiry office was a specialist department in the police that dealt with missing people and all of the sudden deaths in the city. There were 10 dedicated officers who catered to the next of kin; when a death occurred, they produced in-depth death reports for the procurator fiscal. They also collated and recorded all information about every missing person in the city area and any enquiry made relating to each case documented. They created invaluable databases which officers could refer to and utilize, whenever the need arose.

Taylor looked up from her computer with a great big smile directed at a rather flustered DC Black.

"Glad you could come in, better late than never though, eh!"

Marcus apologised genuinely and pulled up a seat beside Taylor. She was looking as polished as ever, her tight fitting suit and long spiralling hair covering her shoulders, her scent intoxicating - any man's dream, if you didn't mind never reaching your goal.

"How long have you been at it?" Marcus, realising what he had just said, was leaving himself wide open for Taylor's reply, which followed quickly.

"No, how long have you been at it more like?" Her laughter escaped and she patted him on the shoulders, as if to say *that's my boy.*

"Let's get down to business. We are looking for women, I'm not sure that the accused will have a certain age group, as we only have one victim."

"That we know about!" added Marcus.

"Although I do think it will only be women, the man at the house was not planned, he just got in the way, poor old soul."

"How many do we have?"

"What, in Edinburgh or Scotland? Who knows how far he's travelled to indulge in his sick fantasies," Taylor replied with a tone of disgust, as her mind returned to Susan and the way he had sadistically left her.

"I think we have about six or seven that have potential, having looked through the files. There are two in Edinburgh, three in Glasgow and one in the Borders that I think we should look at first."

Marcus pointed to the picture of one of the outstanding missing women, a young Polish prostitute; her name was Layla Petrovsky and she had been missing since Halloween a year ago.

"How do we even know if she's still in this country? She might have made her money and gone back to where she came from - maybe just had enough and left, who knows?"

"Well, we'll just have to work our way through all of them systematically and see if anything has been missed or if there is a lead we can still follow. A lot of enquiry has obviously been done and nothing has come to light so far that has made them suspicious enough to turn them into murder enquiries, not yet anyway."

Marcus began his enquiry into Mary Dawkins, a 29 year old music teacher from Edinburgh, who had not been seen since December the year previously, and Taylor took the other Edinburgh case, the prostitute Layla Petrovsky missing since November the same year; neither of them looked overly suspicious, just people who had their own reasons for not wanting to be found, or on the other hand, other people who didn't want them to be found, but it was a start.

On Layla's report it had been her pimp Nicky who had reported her missing, not because he cared, but because he was losing a lot of money. Layla was a pretty slim thing with great earning potential as Nicky had beaten her regularly to do everything that the punters wanted: anal, kinky, bondage, sadomasochism, the works, because that brought in more hard cash for him and a lot of pain and degradation for her, but he didn't care about that.

Marcus and Taylor went their separate ways. Marcus headed to the west side of Edinburgh to look into Miss Dawkins missing from the Cramond area, a very affluent area of the city with large houses and expensive cars, two golf courses and a beautiful river walk on the resident's doorsteps. The Almond cascaded for miles, all the way down to the waterfront marina where enthusiastic yachtsmen moored their treasured boats. An area where there wasn't a lot of crime, unless people took the time to travel to commit it. Marcus stopped outside the home of Miss Dawkins and walked confidently up the driveway. Just as he was about to knock on the door, it was pulled open by a young man in his late 20s with skinny features, sloping shoulders, messy hair, big eyebrows and a weak jaw. Marcus introduced himself and asked if he could come in and ask some questions.

DS Nicks arrived on the east side of Edinburgh at the high flats near to the docks, the exact opposite of the area where Marcus was making his enquiry. She got out of her car and immediately spotted a group of teenagers loitering at the entrance to the tower block that she wanted to enter. The flats were twinned, two pillars looming in the night and each had 20 floors. They both had bold yellow and blue paint work on their exterior walls, with brightly lit red beacons at the top as they were on the flight path to Edinburgh airport. The lower floors were decorated with obscene pictures of genitalia and swear words from the local budding artists and poets, filling in their time before they had the opportunity to rob someone or cause an unsuspecting passer-by a heap of misery, just so they could have a laugh and boast to their mates about their exploits, or get hold of someone else's hard earned cash.

She strode boldly towards the entrance, not showing any fear or intimidation to the group that stood there menacingly, knowing these people fed on any little sign of weakness.

As she walked towards the door, the loudest bold boy wolf whistled at her and leered at his mates saying, "I'd like to get myself a piece of that. He grabbed his crotch, thrusting it towards her.

She ignored him until she reached the door, underestimating them a little, thinking that they didn't have it in them. She was about to pull it open, when a foot appeared and stopped the door from opening. Taylor turned round quickly to end up face to face with the loud cocky male, her pulse was now racing as she was well aware of what could happen. She pondered for a moment whether to reveal she was a cop or not, as sometimes this could provoke the situation even more. Taylor stared right into the male's eyes, which were equally locked on hers. He was slightly taken aback at her confidence and lack of apparent fear. There were five other teenagers in the group; the main instigator was the same height as she was. He had a strong wiry build, short fair hair, stubble on his chin and was dressed in dark sports clothing, although there was no chance of him playing sport. It was almost like a uniform for the kids on the street, unidentifiable with similar brands of clothing to limit the likelihood of being identified for the crimes they had committed or were about to commit. Taylor took a bold step towards the lad and fronted up to him, his five mates astonished at her bravery, with not a word to say. Taylor politely said to him, "What the fuck do you want? Get your foot out my way or I'll twist your fucking bollocks off!"

He spluttered a bit, not sure what to do. Most people didn't react in this way; she was dominating his space and making him look like a tit in front of his mates.

His decision was made and he put his hand up to her face to try and shut her up, shoving her backwards, using her face to push and show her who she was messing with. Without flinching Taylor grabbed his fingers and twisted them right round, his wrist and arm following, and before he knew it he was on his knees begging her to release the goose neck grip she had on him. She told his mates if they came any closer she would snap his wrist and she meant it wholeheartedly.

At that unfortunate moment her personal radio went off; it was the control room requesting a welfare check on her, the timing was that shit it put her welfare at even more risk. Taylor couldn't respond as she would not let the teenager go and his mates were still there loitering in a menacing way. The message on the radio was repeated, again with no response, and this made the youths uneasy.

All personal radios had GPS tracking and Taylor's exact location would be shown on the main computer. Units were now being immediately dispatched without any radio confirmation, a fallback which was necessary for situations like this.

The boy, who was now on the ground, yelled out at his mates to get the bitch and kicked Taylor hard in the shin. She reacted with a brutal twist of her hand and an unearthly snap was heard simultaneously to the slapping sound against her jaw. One of the males standing watching had finally grown a set of balls and punched the slim, defenceless and outnumbered lady in the face whilst slurring, "Pig bitch," as he did so. The guy on the ground was still rolling about in agony as his wrist was clearly broken as promised, but the others now closed in on her, stepping forward in turns to slap and kick her. Taylor punched one of them square in the jaw and grabbed another by his unkempt hair and twisted her hand quickly and powerfully, as the other two continued their attack on her. Taylor was starting to wonder if her bravery had been a mistake and thought she might not come out of this too well.

At last, after what seemed like an age, but had only been minutes, two cop cars screeched to a stop pulling up beside them, mounting the pavement as they did so, and four officers leapt out with their batons drawn. Two of the teenagers scampered away, but were hotly pursued by two cops. The other two stayed put, one because he was too fat to have a chance to get away and the other still had his hair trapped tightly in Taylor's grasp, the whining hero lay on the floor with a broken wrist, screaming that he was going to sue her. Taylor just looked down at him and said, "Self defence, you prick! You reap what you sow you arrogant little twat!"

Taylor was clearly shaken up. Another cop car arrived after the confirmation that there were numerous assailants involved. This was relayed to the control room by the cops first on the scene when they arrived and saw what was actually happening. They quickly took Taylor aside, noting that she had a burst lip, facial bruising and swelling and an obviously bruised jaw.

"I'll call an ambulance for you Serg," the young constable said in a soft and calming manner.

"No thank you. I won't need one. There are far more worthy candidates for their services than me, but thanks for your concern anyway."

"Come and sit in the car then and get your breath back. You've had a pretty scary situation to deal with back there," the young cop said politely as he led her to his car and opened the front passenger door to let her in. She took a seat, taking a long deep breath as she finally allowed herself to take in what had just happened to her and how much worse it could have been had the backup been another minute later.

Police vans arrived and an ambulance too, for the male with the broken wrist and all of the other young males were rounded up and caught and arrested, although one had to be taken to the hospital first of course. The arrest was possible due to an old lady who had witnessed the whole incident from her flat across the road, which corroborated Taylor's version of events, but unfortunately the lady didn't have a phone or she would have called the minute it had started. This was lucky, because in Scots law, there had to be two forms of evidence to secure a conviction or to prevent others from falsifying evidence and creating their own version of events, preventing innocent people who were the victims of crime from getting into trouble for others' wrongdoing and suffering twice at the hands of their abusers.

Marcus pulled up behind the vehicle that Taylor was sitting in and came running towards her, his face contorted with the worry of someone who truly cared as he approached. He opened the door, knelt down and took Taylor's hands. "Are you alright, what the fuck happened here? That's it, I don't care how bold you think you are, from now on we're doing things together, especially coming to places like this!"

Taylor scowled at him with a petulant expression on her face, a mixture of *you're not telling me what I can and can't do* and *you're exactly right, I'm a fool for going it alone to get things dealt with quicker.*

She stepped out of the car as another officer approached her, the team Sergeant Anderson, who stated in an apologetic manner, "You will be required to give a statement." He hesitated and then said, "Under caution though - the guy whose wrist you broke is making a counter allegation against you."

"Fine! Twisted little prick, but I expected that. He brought everything that happened there on himself. I warned him and the rest of them, but he started on me and they just started to pile in. What else was I supposed to do? Release him and make it even more easy for them to attack me? No fucking way."

An hour later, after giving her statement, Marcus started to head towards his car and was expecting Taylor to follow, but she muttered, "Aahhemm, mister! Where do you think you're going? I still need to speak to Nicky. I'm not coming back here tomorrow. No way."

"What! You need to be going home, put your feet up and take the rest of the day off. You're entitled to it you know."

"I don't want time off. I want to do what I came here to do. I'm not letting those little pricks scare me off. Come on!"

They entered the lift, a small enclosed metal box, names burnt onto the ceiling with lighters and the stench of stale urine overpowering. Dried saliva on half of the buttons and a used condom in the corner to join them as the metal doors shuddered closed. Clanking noises sounded all the way up, until the lift groaned as it stopped abruptly at the 17th floor. The doors opened and the floor was split into two sections, one at either side of the corridor with external security doors leading to each set of three dwellings: a futile attempt to stop house break-ins and intimidation.

At the security door Taylor stopped and paused for a minute, almost as if to gather herself back together again. Marcus dared to put his hand on her shoulder in an attempt to offer her some moral support as he had never seen her shaken like this before. She straightened up and looked at him. Her eyes softened and she said, "Thank you, I'm okay you know. I'm just thinking of how bad that could have turned out for me."

Marcus replied, "It didn't, though, and you're a very lucky lady."

Taylor reached for the buzzer and pressed flat number one for a prolonged period, allowing the person inside to wake up or sort themselves out, before coming to the door. Three more tries and the door was finally opened. Before them was a six foot four man, of muscular build with a shaved head and a large diamond earring in his left ear. He was wearing a tight black t-shirt, loose designer jeans and brown Timberland boots with the laces undone. A tattoo of an eye on his neck, just visible from beneath his top completed the look. He had dark brown pupils with an unwelcome gaze which was fixed on Taylor's breasts. He hadn't even acknowledged that Marcus was there, his attention was only for the striking woman that stood before him.

"Have you come to earn a little cash? I'm needing another star for the show," Nicky was careful not to implicate himself with what he said.

Taylor stated in a clear and firm voice, "Detective Sergeant Nicks and DC Black. We've come to ask you a few more questions about the disappearance of Layla Petrovsky."

"What! You've asked me shit loads of questions about that useless bitch already."

"Sir, do you mind if we come in and speak to you somewhere a little more private, please?" Taylor nodded her head, gesturing to be allowed into his flat.

Eventually, he moved to the side and let the two detectives into his place, watching Taylor's every move, leering at her backside as she strode past him.

"Wow! I would like to have a sweet piece of that ass," Nicky muttered.

"I'd watch what you're saying, I've had a really shitty day, and that's enough to get you lifted for a sexual breach, big fella," Taylor said with an edge to her tone, leaving Nicky in no doubt she meant it, and he didn't want any unnecessary attention.

"Was that a little lesson from your man on how to behave when out?" Nicky chuckled pointing to her bruised face, changing his approach to just being rude.

Taylor replied with a vicious stare, threatening him with her eyes not to go down that route.

Nicky sat down on his giant arm chair, covered with a large faux fur. He looked at the detectives and told them to take a seat, nodding his head towards the corner suite, large, black and leather, with reclining seats and numerous pillows, a 50 inch wide screen television on the wall and various other tasteless trinkets dotted around the living room.

"Look, I've told you everything I know, lady. She's gone and she owes me a lot of cash, the little whore," Nicky growled, obviously still pissed off at Layla's premature departure. Taylor took into account that he actually seemed genuine. His anger at Layla for leaving without a word really seemed to grate on him, and it didn't appear to Taylor that he had anything to do with her disappearance.

"Look, I know she was out on Halloween night, and one of the girls saw her at the end of the night and she said to her she was gonna turn a few more tricks cause the punters were out in force and paying good money that night. She saw her turn down towards the links, and she didn't see her come back again after that."

"What's the girl's name that saw her?" asked Marcus.

"Crystal. That's what she's known as. I don't know much about her. I think she's from the west coast," Nicky replied.

"Layla hadn't said anything to anyone that she was planning to leave, which suggests she may not have wanted to go. Everyone tells someone their plans."

"She's not taken any of her stuff, nothing. No make-up, underwear, cash - absolutely nowt!"

Taylor asked, "What about her passport? There's dubiety as to whether you have it or she does, and that really tells a story of its own."

Nicky's expression changed, and it was noted by both of the detectives. They had an eye for deceit; body language was an invaluable tool in gleaning evidence from people, as was knowing when to push things that little bit further. Taylor decided to lead with how the issue would be dealt with. "If you have the passport, that means that there is most definitely something more sinister to investigate here, and we were hoping she had just gone back to Poland. But if you have it, you better start telling the truth. We still have a missing girl on our hands and you would be our prime suspect if she doesn't turn up! Help us out here Nicky. Don't start obstructing us now or we will come down on you with everything we have, starting with a full forensic search of your flat and your detention for further questioning for as many hours as we can request. You'll not be able to operate any longer. You won't even be able to take a fucking piss without us knowing about it."

"Okay, okay, I held her passport from her as security to get my share of her cash for protection and I still have it. I keep it at my mum's house and it's still there. I checked when she went missing but I'll give it to you."

Taylor looked at him, disgust in her face as he had just admitted preventing the girl leaving the country and forcing her to turn tricks for him to give him money. Taylor informed him that he would be getting charged for his admissions but confirmed that it was better than being in the frame for murder.

"Where does Crystal live?"

"She stays in the Magdalane area. I don't know the address, I think it's on the Drive. Just ask around, someone will know her. She's on the junk and she'll be out to get it on a regular basis."

"Thanks for your help", said Marcus. "Why didn't you just say this in the bloody first place?"

"You're under arrest," chipped in Taylor. "You are not obliged to say anything in answer to your arrest, but anything you do say will be noted and may be used as evidence. Do you understand the caution?"

"Come on lady, is there any need?"

"Is that your reply to your arrest?" Taylor asked Nicky.

"Whatever!" he said in a defeated tone.

Taylor explained that they needed to take him to the station to take prints and DNA; lost opportunities for taking samples led to guilty people getting away with crimes on a regular basis. Who could tell what people had done in their past. There were stores and stores of evidence just waiting to find the right match as the future opened up all sorts of scientific opportunities for solving old cases.

"Let's go! We'll get the passport on the way to bottom out that line of enquiry."

"I'm starving!" Marcus exclaimed.

"No wonder. You've had a long day, but this'll take over an hour and then we'll sort something out," Taylor said with apologetic eyes.

Two hours later, Marcus and Taylor walked out of St Leonard's police station, the main custody suite for prisoners arrested in the city. Fettes Headquarters did not have a cells complex. All the procedures had been completed and Nicky was let out and on his way to appear at court at a later date.

"Chinese, do you fancy some?"

"Yep, why not?" Taylor agreed; healthy food just didn't cut it after a day like today.

Chapter 11: Recovering

Susan opened her eyes very slowly. There were three other beds in the brightly lit small ward and only one of them was occupied. An elderly woman lay motionless with many wires and tubes coming out of her. Susan thought to herself, *poor soul*, not even considering how badly injured she was herself. She attempted to sit up but her ribs crunched as she did so, the feeling of crepitus was agony as her bones grated against one another. She made a low whimpering sound as the pain was so intense and to make a louder one would have caused her even more pain. She looked down at her legs. They were bandaged and there was a cast on her left lower leg where her ankle had been broken and her ligaments twisted out of shape. Her knee was also in a brace as her knee ligaments, the cruciate and left medial, had both been torn as she twisted and struggled to get away from her attacker. She blinked again and realised that one of her eyes felt numb and she couldn't see out of it. She cried out loudly, this time not in pain, but in fear of what he had done to her.

A nurse came rushing in and quickly embraced and comforted her by holding her gently and telling her that she was not alone and that she would be alright. She told Susan that she was a very brave woman and that she was in safe hands now and they wouldn't let anything happen to her. Susan experienced a flash back to the attack and her body started shaking uncontrollably. Tears flooded from her eyes. "Why me, why me?" she sobbed, "I've never done anything to anyone, never hurt a soul. Why did he do this to me, why! Ouch, my chest feels like there has been a herd of elephants on it."

"They had to open you up Susan. He sliced through the wall of your heart muscle, punctured your lung. How you survived is a miracle, but you're okay now. CPR for 30 minutes will have also caused some bruising, my love. It will all heal in time and you will be strong again. You'll have to stay with us for a while though, until you get your strength back."

"What about my cat, Baxter! I have to get back for him. God, did they find him? Do you know if he's okay? God, what if that man got hold of him. He'd have killed him."

Wendy, the nurse, told her, "I believe the police found a cat in your house. Could that have been Baxter, unless you have other regular feline residents who utilise your facilities."

"Where is he?"

"I think they put him in the cat and dog home for temporary accommodation."

"Thank god, at least he's safe. Imagine if that beast had got hold of him. When can I get to see my cat. I want to see him, I need to hold something."

The doctor was doing her rounds and spoke confidently to Susan. "I'm so glad you're on the mend, Susan. A couple of weeks and we'll get a physiotherapist assigned to you to get that leg back into shape. It would have been sooner had we not had to take care of your chest first. We can't have that put under any more unnecessary strain. We have a fine young chap lined up to take good care of you. His name is Andy Milne. He's very good at what he does. You'll be in safe hands with him. Oh, and he's very patient, and handsome." Dr Macgregor gave Susan a wee smile, her eyes filled with warmth and respect for her patient; she was well aware how hard the team had worked to save her, and just how strong her will to live must be. They exchanged a friendly smile and the doctor left the room.

Chapter 12:
No Mistakes

A wintery night in February, John put several implements into his black rucksack to carry out his evening's pleasures before leaving his house. He had carefully planned his route to the Dean area of Edinburgh, another affluent district, where only the wealthy and students in multi occupancy flats could afford to live. Anna Watt's house was a three storey town house, probably worth £1.5 million, with ivy climbing up the outer walls. The rear garden was a haven for privacy, foliage and fencing preventing neighbours interrupting anyone wishing to commit a crime unnoticed. The time was 11.35pm and the house was now in complete darkness. He had been a standing in the rear garden for over two hours watching Anna go about her daily business. He located the phone wire and cut it, having made sure that Anna hadn't been alerted that there may be a problem if she made a last minute call before bed. Eventually the lights had gone out about 11pm, and he gave her enough time to slip into a deep sleep, hoping to avoid being heard as he broke in at the rear kitchen window as quietly and efficiently as he could.

Unfortunately, Anna was not asleep; she was lying in her bed reading with a small bedside lamp on. Her bedroom was to the rear. Thick winter curtains draped the windows preventing the light escaping outwards into the garden. John's footsteps were light on the ornate tiled floor, his shoes rubber soled to prevent any unnecessary noise. The kitchen was large and modern with an Aga stove and central breakfast bar, which he almost walked right into. The room was dark and he daren't use a torch in case he disturbed his quarry, which he thought lay asleep unaware of his presence beneath her. He carried on making his way through the luxurious house to the front, where he assumed the stairs would be. The floors were polished and immaculate, which caused his shoe to give a light squeak as he turned to grip the solid oak banister as he took his first step up the stairs.

The hair on the back of Anna's neck rose up like flowers in the morning sun. However, this was no pleasant moment. She listened hard, straining to hear the noise again. Her heart hammered in her chest and a trickle of sweat appeared on her temple as she rose from her bed almost levitating, all of her senses screaming out danger.

He stood absolutely still at the bottom of the stairs, also listening, wondering if he had woken her. Anna was upstairs and he downstairs, both of them trying not to breathe, straining to catch the other moving. Anna tried to convince herself that she had just heard the house creaking as it cooled, with the warmth subsiding, but her true animal instinct told her to be frightened, and only a fool ignores nature's tools of fight or flight. Now convinced there was someone in her house, her mind flashed to her phone, *holy shit, I left it in the hallway.* "FUCK!" she whispered to herself.

His head tilted to the side as he heard movement up above him and he knew that one twist of fate had given his prey the upper hand. He moved up the stairs quickly, three at a time, quiet but now not worried about making a noise. He knew she knew he was there and now he had to minimise the damage caused by his clumsy movement. He pondered for a moment. Should he leave now and cut his losses just in case she'd got word out? He could always choose another fair lady. *No, no way, she's mine! No other rich bitch will make me look a fool again.*

Anna gripped herself round her waist as she tucked herself into the middle walk-in cupboard behind her collection of coats and suits. In her hand, she clasped a small baton that she kept beneath the bed. Her hand was shaking as she could hear whatever was in her house making its way towards her like a wild beast closing in on its quarry. She held her breath as the footsteps slowly approached, tears in her eyes, her mind full of thoughts of what had happened to the poor woman who was attacked in her own home last month. *God no, please no. Don't let it be him.* John entered the room and turned on the light; he knew she knew he was there, and that he was going to kill her; he knew she would see his face and he would make sure she would not live to tell anyone about it. With the lights on he would find her more quickly and that would unnerve her and frighten her that little bit more. *She won't want to see my face. She might think I'll let her live if she has nothing to tell, silly girl.* A grin appeared on his face, cruel and unfeeling. He was enjoying the thought of her fear.

He looked around the room. The lighting was subtle and warm, the colour scheme sensual, very fitting for a beautiful woman's bedroom. The bed was luxurious and the room full of expensive ornaments. A deep pile soft rug covered the solid wood floor and a whole wall was taken up with a row of deep wardrobes, ample room for storing vast quantities of designer clothing and a petite, terrified woman.

John's eyes narrowed as he looked toward the first set of doors, his mind focused on what came next. Anna's hand tightened round the baton, the other hand covering it to strengthen the grip. The door opened beside her. She was aware that he was looking in the first cupboard and hers would be next. He moved across. She could hear his breath. The door opened slightly and she pressed her back further into the wardrobe, her heart pounding, waiting for her moment, waiting to strike. He hesitated too, knowing she could have a weapon and may actually be able to hurt him. Neither one of them was breathing, both suspended in animation, one in fear of her life and the other in fear of the unexpected. John's anticipation quickly turned to rage, hostility beyond restraint. He swung the door wide open, allowing the light to flood in. Anna's vision was momentarily affected but he couldn't see her yet, all he saw were her clothes. Two seconds later, as he pulled the clothes roughly to the side, he felt a painful jab pushing in under his chin. It was all Anna could do; she wasn't able to swing her arm round to strike with any force from her crouched position. John stumbled back holding his throat. His breathing was disturbed as the pain shot through him, stopping him momentarily. Anna leapt out of the wardrobe, her arms raised above her and she swung again with all her might. This time she hit him full on, right on his temple. He reeled backwards as she ran past him and down the stairs as fast as her legs would carry her. John was momentarily stunned but being a strong man was not easily stopped. He turned and gave chase following Anna down the stairs. She was at the bottom and trying to get out the front door, but there were so many locks to keep her safe in her own home that she couldn't manage to undo them all before he was bearing down on her. He grabbed her hair tightly and pulled her to the floor, viciously dragging her backwards towards the kitchen, her feet scraping along the shiny flooring, her heels squealing as her skin burned with the friction. Blood oozed from her fingernails where they were ripped to the quick as she frantically tried to claw at the oak floorboards in a desperate attempt to stop him pulling her towards him. His face was now horribly twisted with rage, a red swelling above one eye with blood on his face and in his eyes making him look even more sinister, his expression dark and lacking any emotion. His fist twisted her hair tightly round and he pulled her up onto her feet, before slamming her face forcefully down on the breakfast bar. Papers and fruit spilled onto the floor as Anna fought with all her might to try and free herself. He simply yanked up her night gown exposing her bare backside. She screamed and struggled even more ferociously knowing what was coming next. She would try like hell to stop him. She kicked out at him, over and over screaming, "Leave me, leave me alone, please, please. I beg you. Please don't, not that, please not that!"

He undid his trousers. He was rock hard, her struggle for survival arousing him like never before. He held her still with ease and forced himself deep into her as she screamed out in agony. Her cries pierced the night air and he slammed her face down hard onto the counter to silence her, her teeth smashing against it, three scuttling onto the floor, blood now pouring from her broken face. Harder and harder he thrust in to her, rage spilling over as he bit her savagely on her back, tearing her flesh while pummelling her body with his flailing fists. She tried in vain to scream again but she was so winded she couldn't draw breath. He pulled out of her and she gulped but the attack continued. He began to molest her anally, her thoughts now dulling as they became tangled up with the floods of pain coming from all over her.

Spent, he withdrew from her, shoving her hard onto the floor, his hatred spilling over as he walked over to get his bag and pulled out some rope, Anna lay still trying to gather herself, trying to catch a breath. He looked over at her, making sure she wasn't about to escape. Their eyes met and he growled towards her, "Take a good look, cause I'm the last thing you'll ever see." She closed her eyes, not daring to incite another onslaught from him. He looked down into his bag and Anna noticed her spare phone lying on the chair in the corner of the kitchen. She saw her chance. She looked up at him; he was taking a large hunting knife from the bag, a huge sex aid and a scalpel. She couldn't stop herself vomiting and he just laughed at her, his eyes filled with disdain. "You pathetic cow! I'll be through in a minute, don't be so impatient," he said, smirking at her.

She quietly but efficiently moved toward the phone. Fingers trembling, she dialled 999. "HELP ME! 4 Dean House," was not heard properly as the call was answered.

"Police, what is your emergency?" came over. Anna gave a guttural howl as the knife was plunged deep into her back.

"Hello, hello, I'm still here, are you alright?"

Anna was thrown over the floor as he smashed the phone off the wall. "You stupid fucking bitch, I was going to have so much fun with you, and now you've gone and spoilt it. You bitches are so fucking lazy."

The call taker quickly rewound the tape to hear the initial call, got the address from it this time and immediately despatched a set to check it out. Only one, however, because numerous crank calls were received daily and the nature of the call was yet to be confirmed.

John pulled Anna's head right back, yelling at her, "Open your fucking eyes you slut, open your fucking eyes, bitch," and as she did, he showed her the large hunting knife and whispered in her ear, "I had so much more to show you, to give you and now it's all over." The knife sliced deep into her neck, the downward pressure so immense that arterial blood sprayed round the room, her carotid artery severed as he started to savagely stab her in the back, again and again; she was still aware of what was going on, her pain now beyond belief. He stood over her and looked down. The pool of blood was growing round her, flowing and gently spurting as her blood volume rapidly dropped. Unable to move, Anna simply sighed in defeat, her eyes bulging at the inevitability of her own death, sadness filling her head at the way her life had been taken from her as one last breath gurgled from her throat.

He was smiling as he grabbed his things, a little tense that her call might have been received. This was confirmed when he heard sirens in the distance. He fumbled with the zip of his bag as it jammed preventing it from closing. "Fuck!" he exclaimed in anger and frustration. He threw the bag away and climbed up over the rear fence, knowing the cops would go to the front door first. He knew where he was going and the route he must take to avoid any attention or trail.

Officers arrived a minute after John had left the scene; the dispatcher had had the foresight to have a free dog van sent there as well, and as the first officers at the scene shouted through the letter box, the dog handler and his dog went round the back, the dog barking furiously towards the rear fence, a scent driving it crazy. The two officers at the front made a quick decision to force the door. They had already brought the equipment from the car, and started to swing the ram at the door. It took several attempts to break it open as it was a solid wood door. On entry they turned on the lights, checking the living room first and then the hallway. There were signs of a disturbance leading to the kitchen, and once there both stopped dead in their tracks. The scene before them was horrific, like something from a horror movie. Blood was spattered all around the room, and on the floor was a small framed woman drenched in blood with a gaping wound to the front of her neck. They raced towards her and dropped to their knees to check for signs of life, shouting to the cop in the garden that there was a body inside. "She's still warm. I'm calling an ambulance. He can't have had that much time to get far." They began CPR, hoping and praying there was a chance although the injury and the blood told its own story. Every compression created a fresh spurt of blood from Anna's neck; the officers did not bother about the blood covering the woman's face, they just wanted to save her.

The dog handler had found the bag and the dog took a deep sniff at it. It growled towards the back door and made for the rear fence. The handler lifted the dog over into the next garden with the extended lead on and, following her over, they sped on to the next garden and the next, eventually coming to a high brick wall. The handler looked up. "No fucking way did he get up that!" The dog pulled towards an open gate that led to the road; there were still people about and the dog had to remain on the lead for their safety, unable to differentiate between good and bad people. It ran up the street for a further fifty metres, nose to the ground, stopping dead at another garden, high fenced with spikes on the top, a jacket strewn over them to prevent injury, a sign that this was where he had gone. There was no other way through so they made their way to the other side of the vast property and garden. A gate to the rear opened into the street. The dog stopped. The street was a thoroughfare to the town and at least five or six people had just walked down it, spoiling the scent and confusing the dog.

"Fuck! Fucking lucky bastard. Good effort girl," the handler said as he leant down to praise his dog.

Out of breath, John crouched down further along the road, watching the copper look around him, the dog circling on the lead. He thought to himself, *fuck me, that was close, too fucking close!* He knew that scent could be spoilt by others walking over it. Luckily for him the bars in town created a constant flow of pedestrians in the area at that time of night. He stayed put as the sound of sirens filled the air. He knew the streets would be searched by numerous police vehicles passing by; he couldn't risk being seen this close to the scene, his clothes had blood spray all over them. He made his way through the rear gardens, trying not to make any noise that would bring him unwanted attention; not his plan, but it would have to do as he moved quickly and discreetly through the night.

He had to duck down several times when he saw open curtains and people near to their windows and as he crossed over streets; every second vehicle driving past was a police car. They were hard at it but the trees and bushes gave anyone in dark clothing a chance of concealing themselves from view; their chances of finding him were now unfortunately low without a helicopter and that would have to fly from Glasgow.

Home at last, his body shook, every fibre touched with the thrill of the evening. Nearly being caught was exhilarating, totally exquisite. He leant on the table on top of the barrel, and started to talk to his wife in a low voice, "Look what you've started. This was your doing. If you hadn't left me I wouldn't have to teach them respect, but I'm not finished yet." He patted the surface of the table and took a beer from the fridge. Slumping onto the couch, he gulped greedily at the drink. His head rolled back and his eyes closed.

Chapter 13: Searching

The Major Crime Unit, CID, uniformed officers and an ambulance crew were at the scene. The Scenes Examination Branch was also there, busy suiting up for the night ahead. Taylor and Marcus were also present in their white suits. They stood in the hallway, staring dumbfounded into the kitchen, Taylor looking at the horror scene before her, her hands trembling with rage and sadness. The feeling of failure inside her was now overwhelming. "He's laughing at us you know, he's taking the fucking piss, the arrogant savage."

"We're doing everything we can, Taylor!" exclaimed Marcus. "We'll get him. He'll make a mistake sometime; these assholes always do!"

They went up to the bedroom, wardrobe doors open, bed unmade, an open book at the end of it. Taylor instantly noticed the baton on the floor and a couple of dots of blood on the carpet and the wall. "She hit him and it must have injured him. There's blood here and a bit there, showing that it was a decent shot. Poor soul - she fought hard to survive."

"There's DNA evidence in abundance again, enough to open

up his own lab, and not a thing we can do with it until he fucks up or we catch him."

As Taylor walked around the crime scene her eyes watered with the grotesque signs of savagery all around her. She tried putting herself in Anna's place, the terror she must have felt, as something, someone, that beast took her life from her. The signs of her struggle for survival, to try and escape from her captor, were everywhere. There was blood spatter up every unit and a pool of blood on the floor. His tools for his night of crime painted vivid, cruel and painful thoughts; Anna's death had been hideous but all the things he had planned for her would have been even more horrific to endure, and then certain death anyway.

Taylor and Marcus left the scene and headed back to the office, silence taking over as they drove the short journey down to Fettes headquarters. The atmosphere was tense as the cobbled streets rumbled beneath them, the car tyres bouncing over them and giving therapeutic vibrations. Old four and five storey town houses rose above them, curtains drawn from the horrors of the night and those inside feeling safe within. With wealth surrounding them, it was a place that the people who lived there believed to be safe, but evil was just next door.

As they waited at the security gate, Taylor turned to Marcus staring at him, eyes filled with despair and emotion. "I can't believe this is happening in our city. Things like this only happen in the States and in the movies. He's not going to stop you know. We have to stop him. This is just the beginning and it's just going to keep on happening."

"I think we need to push the missing person thing further, we need to get a break at some time," Marcus said wishfully.

"I feel useless, totally helpless. We're failing the women of this city and there is fuck all we can do about it apart from sit and wait for this asshole to fuck up. We're doing all the usual things but he seems to be one step ahead."

Once inside the building, Taylor slumped down at her desk, her trays laden down with paperwork relating to the many other poor souls waiting to be helped. She cupped her face in her hands, eyes shut, head forward, her mind racing round everything that had happened and the ton of shit from the bosses that was heading her way. Things like this hit the press like a freight train. The people of the city would not feel safe in their own homes and they'd want the police to reassure them that this man would be caught, which was something they weren't able to say without embellishment. Marcus planted a coffee beside her on the desk. His eyes looked tired, his five o'clock shadow very obvious as it was nearly morning.

Workers on the early shift started to come into the building. They nodded their heads at each other as they passed the office, some would make the usual sarcastic comments about milking the overtime, others would show a little more sympathy for them, as they both looked totally exhausted. The stress of the enquiry was visibly taking its toll on them.

Kay entered the open-plan office, her hair a little windswept, her eyes bright and alert. She looked over at Taylor's desk, something she could not help herself doing these days. The sight she saw was not one she expected; Taylor looked like shit. Her hair uncombed, she had obviously been up all night. Her eyes had dark circles beneath them, the whites of them were bloodshot and expressionless, her face painfully etched with sadness and stress. Taylor looked up slowly to see Kay looking directly at her. Her heart throbbed as their eyes met but she did not react. Her tired frame and worn out mind were unable to visually respond; her thoughts were too scrambled at the uphill struggle that lay ahead to stop this guy.

Inspector Findlay stormed in to the main office a few steps behind Kay, his stare directed at Taylor, his hand gripping that morning's Scotsman newspaper with the headline, KILLER STALKS THE CAPITAL, THIS TIME HE SUCCEEDS". The story captured the terror of the attack, the sadness at his success on his second attempt and the fraught battle that Anna Watt had braved to try to stay alive. The paper was always ahead of the game, the reporters knowing a little more than they should and were given because of some money-grabbing fool looking for a quick buck, risking their careers to expose just a little more information than initially offered and sooner than it should have been released. It would all be shared in good time, just not at the crucial investigation stage. Unfortunately, such articles gave the weird and disturbed cranks of the world the information they needed to make false claims, taking ownership of another's deviance. Findlay, although blustering with rage, still had time to look down at Kay's pert little bottom as she left the office through the other door. This was noted by Taylor who shook her head in despair that he was her boss.

The inspector strode over to Taylor's desk and stood directly above her, staring down at her oppressively, trying to intimidate; not a wise thing to do with Taylor, especially not that morning. She looked up at him with disgust etched in her face. His eyes were filled with anger, an expression of blame on his face - blame for Taylor, not himself. *What! What the fuck are you staring at,* she thought angrily. "Yes," she said in a slightly disrespectful tone due to the body language he was displaying.

"Have you seen this, this fucking piece of shit? Who the fuck in your team opened their big fucking traps? This is a piss poor outfit, filled with loose mouthed fucking arseholes that have exposed every fucking minute of our progress, or lack of it, in minute detail. You better find out who the fuck it was or else. Find out who can't keep their god damn gobs shut around here. No fucking wonder he's fifty steps ahead of us every time. Useless twats."

"That was a motivating little pep talk," Taylor seethed at Marcus as Findlay turned his back on them. "And, I can't believe it was one of us that blabbed. It was probably that fat bastard himself and he's just covering his own back trying to look innocent."

Findlay waddled back over. "How's the enquiry going anyway? You've got a hundred-odd officers on it and you've come up with fuck all. You'd better get your finger out of your ass or you won't be taking charge of this enquiry much longer, lady."

"Surely you can't blame me for this. We've followed up every fucking lead and some. There has to be a breakthrough sooner or later. He can't leave that much crap behind him and not fuck up at some point, boss."

"For your sake, he'd better." Findlay was about to march away from Taylor, when she stood up straight as a board, her eyes filled with pure rage, and spoke, her fury untethered and wild, her words sharp and to the point.

"You listen to me and listen properly. I have already worked my fingers to the bone here and I am giving this everything, every bloody minute I have. I can't sleep and I feel helplessly sick that we haven't come up with anything yet, but it's not for the lack of trying." Taylor pulled down at her blouse in a gesture of rage.

"So don't just sit there worrying about the lack of results, waiting for your piece of luck to strike. Start working this case to get some luck."

"That won't happen if you're gonna act like a fucking arsehole all the time. We're doing the best we can, which is more than I can say for you, sitting waiting for us to get you the success you want, with all due respect, that is, Inspector!"

Findlay's mouth was agape, disbelieving of what he had just faced, but he couldn't think of what to say back and his hesitation was enough for Taylor to claim victory. Findlay paused a little longer and eventually said, "Take the rest of the day off. You need it to sort your shit out. One more episode like that and you'll be back to uniform before you can say jack shit." He pointed at Marcus. "That goes for you too. You both look like shit."

Findlay stormed over to his office and slammed the door behind him, the walls shuddering as he went. Marcus looked at Taylor, his face astonished at what had just happened and what Taylor had said. Taylor looked up at him, about to speak but he cut in and said, "Well done girl. You certainly let him know how you feel and that he is a complete and utter asshole."

"He deserved it. How fucking dare he speak to me like that? That fat bastard hasn't even lifted a finger yet, lazy twat!"

"I'm going home. You'd better do the same. He's right about one thing - we've got a lot of work to do. We owe it to them."

"Sleep well and say hi to your wife for me," Taylor said kindly to Marcus.

"I will," he said, and smiled at her as she left. Taylor sat in her car and cried, her chest involuntarily moving up and down, her exhaustion spilling over into emotion, her sadness a mixture of painful thoughts of the murder and the feeling of total loneliness. She turned the key in the ignition and her phone beeped. It was a text, short and to the point: "Come to mine for dinner tonight, you look like you need a shoulder, Kay x."

Taylor took a deep breath, sighing loudly, a little comfort now within her allowing her to relax and drive to her house, a lot of what she had felt a moment ago now lifted from her weary shoulders.

Once inside Taylor took off her clothes at the door, the pile portraying what she felt. Fatigue engulfing her, she walked into the bathroom naked and stared at herself in the mirror. The face looking back at her was unfamiliar, the ageing bruises from the assault the week before still visible of the commitment to the case. She looked sad and tired. How low she felt was new to her, her usual success unapparent with this enquiry and the pressure was visibly bringing her down.

She walked through to the bedroom, slipped into bed and lay on her back motionless, her eyes open staring at the ceiling, her mind racing with the thoughts of her long night. Her hands gently stroked over her body in an attempt to comfort herself, but there was nothing to shake her negative mood. It was 9.30 am. Her eyes finally gave in to her tiredness and sleep took over, giving her mind peace at last.

Chapter 14:
The Beginning

Evening came. Taylor stood in the shower, hot water covering her body, the relief of it penetrating her soul, her mind drifting off to the evening ahead. She pulled on loose fitting jeans, a nice set of underwear and a tight fitting white t-shirt. She sprayed herself with a unisex scent which was subtle but had a sensual aroma. She pulled on a long warm black coat, affording her the warmth a winter evening required but allowing her to be under-dressed beneath.

Taylor picked up some nice red wine and a bunch of flowers and made the journey to Kay's house. Eventually she found it, the number obscured by a lively shrub which prevented it being seen from the street. The house was modest but modern, a single storey building with large windows to the front.

She rang the doorbell rang. There was no answer. She tried again, tapping her foot against the step, not allowing herself to think the worst. The door finally opened and Kay stood in the doorway, her arm raised as she leant on the door frame, her face subtly made up, her features striking and her smile a little cheeky, but warm and inviting. She looked down at Taylor, a forlorn and tormented soul, not the lady she had shared a night with not so long ago. Kay was wearing casual trousers, which fitted her neat figure, and a loosely hanging blouse that clung to her in all the right places, her nipples stiff with the bitter cold of the night. The low cut neckline revealed her perfect breasts.

Taylor glanced up at her, smiled back at last and stepped forward as she was invited in, Kay taking her coat from her and gesturing her through to the living room. Taylor was about to speak when Kay took the back of her head and kissed her on the lips, open mouthed and full desire. Their passion was overwhelming. Kay had not realised just how much she wanted Taylor. Their kisses were powerful and uncontrollable, Taylor's stomach twisting with knots of lust, her hands taking hold of Kay's hair, gently pulling her head further back allowing her tongue to delve into Kay's mouth. Kay moaned loudly and her breathing got louder. She took hold of Taylor's hand and led it towards her navel, guiding it beneath her panties and pushing it downwards wantonly. Taylor took over and her fingers now moist with Kay's pleasure entered into her. Kay's legs wobbled at the force of desire, the need to be taken over and over again. Kay was pushed against the chest of drawers and lifted up onto them. She wriggled out of her trousers, her panties now on one leg as Taylor's relentless fingers, plunged deeper and deeper. Kay gripped her neck, moaning loudly, her breath stalling as the pleasure heightened. Taylor's free hand grasped at her blouse, unclipped her bra and releasing her breasts. Her mouth now covered her nipple, sucking hard as her fingers slipped out of her and over her, then re-entered her with more vigour, repeating the motion to Kay's pleasure. Kay whimpered softly as the pulse below was released with such force her face flushed a deep red, her orgasm curling over and over, a deep gripping sensation pulling Taylor into her. Taylor maintained her thrusts, not allowing Kay to come back down from her climax, creating a new warmth, a new need; Taylor wanted to take Kay again on her terms and give her a quicker and more feverish orgasm that rocked Kay to the core. Taylor dropped to her knees between Kay's legs, taking her into her mouth, devouring her sweet pleasure, caressing every inch of her intimate flesh, her aromatic luscious scent drawing her into her. Kay gripped her shoulders so tightly Taylor jumped back a little but carried on until she eventually let go again; this time

Kay's orgasm was so intense her body went into a spasm; she was completely overwhelmed by the power of the climax she had just experienced. The embrace that followed was needy for both of them, warm kisses filled with emotion and feeling. Taylor reached out her hand and helped her down from the chest and gestured towards Kay's leg, her panties on her ankle. She smiled at her with a genuine warmth and they began to laugh together. Kay held her again and said, "You need to laugh more. Don't let all this shit with the investigation bring you down. You looked a real mess this morning."

Once they had put their clothes back on and poured some wine, they leaned back on the sofa, totally relaxed in each other's company. They put on some soft music and talked and talked and talked. Each of them enjoyed the stories the other had to tell, listening and gesturing, an affection growing as the night moved on. The pain of the last few weeks paled into insignificance as the evening went on, both of them realising just how much they liked each other.

Kay got up and headed to the kitchen. She was opening another bottle of red wine when Taylor reached round her waist and kissed her neck softly from behind, their bodies swaying a bit. Kay breathed deeply and reached up round Taylor's head and neck. They shared a deep, passionate kiss. Taylor pushed Kay gently against the fridge, their kisses powerful but sensual, once again the need for each other overwhelming. Taylor placed her hand firmly against Kay's intimacy and Kay helped her by obligingly undoing her trousers again and letting her in. "You're so wet," Taylor exclaimed.

"That's your fault for being so damn hot." Lust again took control as she entered slowly into her once more, Kay's bottom cold against the fridge door, creating an unexpected thrill. The sex this time was frantic and rushed, desire getting in the way of slow gentle loving. Sweat trickled down Taylor's cleavage as she fulfilled Kay's need more than once. They headed through to the living room and Kay landed full weight onto the sofa, one leg over the arm, her arms outstretched as Taylor followed her; over and over again Taylor pleasured her, on her front, her back - any way their bodies let them be loved, both of them wrapped up in each other's desire, both of them enjoying the pleasure that the other brought. Once spent, they lay back on the wide and comfortable sofa, arms round one another, the wine and exhaustion pushing them into a well deserved sleep where they lay.

Morning came too quickly. Taylor rubbed her neck, stiff from the night trapped under Kay's arms, her head twisted against the arm of the sofa. Kay got up and walked to the kitchen, deliberately wiggling her bottom as she left the room. She glanced over her shoulder hoping that Taylor's gaze would be upon her, and it was. A smile sneaked across her mouth. Taylor stared at her, aware of the warm sensation of fondness within herself. She rubbed a lock of her hair pretending that it was just a casual glance. Kay brought through two iced fresh oranges, a gift for Taylor's dry palate, a sign of the fevered evening before.

"I've got to go," Taylor said apologetically to Kay, "The boss said an evening off, not the week which means work, work, work, so no rest for the wicked!" She got up from the sofa, and Kay gave her a smouldering kiss on the lips which Taylor returned with equal affection, softly pulling away and making her apologies.

Taylor started the car and headed home to shower and change her clothes. As always she revved the engine more than necessary, driving a little quicker than acceptable for a police officer and offering a few choice words to those who dared get in her way. Her phone rang. It was Marcus; his voice sounded excited.

"There's been a human bone found out in a copse of trees in East Lothian. They're testing it for DNA as we speak. Someone's dog found it and was about to eat it as a treat."

"Why didn't you call earlier?"

"I'm only just in myself. The night shift has been on it."

"What size of bone was it?"

"They said it was a forearm. It still had decomposed flesh on it and other bits of bone."

"I'll be in as soon as I can, I need to get showered and changed."

"Why would that be?" Marcus said in a glib way.

"Very funny! See you soon."

Hair still wet, Taylor headed into the office. There was a frenzied buzz in the air, one of excitement at the bone being found earlier. This was the first decent lead since the enquiry began. Marcus was sitting at his desk, a picture of his wife and son taking pride of place beside the computer. Inspector Findlay furiously paced up and down in his office. He desperately wanted a result in this enquiry, something that would show him up as competent and successful, which he was not. It would also take off some of the heat as those at the top were having to keep the needy press off their backs on a daily basis.

Taylor's head spun and her double-take was apparent as Kay walked into the office not long after her. Marcus, very aware of the keen interest in Taylor's eyes, informed her that more civilian staff had been brought in for the extra enquiry, which needed to be collated and filed using the Holmes system; this ensured that every lead was followed up, logged and any other action required to be carried out was created and filed through the process, making it easier to link and recall information when necessary. Marcus smiled at Taylor, her face obviously flushed with the acknowledgement of Kay's arrival. Taylor looked at him, her eyes telling him to button it. Kay passed Taylor a glance as she sat at a desk in the far corner of the office; very subtle, but Marcus and Taylor caught what it meant.

Findlay popped his head out of the office. "You two," his head nodded toward Taylor and Marcus, "Get down to the site where the bone was found. They've got search teams out there already. Take a look at the search parameters and see if they meet what we need, and if the search needs to be widened, then do what's necessary. Who knows how far that bone has travelled."

Taylor reached for her jacket, her face a picture. "He speaks to us like we're stupid little kids, as if we weren't going to go to the scene. He states the fucking obvious all the time. That dick is trying to regain the control he lost years ago, fucking asshole."

Marcus drove up through Musselburgh just outside Edinburgh, past the race course, then out past Wallyford and onto some of the single track roads that led to the outlying farms that sat remotely on the hills.

"We're fucking lost, you!" Taylor glared at Marcus.

"Calm down there boss lady. Three more lefts and we might be close."

There was field after field of crops, fallow fields and boundary fences, sheep and cows in abundance, a farm house here and there, perfectly remote for a dumping site; remote and private and no street lighting for what might have gone down many weeks ago. The chance of being disturbed here was very unlikely. A few more turns and they saw several protected police vans parked at the side of the road, police tape marking off areas where the public could no longer wander, restricted by the powers that be in an attempt to salvage what evidence they could.

Large areas of trees and fields had been sectioned off, areas made into easily identifiable grids for plotting all of the finds ensuring nothing was missed. Lines were taped at the outer edge of areas that had already been searched and the exact site of every item found plotted, easily identifying and describing the layout of the scene for those who did not have the luxury of attending at the site but could only view photographs taken.

Taylor introduced herself to the police search advisor, Sergeant Brown, and asked how things were going. He replied, "The area here is so vast it will take days to find a deposition site, that is if he even dumped the body round here. There are also large areas of brambles and thick undergrowth just over there, which will slow things down even more."

"Serg, Serg, come and see this!"

The cop that came rumbling over was six foot four, with a muscular build and extremely sweaty. They'd been searching there for nearly four hours, only stopping for a swig of water here and there. The cops in the specialist support unit tended to be large in build as search was only half of what they were required to do. They were also responsible for drug raids, crashing doors, crowd control and high profile arrests, which required a more robust presence. Each and every one of them hoped that they would be going through the door of this killer sometime soon; it was insulting to them that such a sadistic arsehole was still walking about free, terrifying everyone in the city. "What have you got, Dan? Better be something good!"

"Don't think you'll be too disappointed, boss. We've all withdrawn using a single track for exiting, trying not to trample any more than we might have already. It's this way, just over the brow of that hill. About what you'd expect really if he had to carry her from the road down there."

"What? You can tell it's female?"

"I'd say so but she certainly ain't looking too pretty anymore," he quipped with typical cop humour.

Taylor marched through the undergrowth, her nice leather boots taking the brunt of the undergrowth. Marcus held up the bottom of his suit. The search team smirked as they arrived, enjoying the detectives getting their nice clothes dirty for once, usually so clean cut and thinking they were above everyone else. The search officer pointed the way and said, "Follow your nose, boss. You'll find her."

"Well done you lot. About time you earned your wages for once," he said sarcastically. Single file, they made their way to the disturbed earth, the smell escaping from it was a putrid stench that was unmistakeably that of a corpse. Taylor retched a little, the red wine from the night before not helping her slightly weakened stomach. One of the search cops leaned over to his mate and commented, "What a lightweight. You'd think they would be able to handle a smelly body, with all the shit that they supposedly deal with."

Taylor turned and glared at the group of men standing at the edge of the taped outer cordon, trying to work out which one had just commented. All of them stood there with fixed grins on their faces, silent mirth at the princess that stood before them, the rivalry very apparent between the different sections within the police.

Taylor leaned forward and openly boaked at what she saw. There was a skull exposed, with long blonde hair showing. Flesh was missing where predators had tried to rip it away from the bone. The lip were gone and teeth protruded. There were maggots in abundance and patches with no flesh at all. There was also a stump visible where her arm had been pulled from the earth and detached at the elbow, probably twisted off by a hungry fox. Taylor turned to Marcus. "Poor cow, fucking animal just dumped her like a piece of trash, and the lazy bastard spent very little time trying to hide her. He's not frightened of what he's done, that's for sure. He's almost showing her off."

Marcus got on the phone to get the Scenes Of Crime Unit down to put up their tents and comb the area for every little piece of forensic evidence that may have been left at the dump site. The search teams were redeployed to the outer peripheries of the area to carry out further searches until the body was examined, extracted and all of the evidence photographed and lifted.

Chapter 15: Connection

The corpse was remarkably well preserved due to the peat like earth it had been found in. This appeared to have created a natural refrigerator and had kept certain elements viable for examination and only once exposed did the infestation of maggots begin. Blood was extracted from remaining veins and urine from the bladder. Marcus grimaced as the needle pierced the deflated eyeball to take what vitreous fluid remained; he started to rub his own eyes as if the needle had gone into one of his. Taylor looked at him, her own stomach queasy with the sight before her. The blade making the Y-incision on the corpse's chest cut cleanly through the flesh. The crunch of the rib spreaders sent shivers to their bones, the stench of the exposed inner organs enough to make anyone feel sick. The pathologist took out all of the internal organs that were still intact in turn, cutting, slicing, weighing and examining them for any abnormalities; some of them were more decomposed than others. Then to the genitalia, her vagina and rectum were very much intact with very little decomposition. He swabbed them for signs of sexual violation, although the tears on the anus and visible trauma to the vagina left little doubt that she had been brutally tormented. Some were recent and others historical. Portions of the outer flesh on her back showed quite clearly that there were bits of skin torn away with tooth imprints apparent.

Taylor pointed to them and said, "DNA, will it still be viable? He must have had his mouth there."

The pathologist looked up at her and said, "I would say so. DNA is very durable and whoever did this didn't try to cover up anything. The internal swabs show sexual activity to the naked eye, before we've even tested them. We'll rush through the results and have a profile for you within a day or two. I take it the boss will make this a hurry up job, with the highest of high signatures, to give this a priority ride through the system, because we are really backed up at the moment."

"You guessed it. The Chief Constable is on this one and his head will be on the block for results. This is the biggest thing to hit Edinburgh for years and although we could almost recreate this guy with all we've collected on him, we're not doing too well on the catching him front."

Hours later, they returned to the office where they found confirmation of the identity of the corpse; it was Layla Petrovsky, the missing prostitute. "Fuck me that was fast, even for our lot. Now we just have to see who the culprit was, not that we have any doubt who it's going to be."

"She was obviously his first and he enjoyed it, enough to take it up as a career."

Kay walked out of Findlay's office; her skin almost visibly crawling from his unwanted attention. Taylor's face turned red and it was not with desire. An inner rage rumbled inside her. She stood up and was about to make her way across the room when Marcus took her wrist. "Don't! She's a big girl and she can handle him. Anyway what's it to do with you anyway, lady? Just remember this is a disciplined organisation and even though he is a fat prick and an overt sleazeball, he can still put the boot in and screw with your career, so let her fight her own battles. And if you're with her, that just gives him all the ammunition he needs to put you in a box out in the wilderness. And, have you forgotten that this is still very much a boys' club and you're halving their odds of getting laid?"

Kay looked over at Taylor, aware of the reaction she had stirred. She smiled at her and made a gesture of repulsion in the direction of Findlay's office to let Taylor know things were alright. She looked tired, everyone did. Taylor smiled back, so did Marcus and Taylor slapped his shoulder as she saw Kay turn away quickly, obviously feeling exposed at someone else sharing their glances. Investigations like this always took a lot out of everyone. They barely saw their homes and families as the demands placed on them were pretty heavy going but the pay was good, not that there was ever any time to spend it.

Findlay came out of his office, coffee stains on his tie and shirt. "Fucking slob," Taylor exclaimed. Marcus was on the phone to his wife making excuses for his inability to return home any time soon.

"Hey, I need to make up a press release for the boss," Findlay barked. "You two can get on with that just now and try and not cause too much fear and alarm in the city. Tone it down as much as you can!"

The minute he was gone Taylor slammed her hands down on the desk, pens and paper flying everywhere. "That lazy fat glory grabbing fucker. Why can't he do his own fucking work? Why the fuck should we have to do it? We've worked our fucking asses off for days and he's just climbed on the band wagon and taken all the bloody credit."

Findlay turned round and said, "Oh and good work with the follow up on the missing persons. That's what's got us this far. Keep going on that line of enquiry. I think there may be more so once you've finished the press release you can carry on with that."

Marcus acknowledged Findlay before he returned to the office but Taylor couldn't even look up at the Inspector for his lack of respect for her position and her rank. Although still a lowly Detective Sergeant, he should give her the courtesy she deserved. She was a very thorough worker and usually got great results.

Taylor headed to the ladies' toilet, unaware that Kay was already there getting ready to head home. She got to the mirrored area and stared at her reflection. She dropped her head and yelled out, not concealing her rage at all, the frustration making her furious. She heard footsteps behind her and felt a little embarrassed at her open outburst until she felt an arm closing round her waist. Taylor was about to turn and push whoever it was away when she felt a warm mouth close round her ear. She looked up in the mirror to see Kay smiling back at her.

"Don't let that sleazy creep get to you, he does it to every living, breathing female. I'm nothing special, but you are." She leant forward and placed a tender kiss on Taylor's soft lips. Taylor looked at her, anger turning quickly to warmth. She was about to kiss her back when the door opened and two PCs came in chattering. They dumped their belt kits on the floor as they headed to the cubicles, barely glancing up at the two women at the mirrors, totally unaware of what was going on as they passed by muttered an acknowledgement, "Serg."

Kay squeezed her hand and said, "I'm off home. Call if you want to or need to. Take care and don't let him make you work too long." They sneaked a silent but passionate kiss and Kay walked confidently to the door and glanced back, smiling as she left. Taylor rested her bottom on the shelf where the sinks were set and leant there, thinking. Her phone beeped. It was a message from Marcus: "It's been confirmed. His DNA is all over her. How many more do you think he's killed?"

"The bastard; the fucking hideous, dirty bastard." Taylor's head shook with disgust.

Chapter 16: Photo Fit

Susan winced as she attempted to walk with her sticks. Andrew gently held onto her arm as she looked like she was about to fall to the side but she steadied herself and thanked Andy anyway. He reassured her and told her how well she was doing and that her progress was better than expected. She made her way to a chair in the corner and plonked herself down, unable to support her own weight like she used to. Tears welled in her eyes, her exasperation showing as well as the fear that she wouldn't be able to live a normal life ever again. Her youth and her physical ability had been stolen from her in one fateful evening, her fear of tomorrow marring every single day since then and his face constantly intruding on every peaceful moment.

The physiotherapy room was well kitted out and all the equipment was state of the art. Numerous physiotherapists were assigned there. They were specially trained to deal with every physical disability imaginable and the various methods of rehabilitation utilised to get injured joints and muscles back in working order again. Andrew was one of the hospital's most experienced and enthusiastic physios, who still treated every patient as a personal challenge. He still genuinely cared; his work was not just a job to him. He felt very strongly for Susan. She inspired him with her positivity and fighting spirit after what had happened to her.

Susan was still in hospital - her recovery was slow as her injuries required intense medical intervention and specialist help - but she was on track to make a recovery that would allow her to live a semi normal life. That didn't bother Susan. She was just terrified in case he revisited her; she was apprehensive about going home and felt safer in hospital because there were people all around her, which gave her comfort and reassurance. But was she really safe?

Susan was sitting in her four-bedded ward, although she only had one room mate - an elderly woman, Mary, who was admitted after a fall. Mary had a broken hip and ankle but was very kind and still very much with it, regularly chatting with Susan about their beloved cats, Baxter and Hobbes; both were being looked after by relatives until their faithful owners recovered. Susan leant back to rest for a moment, relaxing as she listened to the birds that sang just outside their window. Quickly, she drifted off to sleep, a place where she used to find solace, warmth and relaxation. Now her dreams were invaded with his face, his dark eyes and sinister voice that coldly taunted her. She could smell him. She feared him and every injury that he had inflicted upon her seemed to open up and tingle with pain as he crept into her thoughts, a constant reoccurring torture. She started to toss and turn, each move more animated than the other. Sweat covered her body, her nightdress stuck to her and she let out a loud scream as the blade plunged deep into her once again, her scars aching as if the assault was still happening to her for real, all over again. Two nurses came rushing in. Emily was a third year student and Ann the sister on the ward; each took a side and tried to soothe her. Susan's arms were flailing, trying to fight off her invisible attacker. Emily took her arm and spoke gently into her ear, trying to comfort her and bring her out of her nightmare. Ann took a tighter grip of her other hand as she had been around long enough to know how much damage one of those loose arms could cause and it certainly wouldn't be the first black eye she'd had from a patient. Susan was still obviously distressed, her breathing heavy and erratic as her eyes opened, wide and petrified like an animal about to be slain.

"You're okay Susan. It's just a dream, it's just a dream. You're safe. We're here; we won't let anything happen to you, I promise!" Emily said as she comforted Susan with her warm embrace.

Ann released her grip and also spoke softly to her. "Same nightmare dear? We'll have to try and do something about that you know - hypnosis or something. We're going to stop him ruining your life once and for all!"

Susan turned her head slowly towards Ann, a pitiful smile appearing as she squeezed her hand in response to the strong words. "I won't ever be safe if he is still alive, will I? I'm the biggest mistake he's ever made and his biggest threat. I saw him, I fucking saw him!" she yelled at the top of her voice. "He knows that, and I can feel his hatred running right through me every day. I am the only one that can identify him so what does that make me, eh? Yes, you're right, a sitting duck. The police can't be with me 24/7 can they, and they aren't making much headway in catching him at the moment!"

Ann shook her head in sympathy and acknowledgement. Susan was right on every count and to lie to her now would be condescending, which Ann was not prepared to be.

Emily squeezed her shoulder and gave one of her infectious cheeky grins. She said, "As long as we're here, you know he'll have a fight on his hands. There's more of us than him and women are full of surprises as we well know. We can also fight dirty."

"You're a survivor, believe it. You lived for a reason, and there are thousands of people out there wishing you well and commenting on your bravery," Ann stated as she squeezed the life out of a pillow, obviously simulating what she would do to Susan's attacker if she got the chance. Ann looked over to the other side of the room. Mary's face was a picture. She had rung the emergency alarm and had given a feeble shout for someone to help but Susan's screams had alerted the staff a little quicker.

Ann asked if Mary was okay. She nodded and looked sad as she said, "I wish I could help her more. I can't even get out of bed to comfort her, I'm so sorry."

"Don't be," Ann said. "You just being here to listen and talk to is good for her and she likes you. Can I get you anything?"

"A gun!" Mary replied with a wry smile.

Susan heard this and she too agreed. They all had a laugh, and tried to think of better things, their humour a tonic for Susan.

Just then there was a chap at the door. Susan, Mary and the two nurses looked up to see DS Nicks poking her head round the door, quickly followed by DC Black and another woman with a sketch pad. "I hope we're not intruding and that you got the message I left saying we were coming today." Both detectives could see that they had come at a less than favourable time and that Susan looked a little worse for wear.

"Yes, I got the message," she sighed, "but I don't know how much help I can be. I'm trying my best to put him out of my mind and, as you can see from the state of me, I'm failing miserably!"

Ann smiled at Susan and led Taylor out of the room. Taylor asked what had happened, and the sister explained about the recurring nightmares and the stress Susan was still under, both with her physical recovery and mentally. Taylor gave a sincerely sympathetic look and said, "She's our best hope though. We have DNA coming out of our ears but he's not on any of our databases, and she can identify him; it's crucial that we do this. We need to stop him before he does it again!"

Ann looked down and said, "I know, that's why she's so worried but it's so hard for her just now. He's still haunting her, terrorising her from within, and she says she can feel his hatred. Pretty spooky, huh?"

Taylor went back to the ward. Susan was sitting up speaking to Marcus and the artist that was going to compile an E-fit for the next episode of Crimewatch, to be aired within the week. Taylor pulled over a chair, the feet scraping on the floor with a dull screech. Everyone looked up at her with painful grimaces on their faces. Taylor's face went a little red and she politely apologised to them for her interruption. She introduced herself to Susan and made sure a full explanation was given to her about what was about to happen and how the sketches would be utilised. Taylor's eyes met with Susan's; Susan's were pleading for help and reassurance and Taylor's longing to solve the case, to stop this monster killing another innocent woman. From that meeting of minds there was a silent trust created. Susan could tell Taylor was a strong woman, unafraid and confident and 100% committed to catching him and putting him behind bars. She trusted Taylor to do her job.

Susan was trembling simply from the thought of describing the man who had ruined her life completely. Marcus calmly reassured her, his words kind and strong, his eyes honest and protective. Susan said softly, "I don't know where to start. I don't want to remember him, it makes him too real." The sketcher told her to take her time and start with the feature uppermost in her mind. Instantly she remembered his eyes, his piercing evil eyes, and she started to visibly shake.

"Piercing bright blue, the whites showing the full way round, dark thick eyebrows, straight nose, unclean teeth, stubble with a thick jaw line and foul breath and a creepy countenance." The sketcher joked that the breath would be a little difficult to draw and Susan smiled too, though the pain she was obviously in was uncomfortable to watch; terror churned inside her as the picture began to form on the paper. She carried on. "He was tall, over six foot two, and he had huge powerful hands and his arms were strong and muscular, especially his forearms. His body didn't match his arms though. His stomach was not taut and a lot more slovenly. He had a paunch and it showed over his trousers."

"Sorry, Susan, just keep to his face for the sketch. We'll get to the rest of him later. What about his hair?"

"Sorry, dark shortish hair, dishevelled, unkempt and unwashed. It smelt foul, just like the rest of him!"

Susan went on to describe every minute detail. She could remember everything. It was all flooding back to her. She was starting to speak more quickly and getting stressed. It was Marcus who noticed that she was almost slipping back to the night she was attacked. He didn't want her to feel that way. He put his hand on her shoulder and said to her, "Stop! Don't say anything else just now. Take a rest, breathe. Yup that's right, just breathe, nice and slow."

She had jumped back at his touch, freeing her from her trance-like stupor. The sketcher looked up and saw that the perfect details she was drawing were taking their toll physically on the poor woman. The sketcher had been so focused on the drawing that she had barely looked. Susan was now crying and her shoulders were shaking, moving up and down uncontrollably. Taylor gestured to the sketch artist to leave the room to let Marcus do what he was good at, genuine comfort.

Susan looked up and saw the warm and kind side that a man could have, the exact opposite of what she had just finished describing.

"I wish you could stick around here forever. I just feel frightened and alone all the time. You make me feel safe which I haven't felt for so long."

Marcus smiled at her, a warm sincere smile. Nothing false about him, just genuine emotion, a truly kind and honest man, strong and loyal. He struggled to answer her desperate request without hurting her feelings or making her even more insecure about the way she felt already.

He held her hand and looked at her straight in the eyes and said, "We promise to do everything in our power to catch this guy. It's been sanctioned that you can have a cop here 24/7, which is practically unheard of within this penny pinching organisation, and Taylor and I won't stop hunting your attacker until we have him behind bars or someone kills him."

Susan smiled a little at the thought of his death, and said, "That would be nice. Then I could maybe sleep a little better."

Marcus smiled too. He said, "There are rules though. Let's not go breaking too many of them or we'll all end up behind bars."

Two cups of tea and a chocolate biscuit later, they resumed their drawing. Susan was now much calmer and her spirits seemed a lot better; she appeared more confident now, after spending some time with Taylor and Marcus. They explained all that they could and what they were allowed to divulge. It gave her a boost, knowing how much physical resources were going in to catching him and to protecting her. Taylor explained that once they had the drawing, and if it was anything like a true likeness, it would be shown on the news and on the next edition of Crimewatch, both of these programmes reaching out to a multitude of people and affording those who might know something a chance to come forward in total secrecy; every single lead would be followed up and referenced, with any other links creating even more follow up enquiries after that.

Half an hour later, Andrew the physiotherapist was passing and popped his head in. "I hope you're remembering our appointment later today, young lady?" Susan looked up and smiled, her face flushed a little as Andrew looked straight at her.

"Did he see. Could he have been that perceptive?" Susan thought to herself. Marcus smiled at her. He had also spotted it, the slight flush in her face and the affection in her eyes towards the man that stood smiling in the doorway.

She spoke quietly back to Andrew, trying to play it cool. "Yes, I'll be there. 7.30 pm, was it?"

"Don't be late, we've got lots to get through, and bring your positive head." He turned and left with a noticeable smile on his face too and an obvious spring in his step.

The sketcher added a final piece of shading round the eyes and looked up at Susan. "Are you ready for this?"

Susan took a deep breath, and said, "Yes, it's now or never."

Marcus took her hand as he could see that she was uncomfortable with having to look into the eyes of the monster once again. Susan's eyes were wide and focused. She held her breath as the pad turned slowly round towards her. She gasped at the unmistakable face before her. The eyes were an exact copy of those of the killer; his mouth, his stare all captured almost identically, all done by the skill of the woman holding the pencil and pad.

"That's him, that's fucking him! It feels like he's here in the room, I can't look at it any more. Please take it away. It's a perfect likeness to him. It's hideously similar and I don't want to look at him, if you don't mind, sorry. Please take it away and do what you have to do, I can't look at him anymore."

"No problem, we've got what we need and we'll keep in touch with any further developments," Taylor said respectfully. The police and the sketch artist rose to their feet. They said their goodbyes and Marcus deliberately delayed just long enough to give Susan another reassuring smile before they went out of sight.

Mary, who had been sitting quietly in the corner, said kindly and slightly mischievously to Susan, "He's a fine looking young man, isn't he?" A wry smile covered her old and weathered face, warmth and kindness in her eyes.

Susan smiled back at her and told her, "Don't be so naughty, Mary. He's married and he's just nice, nothing more than that, and anyway, he made me feel better. He made me think they may actually catch him and I trust him."

"No, not him, the handsome physiotherapist, I saw the way he looked at you and you him." Susan just smiled, gently twisted her hair and shook her head, breathing out heavily.

Marcus turned to Taylor in the car park, as they waved to the artist as she sped away in her car.

"This picture's going to nail him you know! Because, if it's as good as she said it is, then someone has to know where he is?"

"Let's hope so. Hungry?" Taylor smiled, licking her lips.

"Starving!" he replied, "I don't know why I ever ask you. You're a gannet."

They arrived back at the station, both guarding their pizzas from the prying eyes of those who were still on duty. Findlay waddled towards his office; Marcus looked up at Taylor, mirth in his eyes as he dived to shield his pizza completely from his overweight boss, hinting that he would be first to steal some to feed his greedy appetite. She laughed heartily too, a full on belly laugh, as she knew the greedy capabilities of fat Findlay and his over indulgence with food. Pizzas intact, they ate happily, more so because they knew Findlay's belly would be rumbling with the mouth-watering aroma. The E-fit picture was safely in their folder. They'd show it to Findlay later, once every trace of the pizza was gone. They didn't want any distractions, not with something so vitally important.

True enough, on showing Findlay the sketch, his face did actually crack a smile. They could almost see him thinking ahead to the solving of the case and all of the accolades that would wrongly come his way.

"Get this scanned immediately and run it by the Super. Then get it off to the press office with the instructions for disclosure. Pronto! Come on then! What are you both waiting for? Chop, chop!" he said in his usual condescending manner.

Taylor turned and left, barely acknowledging the rotund piggy eyed, Inspector. "Money wasted, that is. He's such a useless prick. What do you think?" Marcus nodded in agreement and followed her through to the scanner, their short lived humour now totally subdued.

At that moment Kay came through the double doors and into the corridor. Taylor's eyes met hers and both made polite greetings, although Taylor's face turned slightly pink with hidden affection. There was an intensity in her eyes that her perceptive partner noticed straight away. Kay continued walking till she came to the next door. She turned her head and gave a backward glance that had unmistakeable affection in it.

Taylor looked at Marcus. She said, "Shut it you!" and smiled.

"You are, aren't you, you lucky mare? You are one lucky lady. You're like the cat that got the cream."

Taylor looked at him, her eyes confirming his suspicion. "She is hot, isn't she? And you're right, but it's not for others' ears."

"How long? When? How? I thought she was straight."

"So did I. It was after the last night out. She kissed me! And of course, being me, obviously I couldn't resist." A smile covered her whole face, a bit like a Cheshire cat. Marcus looked at her. This time he saw true affection in Taylor's eyes, not the look he usually saw from the predatory womaniser.

"You really like her don't you?"

"Yes, I do and it freaks me out a little because that makes me vulnerable. She can hurt me and distracts me every time is see her."

"No wonder," Marcus agreed, obviously very aware of just how attractive Kay was.

"Come on! We've got work to do. We can talk about things if you let me buy you a drink later."

"You're on but I'll have to phone my wife to let her know."

"Hey, you never know. I might have to start phoning home and explaining myself too one day."

Marcus rolled his eyes at her and went to his desk. "That'll be the day!"

Chapter 17:
Visiting Hours

John sat at home staring at the drum in the kitchen, the portable telly chatting away to itself in the corner. The news was on and his escapades might feature. His head tilted as he listened. Blah, blah, blah, the reporter went on and on about Afghanistan. Eventually, the third item of news was about the general investigation in to the two murders in the city and the progress being made, *or not,* he thought. The mundane report ended with a headline: POSITIVE NEW LEAD. The news reader stated that it could change the direction of the whole enquiry, which could only speed up their progress, although details could not be revealed at this time.

John immediately stood up and punched the wall three times in quick succession. The plaster buckled beneath the force. "FUCKING BITCH," he shouted. He went to the bathroom and took a quick shower, shaved and put on an old set of blue overalls and headed out using a back route to the hospital. He was careful to park his car, a good distance from where it could be picked up on any of the CCTV cameras.

He had a tool bag with him and wore a plastic badge with maintenance operator embossed on it. He went to the rear of the hospital to the staff smoking area, lit a cigarette and waited patiently until someone else came to join him. He didn't have to wait that long. A nurse came out, shook her lighter and spoke to him, "God I need this one, what a day it's been."

He didn't answer; he just stared right at her coldly. She looked up at him; he just kept staring at her. Her blood ran cold as she looked back into the eyes of a mad man. A feeling of nausea rose up in her instantly as she recognised the eyes, eyes that she had seen less than two hours before on a piece of paper shown to staff prior to them leaving. John had not intended to start the night with such pleasure but he had clocked the fact her demeanour had changed and she had become uncomfortable in his presence. The first blow came down on Ann's temple with such power it knocked her to the ground, smashing two teeth as her face hit the concrete with the force of a sledge hammer. The second blow came from his boot, which crashed down onto the back of her head, forcing her face into the ground once again. She lay there, still. He took her entry key and, heaving her body unceremoniously onto his shoulders, opened up one of the industrial bins and threw her in. Her lifeless body lay discarded along with the rubbish. He moved some bin bags on top of her to cover her up and slammed it shut, concealing her inside. He could not hide his pleasure as he entered the ground floor of the hospital, a smirk etched on his evil face.

He walked through the corridors with confidence, a cap on his head, which matched the colour of the overall he was wearing. He did not look out of place at all. He looked around in each corridor checking for cameras and selected the routes with none, or with a little careful evasion required if there was no other option. He could pass without his face being caught fully as the brow of his cap covered a good portion of his face from the cameras above. Not one person checked him out or even gave him the time of day. *Ignorant bastards,* he thought to himself, *serves them right for being above it all.*

Emily looked at her watch. Susan was at the physio and Ann was really milking her time for her ciggy break tonight, although there was never any issue with Ann's time keeping or work rate. They had a really good working relationship and Ann could have stopped to talk to someone as she was a real salt of the earth and loved a blether.

He walked through the corridors, painstakingly checking the names on every ward. He tried floor after floor but with no joy, and he certainly wasn't going to ask anyone; he wasn't that stupid. Eventually he walked past a small room, and there it was: Susan's name, alongside Mary's. No cops and no nurses, just an old dear sleeping in the corner. He went into the room; he was quiet, not wanting to disturb the woman in the corner. He desperately wanted Susan to know that he hasn't finished with her yet. He took out his knife and sliced into her pillow. He cut his hand deliberately, letting his blood drip onto it, enough not to be missed. Mary's eyes opened in the corner and she slowly focused on the large man standing over at Susan's bed, but she quickly closed them again enough to pretend she was still asleep as he seemed to sense her gaze and looked up towards her. Her inner senses alarmed her, a prickling sensation of fear prevented her from breathing normally and she was very conscious he might notice this. He turned again and stared straight at her for longer this time. He wondered if the old woman had croaked it as she was ashen grey and appeared not to be breathing. The gap between her lashes allowed her to see him move in her direction, and a warm flow of urine escaped involuntarily from her, terror now etched clearly on her face. Her sharp intake of breath was loud and it rasped. She tried to scream as his huge hand engulfed her neck and gripped her round the throat. It only took seconds for her to pass out, which was enough for him to make good his escape without detection. He had no desire to kill her. She was ill enough already and did not pose him any real threat; he hoped that there was more pleasure to be gained elsewhere, and he knew she would enhance Susan's fear when she recollected for her just who had been there. As he made his way through the hospital, he wondered where Susan could be. He looked at the many signs pointing out the various specialist areas and stopped at the sign pointing to the gym and physiotherapy department. His heart began to beat faster. The excitement of maybe seeing her again made his mouth salivate with anticipation; the taste of her, her scent and her fear, firmly etched on his mind. He made his way there, his stride long and full of purpose.

He turned the corner and came to an immediate halt; a tall policeman stood at the end of the corridor, blocking the doorway to the gym. The policeman looked up and saw the tall man at the end of the corridor. He had noticed how quickly the man had stopped. His suspicious mind and the importance of the person he was there to protect made him move towards the man. Their eyes met; John's were full of hate. The police officer got onto his radio straight away, realising something was not quite right. He kept watch and the man moved quickly out of sight. The cop called Andrew immediately and instructed him to lock the gym. The officer was torn with the decision to stay put or pursue the man, as he was certain he was there for something sinister and, *god knows*, he thought, *it might be the man we're looking for.* He was assigned to protect Susan and if he left her, he could not be sure the man wouldn't do a U-turn and come straight back to the unguarded room.

Susan's mouth went dry instantly, her stomach twisted into a tight knot. Andrew had left her holding onto the bar as he made his way instantly to the door, slamming it shut, locking it and putting on the deadbolts. His heart was pounding too, right through his chest, as he knew what this meant: he was here! He went back to Susan and took hold of her hand and arm carefully but with a firm protective grip and gently assisted her over to the storage cupboard, scooping up a chair as he went, sweat beads now clearly visible on his head.

She looked up at him, tears streaming down her face. "It's him, isn't it?" she said. Her hands were shaking as she buried her face in them.

He took hold of her shoulders, lifted her face and said to her in a calm and reassuring voice, "You're safe here, he can't get in. It might be something else, who knows? This is just a precaution. I won't let anything happen to you."

He reached over for a metal weights bar as he spoke. "Just another wee precaution eh! Better safe than sorry. This bar could stop an ox."

Susan looked at him, fully aware that he knew what was going on and he was trying to protect her from what was outside the door.

The cop ran to where the man had stood, and up the corridor to the stairs leading to the main building, his decision made that he had to pursue him. This might be their only chance. He was slower because of all of the gear that police have to wear; the vest alone, the cheapest available, was heavy and guaranteed to let suspects get a head start. The cop chose to head in the direction of the exit as that was what he would have done if he was being pursued. As he ran, doctors and nurses stopped and stared at the police officer running past; only one pointed out the way in which the man had gone, the rest just stood there watching as if it wasn't real and just an action scene on the television.

Outside the door, John ran over to a small fence, leapt over it effortlessly and into the trees. The cop wasn't that far behind him. *Quite a fit guy,* John thought to himself.

The cop stopped in the doorway. "Alpha November 81 to control."

"Go ahead," the controller replied.

"He's made his way into the wasteland to the rear of the Royal Infirmary. We'll need dog sets to attend and the firearms officers here too ASAP. He's probably armed and most definitely dangerous. He looks really strong."

Once outside, the cop just stood there and stared into the trees; all he could see was darkness. He squinted his eyes to try and focus.

"Fuck, fuck!" he moaned aloud. Then he heard it. A soft groan came from the corner near the exit, over beside the industrial bins.

The hair on the back of his neck bristled. He had to give himself a shake to control the blood rushing through him. He wasn't easily spooked but he felt like he was being watched and there was something close to him, something very much alive. At that moment his radio crackled loudly and startling the life right out of him.

"Shit! I wished they wouldn't do that."

"Fire arms off at the front entrance, where do you want us?" came boldly over the radio.

"Rear exit on the south side, over."

"Help me," a female voice whispered. The cop spun round, his mouth now totally dry, all of his saliva gone. His heart raced as he looked slowly round. He turned to where the bins stood and tentatively walked forward, calling towards them, every nerve in his body tingling as the adrenaline in his system went out of control.

"Is there anyone there?" he said quietly, almost afraid to be heard; he could not believe how spooked he was. *Fuck sake, pull yourself together man,* he thought to himself. Just at that moment he heard a loud crack not too far away from him, in the woods. He turned back and stared straight towards the noise and saw a dark shadow move off at pace further into the trees, northwards.

"He's been fucking watching me, the fucking warped creep," he muttered to himself.

"Help me! Please, please help," the voice came again, slightly louder this time.

He was caught in the middle of a critical choice he did not want to make: Pursue the devil's offspring? Or see what was calling out to him? He was a little unsure of either option. He looked into the woods, gave a loud sigh and turned to the big bins. Tentatively he opened them up one by one to see what was there, unnerved at how desolate it was at the back of the hospital. The firearms boys had arrived and he pointed to the woods, telling them the suspect hadn't left the vicinity much more than a minute ago.

The cop opened the last bin closest to the hospital and looked down into it. His heart skipped a beat. Initially, he couldn't see anything but when he moved some bags his eyes could not believe what they were seeing - a woman's face buried in trash, soaked with blood, eyes staring pleadingly up at him to help. All he could see was bright, blue eyes buried in a sea of red, reminding him of the film Carrie, when pig's blood was poured over her at the end. The woman was wearing a nurse's uniform, she was clearly in a bad way and he thrust himself over the ledge and climbed down to be beside her while calling for an ambulance over his radio. Ann gripped onto his vest with her quivering hand, making sure he didn't leave her, her eyes silently pleading for help, her face disfigured by John's brutal assault.

"What happened to you? Who did this?" Not really thinking, not putting two and two together, the cop failed to connect that the man he was pursuing was responsible.

Chapter 18: Pursuit

Taylor couldn't believe what she was hearing on the radio. "The arrogance of the man, we could've still been there. It's not been that long since we left. We'll have him though. He's bound to have been caught on camera at some point, and the dogs should have a good chance. Come on Marcus, we're leaving. He might still be in the area!"

Four firearms officers sprinted into the woods, weighed down by all of their kit - their side arm, two less lethal options and their main weapon, ballistic vest, helmet and other standard issue wear. They were fit officers, one of the few specialists that were still fitness tested in the force. They were red status, which meant they were fully armed, and had authorisation to take lethal action if required, as well as the right to self-authorise if the situation warranted it.

John was breathing hard and regretted staying to watch his pursuer for that long, although he knew he had the edge, a head start and the upper hand. He had planned his escape and didn't have too far to go to get to his car.

"STAY WHERE YOU ARE. DON'T MOVE OR I'LL SHOOT," was shouted loudly through the night.

"No fucking way have they caught up with me already, I watched them get here and I saw that both sets were still behind me."

Constable Lomond was bluffing, unaware of the knowledge that the suspect had. The young officer remained crouched down, 20 metres away from John, not wanting to give away his position, unaware of how sinister the suspect was. It was very dark in the trees, a slight breeze making the leaves rustle, sending a chill down his spine, as if warning him of the danger he was in. He shook off the sensation, as everyone in life is guilty of doing, ignoring his subtle senses. He repeated the order, louder this time, making his voice sound more authoritarian. He now wished that he and his partner had not chosen to split up as they entered the woods. He was unsure whether to use his radio at this time, in fear of the suspect hearing thus giving his position away, and hoped that his voice could be heard by the others and they'd come to assist him. Constable Lomond's mouth went dry as he looked into the trees where John had been standing. The branches swayed and the shadows deceived but he was no longer there. He had vanished in an instant; the officer had only dropped his eyes for a second.

"Fuck me! Where's that bastard gone? Alpha Mike 23 to control. I'm at the west entrance to the wooded area, about 200 metres from the back entrance and-"

Constable Lomond felt his hair stand on end, just before a dull thud sounded out as John struck him on the back of the head with substantial force, using a thick piece of wood. Constable Lomond dropped like a stone, falling face first onto the ground. John leaned over him to check if he was out cold; the officer didn't move. His radio crackled.

"Alpha Mike 23." This was repeated several times, PC Lomond's colleagues were seeking confirmation of his position. John smiled to himself. He thought about taking the radio to monitor their progress but remembered that the software had been updated. They all had GPS these days and they could just follow him right on home to his house.

His smile came to an abrupt halt when he heard a dog barking from the hospital car park; the police dogs had arrived and they were pretty swift at closing down the ground, unless the handler was a slouch. John turned on his heels and ran as fast as he could in the direction of his car, which was safely parked in a residential street nearby. This time he would be more careful not to lumber into any more enthusiastic young cops. He crashed through the undergrowth, his heart racing. He was starting to worry that the plods might actually catch him this time. He got to the outer wall and climbed up to look over. Several cop cars were arriving and going to the main entrance 100 metres down the road. He knew it was only a matter of time before they fanned out and surrounded the area completely. Heaving his body up onto the wall he took his chance and sprinted over the road into a neighbouring garden, which offered bushes and shrubbery to secrete him. He pulled his feet through the bush just as another siren sounded, the vehicle racing past where he had crossed a moment before. "Close, too fucking close," he rasped, as he pulled himself onto his feet and casually walked further away.

Taylor and Marcus pulled into the hospital grounds in time to hear Constable Lomond's voice on the radio. He sounded like shit. He gave his position as best he could and stated that he had seen the suspect prior to being assaulted, but was unclear exactly where he had made off to as he had been struck on the head.

"He obviously didn't come here on foot, unless he lives around here. Where would you have parked your car?" Taylor said to Marcus.

"Where it won't be noticed. Somewhere with no CCTV and in a decent residential area."

"Name one and we'll start there," Taylor exclaimed.

Marcus slammed their car into reverse and sped to the Craigour area, the nearest scheme. They drove from street to street hunting for his car. There wasn't much traffic around and the evening streets were quiet and almost pedestrian free. Taylor focused on every lane and open garden, hoping for a glimpse of something, knowing the odds were in the suspect's favour as he could hear them coming.

John stood completely still as he watched their car go by; he knew straight away that they were undercover cops.

"Well done," he said to himself. "Good forward thinking but I can see you and you can't see me.'"Get the fuck out of ma garden ya fucking arsehole!" came bellowing out from the window, one floor above him, proving that there were a few rougher people living there amongst the good ones.

"Keep your fucking hair on mate, I've lost my fucking dug!" he replied without hesitation.

"My fucking arse, you're hiding from the feds. I've seen them. They're all over the place and I'll call them right now if you don't get the fuck out of my garden, ya arsehole!" John had no choice but to leave his hiding place and move swiftly down the street to another well covered garden before the cops returned. He could tell that the bloke meant it but wasn't a lover of the police himself.

Marcus turned the car round and headed back the way he had come. There was a big guy standing on the kerb flagging them down, his arms covered in tattoos, a cigarette hanging out of his mouth and a sneer on his face. Taylor brought her window down and asked what he wanted in a polite voice. She was about to give their excuses and carry on until she heard what he had to say. He told them that he had seen a guy hiding in his garden as they drove up the street, and he was only grassing because there was something not right about him.

Taylor asked, "Can you be more specific?"

"He gave me the creeps man. His eyes were pure evil, like, and if looks could kill, I'd be deed!"

"How long ago? Which direction?"

"Barely minutes. He went down to the right and I lost sight of him. I was just checkin' that he was leavin', 'cause I dinnae want him comin' back to ma door. He's a fuckin' scary looking bastard an' all."

"Thanks, thanks a lot. I mean it!" Taylor turned to Marcus her eyes wide and excited. "Come on, we're close!"

John unlocked his car and climbed in just as the headlights came round the corner. He ducked just in time but did not know if he'd been seen. Sweat poured into his eyes, the result of the chase through the woods and the assault course through the gardens showing all over his face. His heart raced in anticipation of being caught, there was no way he could talk his way out of this one with sweat pissing all over his face and no plausible explanation.

Did they see me? Was I quick enough to get down? I'm up shit creek if they did, or perhaps they are.

Taylor was looking to the left and Marcus to the right as they rounded the corner. There were cars parked on both sides, windows with condensation on them, none of them looking as if they'd been moved all night. "Shit it's like a ghost town up here. He could be anywhere," said Taylor. "Call in the last sighting of that guy seen in the garden. It might not even be our guy cause this area can be full of strange folk and robbin' wee bastards."

Marcus got on the radio and told them their position and then they headed in the direction of the high flats at Moredun.

"The last sighting of him was at Craigour Crescent, near number 14, and get a dog set to come along here ASAP and see if they can pick up a scent," Taylor called on the radio. "He's still fucking here. I can feel it in my bones and we need to find that bastard!"

Hands shaking, John raised his head and watched the unmarked car head off towards the high flats. He quickly turned the ignition key and put the demister on full blast, hurriedly wiping enough of the screen to see out. Putting the car in gear he slowly pulled away with his headlights off and headed in the opposite direction of the police. He kept his speed down, although the huge speed bumps prevented any great speed anyway. His heart still pounding, he allowed himself a wry smile as he reached the main road that ran parallel to Dalkeith Road, because the minute he got onto that road, there would be several other cars travelling in the same direction and he could join them and blend in like all the other good people going about their lawful business.

After touring round all of the parking areas of the high flats, Marcus turned back, retracing his route. Taylor had suggested they head back to the hospital and get a full update on what had happened there, leaving the marked cars to take over as the suspect could be anywhere by now. They pulled round the corner back onto Craigour Path, where they had already been, and looked at all of the parked cars one more time.

"There's one fucking missing from over there. Shit we were too quick to leave. We should have got out and walked and physically checked them all out!" She pointed to the recently vacated space.

Marcus turned to her with an anxious look. "It could have been anyone, Taylor. You're just gonna beat yourself up thinking the worst."

"It is the worst. Get the dogs to number 14 and if that mutt stops here where that car was, we've driven right past that bastard and he knows it. Fuck, fuck, FFUUUUCCKKK!" she yelled at the top of her voice and thumped the dashboard, making Marcus jump.

They sat at the space where the car had been and listened on the radio as the dog set called up, confirming that he was at 14 Craigour Crescent and that the dog had indeed picked up a scent, just as they'd suspected. There hadn't been any pedestrians in that area and that was good for the preservation of the scent particles that the dog's nose could pick up. The scent was only left a short time ago. Taylor and Marcus watched as the General Purpose dog, one that dealt with tracking human scent, came round the corner, nose to the ground, heading straight towards the space.

"No, no, no!" exclaimed Taylor as it stopped dead at the spot where the car had been and sat down, wagging its tail.

The handler clapped the dog and threw it a ball, reward for a job well done. He leant in Taylor's window and said, "Serg, the vehicle that left was driven away by the guy who was hiding at number 14 and if he's the guy from the hospital, he's long gone by now."

"Thanks for your help. We should've checked the fucking cars Marcus. Why didn't we do that, hey?"

"Hindsight is a wonderful thing and we did look at all of the cars. There was condensation on all of them. We weren't to know."

"Can you remember what type of car was there?"

Marcus looked at her and said, "A dark one. All of the cars on that side were dark. As for the type, I can't remember, something non-descript!"

"Let's head back to the hospital and see what the score is," Taylor sighed. "We were so close, so god damn close. He watched us, you know, and the outcome could've been so different, all for a few measly seconds."

Taylor moaned as she looked out of the window. "Where are you now, you twisted bastard?"

Chapter 19: Loose Ends

Taylor entered the hospital at the main entrance, avoiding A & E as there was always something going on involving the police and she didn't want to get embroiled in any trouble. She went to Susan's ward and a young police officer stood almost to attention as she arrived.

"No-one's to go in there."

"I'm Sergeant Nicks and I am in charge of this investigation."

"Sorry Sergeant, I didn't know who you were," and he gestured for her to carry on after looking at her ID.

She thought to herself, *at least he's doing his job properly, regardless of what was said.*

At a glance, she saw the state of Susan's pillow before looking over at Mary's bed; the sheets were soiled with urine and the covers dishevelled. She caught a nurse as she walked by.

"Where are they? Are they alright?" she asked.

"They are both okay. Mary is a little shaken up and has been moved to Ward 10 and Susan is with Andrew in the TV room, waiting for the police to speak with her."

Taylor looked at her. "There was a nurse hurt too, was there not? How is she doing?"

"Ann. She's down at A & E with facial injuries but nothing life threatening. She's tough as old boots that one."

"Will I be able to speak to her?"

"I assume so although her mouth will be sore. She lost a couple of teeth but she'll want to tell you all about it. She loves a good story."

□□□

John parked his car in his driveway and moved inside quickly, sweat soaking through his clothes and his heart still pounding. He kicked an old beer can hard against the wall and shouted, "BITCH," at the top of his voice. *I'll get her and she'll wish she hadn't survived. They can't look after her 24/7 and when they let their guard down, she's mine.* His thoughts drifted back to the night he had spent with her, the pain and terror he put her through still fresh in his mind. He licked his lips, saliva glistening on his unshaven face. *I want you again, I want to savour you one last time and this time you will die, but it won't be quick.* He clicked on the TV and put on the news channel; the local news had just finished and he threw the remote across the floor with rage. He wanted to hear them talk about the night at the hospital and his escape. He took great pleasure in outsmarting the police. Easy when you had spent years working alongside them, working hand in hand with them, providing video evidence for a multitude of crimes in the city, and it certainly helped when he knew of every city and view camera in existence and what they covered. He was aware of police tactics; how many there were and timescales for their attendance at call outs. He was blissfully unaware, however, that on that night's news, there had been a press release admitting that there was a dangerous criminal on the loose targeting women. An apparently accurate sketch artist's drawing of the suspect had also been shown along with a large reward for information. John sat blissfully unaware as he slouched back on his couch, his hand now buried in his trousers as he recalled the night he had tortured Susan.

□□□

"Thank you Ann, you've been a great help, and I'm glad you saw the sketch earlier and you're sure it was the same man."

112

"Yes I'm sure. His eyes were so demon like and sinister, I'll never forget them. He was utterly terrifying. The sketch is definitely a true likeness."

Taylor turned to Marcus as they left A & E, an old tramp nearly bumping into them. The vagrant was completely drunk, looking for a place to rest his head for the night, somewhere warm to sleep, much to the annoyance of those waiting for treatment.

Taylor said to Marcus as they walked, "He's totally lost it you know. He wasn't worried about how many people saw him and the risks he took just to get near to Susan were unbelievable."

Marcus agreed, saying, "I think he'll regret this mistake big style. He appeared to want another chance to prove it, and almost at any cost, if tonight's anything to go by."

"The photo fit was being released on tonight's news. Let's see what that will turn up for us and take it from there."

"Why didn't he kill anyone tonight? He had the chance and didn't take it," Taylor exclaimed as they made their way into the parking lot.

"Maybe not enough time to enjoy it or maybe he's playing god with other's lives? Who knows? The guy's a fucking freak anyway. Who knows what goes on in his mind?"

¤¤¤

Peter sat watching the news in his house, staring at the screen when the photo fit came up. He laughed to himself, thinking that John at work wouldn't see the funny side, that the guy terrorising the city was a spitting image of him. It didn't even cross his mind that the guy he shared eight hours a day with was a murderer. *He's such a normal guy. No way could he have carried out all of the things that have been reported. John's just a decent hard working guy, who is just a little lonely and a little awkward around women. It couldn't be him,* he convinced himself. They'd have a right laugh about this at work when they were back on shift together. The girl from the office where John worked froze when she watched the news; she remembered the way she had felt in the lift that day when his eyes had roamed up and down her body like an animal stalking its prey. He had unnerved her that day and she had only been exposed to him for a few seconds. *Could this possibly be the same person,* she questioned herself. Lucy Millar picked up the phone and dialled the number shown on the screen. The phone was answered reasonably quickly and a woman asked what information she had and the basis of the call. Little did Lucy know that she was number 478 to call in since the bulletin was aired on mainstream television. It was amazing how many people saw things when there was a reward to be had, bogging down the police with false leads and fabricated stories to try to get their hands on the money.

Stressed and worn out, Taylor left the office at 2 am and headed straight to a club that she knew would still be open. She ordered a double Bacardi and coke at the bar. She gulped it down and asked for another; this time she held it in her hand and watched the other patrons coming and going, laughing and frolicking with each other, not a care in their cosy little worlds. Taylor's heart was heavy with failure and the events of the night; her mind raced as she thought how close he had got to Susan and the people he had injured in the process.

He could have killed them so easily and chose not to. Why? Is it because he chose who he wanted to kill and derives great pleasure from doing so, even the choice? He didn't need to kill them tonight, so he didn't, and he is controlling what happens, almost like playing games with life itself. Such arrogance.

Taylor jumped as a slim blonde woman came up behind her and tapped her shoulder. "Penny for your thoughts," she said softly in her ear.

"You don't want to know - just a totally shit day should cover everything."

The woman pulled up a tall stool beside Taylor and dragged another over for Taylor to sit beside her. The bar was still quite busy being a Thursday night, the weekend starting early for some and a wee night out for others. The bar was Edinburgh's premier gay night club, a far cry from the old dark rooms with bell entry systems, where people had to hide away from others to be themselves, to be gay. The bar had tasteful décor with modern furniture, booths for privacy and a spacious dance floor with clientèle from all walks of life socialising together, a real good natured atmosphere.

"I'm Sarah." The blonde held out her hand inviting Taylor to take it.

Taylor looked at her and met her hand with hers. She gave

the stranger the once over and managed a slight smile. It had not been her intention to meet anyone. All she wanted to do was unwind and have a drink and think more about the case but, in reality, thinking about it was torturing her. This situation was one Taylor used to thrive on, picking up a random woman and having a one night stand. She loved flirting and loved the chase. Being attractive had always made Taylor a prime target when she was out as people with her striking features and physical frame were few and far between on the gay scene.

Sarah ordered herself a gin and tonic and asked the barman to give Taylor another of what she was drinking. He looked at her and told her it was a double, checking whether she still wanted to pay for a double. She nodded her head casually, not bothered about the double measure. The barman, slim, well built, with a wiry physique and designer clothes, brought over the drinks and smiled at the blonde, aware of what she was up to. He winked in a camp way at Sarah, gestured towards Taylor and mouthed the words, "She's beautiful, and she's a cop."

Sarah sparked up the conversation with small talk and then asked more directly about Taylor's job. Taylor looked at her and said, "I don't want to talk about work." Her stare was a little hostile and she hoped that it might end the topic.

Sarah moved closer seductively and said, "What do you want to talk about then? Or is talking not what's on your mind?"

Sarah had pulled herself closer to Taylor and before she could react, Sarah's mouth touched hers and her hand gently touched her thigh. The kiss was soft and inviting, not forceful, just warm and tempting, so tempting that Taylor responded. Taylor's face was already flushed with the alcohol and now with the feverish needy kiss that they were sharing, a release that she desperately needed. She needed to forget work, forget everything, just for the here and now.

After several minutes of surreptitious sexual contact, Taylor stopped and pulled away. She looked at Sarah and said, "I can't do this. It's very, very nice, but I can't."

Taylor's head spun with the alcohol and the kiss. What was she doing? What about Kay? The Taylor of old would have been half way home by now with the blonde in tow for a night of lustful sex, or maybe it would have even happened on the way home - Taylor didn't usually mind.

Sarah leant forward and tried to kiss her again, her soft inviting lips glistening and a subtle show of her tongue. "Yes you can do this, that kiss was real and you wanted it then, and you could want it again."

Taylor allowed her to kiss her again. She was struggling with her old self. She was at a low ebb, tipsy and stressed and this could be the pick me up she needed. Sarah stood and pushed herself between Taylor's legs, putting her hands on Taylor's thighs. They moved further up her legs. Taylor's suit trousers were of a thin material and she could feel a tingle where Sarah's hands had been and where she wanted them to go. They gently brushed over Taylor's pussy with a tempting change of pressure. Taylor circled her arms round Sarah's waist and pulled her close, her face now leaning against her breast. She could feel the taut nipple on her cheek, and she could feel the need growing between her legs as Sarah's hand rubbed against her, skilfully teasing her. She moved her head round allowing her mouth to brush against the nipple, flames of lust burning deep inside her, urging her to take what was on offer.

"I can't do this, I won't do this. I'm so sorry, I have to go." Taylor created a space between them to enable her to stand. She gathered her things and headed for the door. Sarah sighed, "Your loss," and smiled as Taylor's statuesque figure exited the club.

Taylor wrapped her arms round herself, her work suit giving little warmth in the chilly night air. *What was all that about? Why did I just do that? Hmmmm, very nice though.* Taylor looked at her phone to see if there were any messages.

"Shit," Taylor sighed, Kay had sent a text and would wonder why it wasn't answered. *Fuck it! I'll just avoid her tomorrow so I don't have to answer any straight questions.* Kay was not the sort of woman that would stand for any messing around. Taylor questioned herself again as to why she had allowed the woman to kiss her, to touch her, and why had she kept it going? Because she was human and needed comfort, any comfort. All sorts of thoughts were buzzing around in her head. *Why worry now? Because I've never cared before. Nothing really happened anyway,* she convinced herself. But it had, and Taylor had allowed herself to be tempted and she had nearly taken up the offer. What were her feelings for Kay? After all, she had stopped herself and gone home, hadn't she? She did care.

"Got any change?" A beggar looked up from just below the cash machine, something the police didn't take kindly to. It was a little unnerving to have someone so close when you took your money out at the bank. Taylor took a step back as she had been lost in her own thoughts and got a fright.

"Asshole! You gave me a fright."

"Sorry lady. I didn't mean to scare you. I'm just hungry an' looking to get myself something to eat." Taylor glared at him and told him he shouldn't be sitting where he was.

He replied, "What's it to you anyway? Are you the polis like?"

She didn't confirm or deny what she was. She took out a pound coin and tossed it to him. "Buy food, not more bevy or I'll come back and take it off you."

"Cheers doll! Anything you say."

Taylor got her money out, flagged down a cab and got in. She made a mental note of the cab number and then slumped back in the seat. The motion of the vehicle made her nauseous and she got out just before her house. The fresh air would do her good as she walked the remainder of the way, thoughts buzzing round her head. Her mind filled with a mixture of despair, sadness, lust and a little light headedness from lack of food and several quick drinks in succession.

oooo

Kay switched off her bedside lamp. Her phone was on the bedside cabinet; she had not had a reply from Taylor. She worried a little and her heart was a little sore as she thought the worst. *Why am I being like this? Taylor doesn't owe me anything. We're not committed, but she's not going to make a fool out of me and I won't be one of many, for anybody!*

oooo

Taylor got to her door, let herself in and went into the kitchen where she took a beer from the fridge; a cup of sweet tea would have been better for her. She wanted to erase the night, her old self and the case but she couldn't do any of those. Three beers later, all in quick succession, her head suitably spinning and her mood more relaxed, she headed off to bed leaning on the walls as she went, lonely and subdued, but pleasantly pissed - just how she wanted to feel.

Taylor felt she had no sooner gone to sleep when the alarm went off. "No, no, no." She sat up and a wave of nausea swept over her. "Why do I do it? Drink and work do not mix, not with me anyway." Her hair was dishevelled and her make-up still on. She sighed and began getting ready. *I'll have to get a taxi into work. My mouth feels toxic. I have fumes for breath and would definitely be over the legal drink drive limit. What an asshole I am. Will I ever learn?*

Marcus was already in the office, clean shaven and immaculate as always. As for Taylor, her suit was slightly askew and her hair not as neat as it normally would be.

"I need coffee," she said. Marcus looked at her with mirth in his eyes.

"Heavy night, huh? Tell me you didn't go out after the shift last night. Did you?"

"I did and I regret it and I don't need a lecture from you either, just coffee and lots of it."

"Findlay's been out already. There have been over a thousand calls since last night. The Holmes team have been working flat out to create actions for the squad to pursue today." The Holmes team was a special unit of officers, who took every call and piece of evidence and referenced it. They created an action for every lead and cross referenced everything to avoid missing any vital connections.

"Great, and there probably won't be more than a handful of genuine ones with real leads to follow up."

Taylor sat at her desk, her head pounding, her eyes heavy with lack of sleep. She stood up to go and make another coffee when Kay came into the office. She looked over at Taylor and Taylor's face flushed as their eyes met, but it wasn't with the usual lust, it was with guilt and remorse. Kay smiled at her although she could feel her stomach churn inside. Was she imagining what she had just seen or was Taylor acting a bit differently? It wasn't the look she had hoped for.

"What's with you today? It's more than a hangover, isn't it?" Marcus asked in a respectful way.

"I didn't, you know. I started to and did enough to feel like a real shit house."

"Are you fucking crazy? Kay will string you up - that's if she ever speaks to you again!"

"I'm a fool with a needy ego. I like the thought that I can do as I like but I've never really had to suffer any consequence before."

□□□

Peter sat at his desk surveying the multitude of screens in front of him, hoping to spot trouble brewing before it came to anything. He jumped as John came into the room, which unnerved John as he wondered if it could be real fear. *Don't be stupid,* he told himself. *Act normally and avoid any suspicion.*

John said, "Are you surprised to see me in here today then?" and laughed.

Peter replied, "Thought you were gonna be off sick for ages."

"Got bored to tell you the truth. What's been happening here, anything exciting since I've been away?"

"Not in here but the city is buzzing with the cat an' mouse chase going on with that guy that's been terrorising the city. Did you even watch the news last night John? Because they showed a photo fit on the late news and it was a bit freaky; it looks a bit like you. You would've shit yourself if you'd seen it."

John froze inside. His guts tightened into a large knot and it took him every ounce of strength to hide the sick feeling he felt deep inside.

He smiled at Peter, "You're kidding me right? Surely there can't be another great looking guy like me about in the city."

This confirmed it in Peter's mind that John was just John. Nobody could be that cool about what he'd just said, if he had been the actual killer. Satisfied, Peter dropped that subject and started talking about football as usual. John had a coffee and was patient, biding his time before heading out of the room.

Sweat beads formed on his forehead as the reality of the situation hit home. *Fuck, they're closer than they think. The filth is in here all the time, it won't take them long before they work out who's who.*

He went to the lift, his stride confident and not in the least bit shifty, and headed for the car park beneath the building. He had made the decision that he had to get some cash and leave his work, his house, and lie low for a while, or maybe forever. He stepped into the underground parking lot an expansive, desolate space with room for over 300 cars, where the sound of your footsteps echoed eerily when you were there on your own. His heart was pounding; he felt like a trapped animal. For the first time since he had started to kill, he experienced fear and terror of being caught. Nausea drifted over him and he felt physically sick. The feelings were short lived when he heard the clacking of heels heading his way. He looked up and saw a woman 20 metres away. She stopped and froze on the spot. The fear in her eyes was clearly visible and she began to shake. *What's wrong with her?* he thought to himself. *Who is she anyway?* Only as she turned away and started walking quickly back towards her car did he remember that she was the female from the lift the other day, the one with the tidy little ass that quite clearly didn't like him. *If Peter was right and that photo fit was good, who knows what she is thinking? Does she suspect me? I can't take the chance.* He moved quickly towards her.

Terror engulfed her as she heard heavy footsteps behind her. Lucy Millar wished she hadn't been so obvious in her change of direction; she should have just walked past him and not even given him a second thought, not even glanced up at him. *Too late now*, she thought, kicking off her shoes and running towards her car as fast as her legs would carry her. Big mistake! Her petite frame and lack of height gave John an instant advantage and he closed the ground between them quickly as he was tall and still quite able. Lucy fumbled frantically in her pocket for the key to her car. It seemed to take ages, her fingers grasping around, hysterically hunting for its familiar shape. *Got it!* Elation overtook her as she thought she stood a chance to escape. Lucy reached the door of her car; she'd managed to unlock it as she ran, her trusty Ford Focus sounding a comforting beep, beep. She grabbed the door handle, pulling the door open as fast as she could, scraping her leg on its the bottom edge, only to have her arm wrenched away with such brutal force it dislocated instantly and pain seared into her shoulder joint.

He stared into her eyes. Pain pulsed down her arm as the truth about her recognition of him and what he was bore down on her. As he stood ominously over her, there was no hiding it. Tears welled up in her eyes and her bottom lip trembled as John raised his hand up in a clenched fist above her head, realisation dawning of the futile situation she was now in. She was about to plead with him but before she could open her mouth, punches rained down on her fragile being. Her head and body were pummelled relentlessly and brutally until she was completely unrecognisable, face deformed, bruised and bloodied. He kept on until he was sure her life had passed from her body. He looked around him, his breathing heavy with the exertion, checking for any witnesses to the savage slaying. Scooping up her tiny body, he popped the Ford's bonnet and dumped her in the boot, shoving her legs round cruelly to fit, showing no emotion or remorse for taking another innocent life. There was a bottle of mineral water in the front drinks holder and a cloth in the door of the car that he used to try and clean up some of the blood from the car and the ground nearby. This would at least conceal enough to buy him a little time to sort things out and possibly prevent detection or pursuit for a while longer, enabling his escape.

He turned and walked towards his own car, which was parked 50 metres away, locking Lucy's as he went. He sighed and thought how lucky that turn of events had been. The girl had known who he was, who knows what she could have done to him? Apart from him stopping her blabbing, she had given him a thrill he hadn't expected today. It was a pity he couldn't treat her to the full package. She had been quite a tidy wee thing and it was a shame to waste the chance of enjoying a body like that. She would have loved what he had to offer. He got in his car and was about to drive away when he remembered her shoes and got back out of the car to retrieve them when another car pulled into the parking lot.

"Shit," he exclaimed, knowing he would have to leave them behind and hope no one missed her for a while.

He drove slowly as he left the car park, deliberately not drawing any attention to himself. He stopped a short distance away, he called his boss at work to apologise for his premature return to work, saying he would need to go off sick again as he had not fully recovered from his illness and had come back too soon. Another believable ploy, which would add legitimacy to his comings and goings and again give him more time to do what was necessary before they caught up with him; he needed time to have one more special evening with Susan. He was a bit bewildered at how quickly things had unravelled so badly for himself.

One minute he was untouchable and the police didn't have a clue and the next they were practically breathing down his neck; all of this because of Susan. How could he have been so careless? He should have made sure she was dead. He thought to himself about the night they'd spent together and his final blow, which would have killed a buffalo, but didn't kill her. *Susan's will to live must be very strong, but not as strong as my desire to kill. I'll have the last laugh and you'll wish you had died that night, you useless bitch. I'll make sure of that.*

He had enough of his wife's money stashed away to start up elsewhere but first he had to purchase a few items to disguise his identity, buy a car and collect a few things from his house. It would no longer be safe to stay there. This time he would be leaving his wife for good; on his terms of course.

He pondered whether to leave everything behind at this time as he could not be sure what the girl at the office had done already; maybe nothing, but he could not take the chance. Even his work colleague Peter had made a comment. Although jokey, it had obviously been such a good likeness that his guilt might have been a possibility and Peter might change his mind, or at least say to someone else who would take it further.

"Fucking bitch, I'll make you pay. Your life is mine. This time there will be no mistakes, and more pain than any human being can imagine." Intent on revenge, he repeated this to himself over and over and had not noticed that he was rocking back and forward in the car. He was salivating, his teeth were gritted and his face contorted into a hideous mask of pure evil and hatred. Only when he heard a horn behind him did he snap out of his trance and pull away at the green light. His driving was a little erratic due to the adrenaline that was still coursing through his veins from the slaying of his colleague. He was just about to pull onto George Street in the centre of town when he noticed a police car pull up behind him and start to follow him. He turned down Frederick Street and made sure he didn't make any more mistakes and obeyed the speed limit. He was in two minds whether to give them the slip or not, but that meant certain capture if he couldn't get away, as any vehicle making off would usually draw a multiple response to ensure its capture; he knew this as he had watched and listened to many pursuits. Police were like dogs with a bone in a pursuit; they just wouldn't let go. They would have checked out his vehicle already by this time and it would come back, showing valid insurance and MOT and there should have been no issues. Maybe they thought he was drunk or something, so they would probably stop him.

He looked at his hands, his knuckles were bruised and a slight spray of blood was still visible on the back of his hand. He was glad of his dark clothing, any blood would be almost invisible to the naked eye or. He licked the back of his hand and frantically wiped the blood off onto his trousers, making sure there was none left to be seen. Inevitably the blue light came on and a short blast of the siren signalling him to stop came straight after. He stopped as quickly as he could, along from the botanic gardens, a very wide road with a popular park on each side and the gardens on the other, a popular destination for families with plenty of space to park, perfect for a vehicle stop. He stayed in the car, trying everything not to rile the officers who would come to the window to check him out.

"Everything alright sir?" the young officer said.

"Yes, everything's fine. Is there a problem?" John knew what the cop was doing; he was trying to get a whiff of his breath to see if he could smell alcohol, so he spoke clearly and directly to the officer with a respectful tone throughout the conversation. "Why have you stopped me, officer? Was it when I stalled my car at the lights back there on the bridges? I was in a little dream."

"You seemed to be a little preoccupied sir, a little angry."

"I was, I was a little pissed off about an incident just before. I was cut up on the Royal Mile by some guy in a black Merc. Sorry! I'm only human." John gave his most sheepish plausible grin. His believable tale as to why he was angry was not uncommon. The young cop believed what he had heard and John's details had checked out. He was about to let him go when the old sweat of a cop lumbered towards the window. He wasn't going to be quite as easily put off the scent and probed John a little further regarding his behaviour. He looked a bit like a jowly blood hound on the scent, hunting down his prey. "Do you like boxing?" he asked.

"No," John replied, "Why do you ask?" knowing fine well why he had asked.

"Look at your knuckles. What happened there, Sir?"

"Nothing really. I've just got a bit of a temper and hit a few walls earlier when something annoyed me at work today," John replied calmly. It was the truth and came across that way to the officer but he still wanted to check him out further and was about to ask where he worked to check that it wasn't a person that had been hit instead of a wall. Neither officer had attended the briefing that morning because they had gone straight out to a grade one domestic call and had not seen the top item on the brief - a photo fit of the suspect for two murders and numerous assaults, who just happened to be staring up at them from his car.

Had they been at the briefing, the game would have ended there and then for John, unless he murdered them both right there in the street, which had crossed his mind. They would have caught the biggest criminal to have ever stalked the streets of Edinburgh, and all because of a minor road traffic issue. John could feel his nerve starting to falter a little as the big older cop stared right at him as if seeing straight through his lies. He was sure this was it and they were stalling him until back up got there to arrest him. He knew his photo fit must have been passed to all stations. Sweat started to gather at his hairline and he hoped it couldn't be seen. The cop turned to the younger one, their heads together. John heard him say that something wasn't right with this guy but there was nothing to hold him on.

Just then their personal radio sounded. A disturbance was ongoing at the Muirhouse area of town, an area well known for drugs, violence and other troubles, fellow officers required urgent assistance. All police not dealing with emergency calls were expected to attend such incidents as no officer wanted to be at the wrong end of an assault with no help coming quickly.

Reluctantly, the older cop told John he was free to go and they got back in their car and sped off in the direction of Muirhouse, blue lights flashing and the siren wailing loudly as they left. John put his head on the steering wheel and sighed; the realisation of what it felt to be hunted was exhilarating and terrifying at the same time; he had truly thought that was it. He had never really given much thought to being caught as he hadn't believed it would ever happen. If only he had killed her, none of this would be happening right now.

He drove to his house, knowing that it would not be long before the police realised their monumental error in letting him go; the place would soon be crawling with them. He smiled as he packed up some things, taking enough clothes to make do, a small flat screen telly, DVD player and half his stash of porn as he would needed something to amuse himself wherever he ended up. "Just need the wigs and I'm sorted. I'll grow a beard. That will change me enough to hide myself in plain sight." He patted the barrel with a twisted sense of power, the decaying corpse of his wife still sealed grotesquely inside, and glanced round at his flat for the last time. He headed for the garage that would buy his car for cash. "No ties or loose ends this time, I'll make sure of that," he muttered to himself.

Chapter 20: Too Late

Findlay stood before the 40-strong squad, his gut hovering above his belt, moving up and down as he addressed the room. This made Taylor feel even more nauseous, a sight to turn even the most hardy stomach. He whined on and on about the lack of progress and that the bosses were snapping at his heels for positive results and a quicker response to all of the leads. *Get off your own fat ass and do some work then,* Taylor thought. *Stop moaning about how badly we're doing when you can't even cope with making a cup of fucking coffee.* Actions were handed out, several were given to each pairing, and each one had to be treated as genuine, even though everybody knew the majority would be false, requiring tons of paperwork, which in turn would create a huge delay in getting down to enquiring into the genuine leads.

"Why can't people give us clear facts, full names and areas of work, instead of leaving us to fill in the blanks," Taylor vented at Marcus. "People always seem to think that what they've said is clear and understandable and that we'll know exactly what they mean, when it's quite clear it's the opposite. Take this one for instance - a guy, who might be called John who works somewhere in the City Council main office, gave her the creeps and resembles our guy. Do people think we have crystal balls or magic wands? No, we don't!"

"Are we taking that one or not?" Marcus looked at her questioningly.

"I suppose so, the others are even worse. At least this one could be something, even if we do have to do a shit load of digging around. One more coffee and we'll head off and you're driving."

"Thanks for that," Marcus sighed in a joking manner.

As they were leaving Taylor glanced over at Kay and attempted to smile at her. Kay looked up at her, her lips curled into a semi smile and she looked away quickly, not wanting to make Taylor think everything was alright, her heart sore from the unknown. Taylor could feel the distance open up between them; it was as if Kay could feel her guilt and read her thoughts. Taylor couldn't even go over and talk to her because of the secrecy of their relationship; Kay would not appreciate her dirty linen being aired so publicly in the squad room. She wasn't ashamed but liked her business to be her own. Taylor and Marcus moved towards the exit and Kay glanced in their direction. She caught Taylor's eye as she looked back into the office, her eyes fixed firmly on Kay with genuine affection and happiness that she had taken the time to watch her leaving. The door swung closed and they were gone. Kay sat back down and stared at her computer, her heart pounding, longing, needing to know what was going on with Taylor. Was she making a fool out of her? Was she just another prize or did Taylor genuinely feel for her?

"She looked up and watched me leave. She still cares so there's still a chance," Taylor tugged at Marcus's suit pocket. His eyes rolled and he said, "Stop fucking her around then. You either want her or you don't. Kay doesn't suffer fools gladly and you need to change your ways!"

Taylor smiled at Marcus, her colleague, friend and confidant, someone she could turn to and trust. Their relationship went further than being just work colleagues, they had mutual respect for each other and shared genuine affection for one another.

Marcus collected one of the spare pool cars from the garage at Fettes, cursing under his breath at the CID officers who had taken their usual car. Findlay had probably offered them it, just to annoy Taylor.

"He's such a dick isn't he, childish plonker," Taylor moaned to Marcus.

"C'mon, you would do the same to him if you were his boss," he smirked at her. She shrugged her shoulders and could see the funny side of things, because she knew she would do so much more. The funny side left her as soon as she got in, the smell of chips overwhelming and the mess in the car a disgrace.

"This is revolting. Some cops are like pigs Marcus. I'm embarrassed to go anywhere in this bucket." She giggled at what she had just said, repeating the word "pigs".

"I'll sort it boss, with a fart, if you get the coffees," he said like a naughty little boy, tickled pink at how gross he had just been. Taylor looked at him in pretend disgust but a fart might actually be slightly nicer on this occasion.

"I've got some spray. It has got to be better than fart or chips," Marcus smiled. "You know I was joking, right? I've never farted in your company!"

Taylor looked again and said, "Just as well, or I'd change partner. Coffee coming up."

They eventually drove to the council CCTV building, an air freshener now hanging from the mirror and a skinny latte in Taylor's hand; the day was just beginning. They had several enquiries to make, the paperwork stuffed semi neatly into their folders, as they set off to find a John, somewhere in this really quite large building.

They pulled into the loading bay at the front and popped up the police sign in the window of their vehicle. They headed to the reception area and gave the name Lucy Millar, explaining that they needed to see her and take a statement from her if they could. The clerk searched the employees list and her place of work and department came up on the screen.

"Third floor, end of the corridor, the door straight in front of you. It will have a white door and a glass panel. She works in the CCTV production department. She should be in today but her time card hasn't been activated. Do you want me to ring up to the department?"

"No thanks, we'll head up there and ask around. Thanks for your help."

"Excuse me, here's your visitors passes. You'll need them to get through the security doors. I'll trust you to go without a chaperone."

"Oh, and we'll need a list of all of the Johns, Johnathons and any other names that resemble that, their details and where they all work and whether they are in today."

"Okay, I'll get on to it," the security man said.

"Do you have photographs of all of the employees, you know, the ones that will go on their ID cards?" Taylor asked, ever hopeful of an easier ride.

"We do. They might not be up to date, but we do have photographic ID for all employees."

"Ya beauty!" Marcus whispered in Taylor's ear; even she gave a joyful little smile.

They reached the CCTV production department and spoke with the supervisor there. He told them that Lucy wasn't in today, which was totally out of character for her. Taylor asked several more questions, the last one being how Lucy usually travel to work. The supervisor pondered for a while and said that he thought she drove in because she was from Fife and was lucky enough to get an allocated space because of her 24/7 shifts. Taylor asked him to call her home and see if she was ill, a basic welfare check.

"Hopefully she won't think we are being intrusive. It's just that if this is out of character, we need to know if she's alright, and if she's well enough, we could head straight to her home address and get a statement from her there."

"I'm Gary by the way. I prefer it to be less formal." He put out his hand and Marcus and Taylor shook it.

"Thanks for doing this for us Gary," Taylor said.

Gary called Lucy's home number. It rang numerous times and he was about to hang up when a male voice came on.

"Hello, Millar, what can I do for you?"

"Hello, sorry to bother you. It's Gary Russo, Lucy's supervisor at the office."

"What's she done now, dropped something on her toe again?"

"Are you saying that she's come to her work today and she's not with you then?" Gary confirmed.

"What do you mean? Has she not arrived yet? She left more than four hours ago and she's not phoned me to say there's been any trouble. Are you sure she's not in some other department working or something?" Lucy's husband inquired, with alarm in his voice. "The police are here to take a statement from her and she's not clocked in today, I thought she might have been off sick and just not called in to us yet?"

"I'll give her mobile a ring. There's got to be an explanation for this."

"Ask her husband what type of car she drives and the registration number and we'll put it on ANPR. That should help us locate it and where it's been," Marcus requested. Gary asked all that he was required to and passed the information on to the officers. Taylor had a very bad feeling about the turn of events unfolding in front of them. They got a description of Lucy and put it out over the city wide radio channel and also over the water to the division in Fife; she was now to be treated as a high risk missing person until proven otherwise.

They headed back down to reception where they spoke with the concierge. He had compiled the list of Johns for the officers and had pulled up the staff photographs. "Marcus, I've got a bad feeling about this. If these photos even look a little like our guy, then this coincidence is one that doesn't look good for Lucy."

"Here they are. There are 23 altogether although most of them have worked here for quite a while."

Taylor and Marcus leaned into the computer and scanned the photos for anyone familiar. Taylor swallowed hard as she looked into the steely, unemotional eyes of a much younger but now very familiar face. His name was John Brennan.

"That's him, that's fucking him. God damn it, he works in the CCTV operations room. No wonder we've never seen him, he knows every damn location of every bloody camera in the city."

"Oh, I almost forgot. These were handed in today - ladies' shoes, size four, nearly new. They were just left in the underground car park. Found this morning they were. I was going to put them in lost property. Do you think you might need them?" Taylor looked at the shoes and her heart sank.

"Where did you say they were found and when," she asked with a voice of concern. "They were handed in pretty much first thing down in the underground car park, just left in the middle of one of the entrance lanes."

"Get some back up, Marcus. We need a search team down here right away and we need to get this building checked for the suspect. Who knows, he might still be here and if cornered a very dangerous man."

"Come on, let's get down to the car park and take a look around and cordon it off. No-one else gets in there."

"Which area of the car park were the shoes found in and how do we get access to it?"

Once down in the lower basement, Taylor shivered as the lift doors opened out into a parking area with space for numerous cars. She was struck by how quiet it was. There was no-one around, everyone was obviously where they needed to be and certainly not here. A cold chill ran up her spine as they walked from car to car, an array of scenarios racing through her mind about what could have happened to Lucy. Her heart pounded as she thought of the photo of John Brennan, eyes cold and evil, even in his work photo. How could people not see what type of man he was, or was that just her intuition kicking in, in the knowledge of what he was now proven to be capable of? Marcus, who was just ahead of her, stopped in his tracks and turned to Taylor, his face pale and concerned. He pointed to the ground next to a car with the registration given as Lucy's. There was a pool of blood and blood spatter on the ground and on the side of the car, a sign that someone had been assaulted or even worse, murdered. The trail went round to the back of the car and there where globules of blood congealing on the ground and on the bonnet of the car. "Open it, Marcus. Smash the window and pop the boot open. There's a button on the dash. She might be alive."

Marcus quickly put on gloves and did as he was asked but his mind was not so hopeful; that amount of blood usually meant only one thing and it wasn't good. Even if Lucy had been alive, several hours shut in a cramped boot would certainly not help her chances of survival.

Taylor stood at the boot waiting for Marcus to reach in and open it, her heart heavy with what she knew was beneath the sealed hatch. Click! The boot raised an inch and it was now free to be opened. Taylor hesitated and took a deep breath to compose herself. She lifted up the boot slowly at first, gasping her next breath as she found herself staring into open eyes, terror and fear etched into them for ever more. What had happened to Lucy and how was now tattooed in emotion for all to see. Her eyes were the only thing that remained semi human. Her head was so swollen it was hard to imagine that sweet, pretty face in her employee photo. Blood had poured from her nose, mouth, ears and eye sockets, the brutality of her attack obvious, cerebral fluid also visible from her nose and eyes. Her body was twisted grotesquely into the small space, jammed in with brutal force and violence. There was deformity in the skull showing the massive force used to kill the young woman. Taylor reached down to her neck and checked to see if there was a pulse, knowing fine well that there wouldn't be; Lucy's opaque, soulless eyes said it all. Tears clouded over Taylor's eyes, her heart sickened and sore with the what ifs. *Why kill her today, why not before? How did he know she had phoned us? If we'd only come here sooner, we might have been able to save her.* Taylor lifted her radio and called for a doctor; although she knew Lucy was dead, she was not authorised to confirm death unless there was a decapitation or advanced decomposition.

"Get a set to go round to the husband's house. He'll need to come and identify the body, and send someone with a heart and some experience. This one is not going to be easy to take in. No one could have seen this one coming. Thanks, over."

"Has someone checked if Mr Brennan was at work today or not? We need to move on this fast," Taylor exclaimed.

"No sign of him now but he was in earlier. His colleague said that he joked with him about looking like the photo fit on the telly."

"Fucking great!" Taylor muttered to herself. *Inadvertently he's set the time bomb off with that innocent comment.*

John had not been seen and he also had a parking space in the same section as Lucy. The picture was now becoming clearer: John was leaving and Lucy was arriving. She had called the police and he knew that his face was all over the news, thanks to Peter. Did they meet by chance? Did she act differently? What let him know what she had thought of him? Fear, perhaps? She'd read the papers and knew what had happened to John's victims and if it was him, coming face to face with him in a secluded area must have caused her to react. He, being the beast that he was, would have sensed this and wouldn't be prepared to take the chance he was maybe wrong. Whatever happened, their meeting was a million to one chance with the timings and information; Lucy had now paid the ultimate price for being human and showing a little fear faced with the devil before her, poor thing.

Taylor looked at Lucy's hand and forearms. They were deeply

bruised and one may even have been broken in her feeble attempt to protect herself. Marcus looked around for more evidence, signs of what had happened, just as more officers entered the basement. Taylor stopped them in their tracks and issued specific instructions for them to protect the area for the Scenes Examination Branch to attend to photograph everything in place and gather evidence. One of the officers stated that there were officers at John's address, but it looked like he'd packed up and left in quite a hurry.

"Fuck! We'll need a full forensic team down there too to search that house. Who knows how many he's killed, because he's certainly got a taste for it now, the twisted fucking bastard."

Taylor took one more look at Lucy's pitiful face before turning on her heels and heading for the exit; she felt nauseous because of the turn of events, more due to her failure to stop it happening than the sight before her. Death and horror was part of her job.

"We have to step this up, you know. He got lucky this time but we were close, so very close and he knows it. Maybe he'll get careless now that we've rattled his cage and flung him out of his comfort zone. He can't hide forever."

Chapter 21:
Till Death Do Us Part

Taylor stepped into John's house along with Marcus and the Scenes examination team; there were signs of the slovenly way he lived all over the floor. Filth covered every surface that was not taken up with empty food cartons or beer cans. Black refuse sacks bulged at the back door. There was a huge collection of pornographic material, although there was a noticeable gap where he had taken the time to choose a few of them to entertain himself when he was elsewhere. His bed lay unmade and the sheets were stained brown with sweat; it had obviously been a long time since they were last changed. Countless other DNA samples were to be found on the pillows, sheets and duvet. Taylor could not believe that someone could live like this and still go to work every day and fit in as normal. It was amazing that people were socialising with him, working alongside him, talking with him and all the time his secret hobby was invisible to them all, and too hideous to imagine for those who at least felt a little uncomfortable around him; everyone knows someone that is a little different, but that does not make them serial killers who enjoy torture and sexual abuse. The Police Search Advisor arranged for the house to be gone through with a fine tooth comb once the scene examiners had finished taking their photos and samples. Every surface, every clue was meticulously gathered, bagged and labelled to be taken off to one of the labs. Taylor walked through the house several times after the examination branch had left, knowing that she wasn't destroying any potential evidence any more. Her eyes kept going back to the makeshift table in the kitchen, an old metal drum with a table top affixed to it, *very strange*, she thought to herself.

"What about the drum Marcus? Even in this shithole, that's not quite right there don't you think? I bet there's something inside that."

"He's a freak, nothing would surprise me, but it's sealed with a good weld and the scene examiners took all the samples they could have from it, none from within it though."

"Let's take it in as a production and arrange for it to be opened. There's no way we could leave that knowing who owned it."

"Any chance we could get a couple of your strongest officers to move this so called table, please," Marcus asked the rather large group of search officers. They looked up at him with their usual do-it-yourself look, but their Sergeant picked a couple of them and they came into the kitchen area to help, their reluctance obvious.

"Where to, boss?" the larger of the two said sarcastically.

"There's a transit outside. That'll do fine, thanks."

They grunted as they lifted it to waist height and started to move towards the door, tilting it a little for it to fit.

"What the fuck is that smell," shouted the officer at the lower end.

"There's something leaking from this and it fucking stinks."

"I know what that smell is and you should too!"

They put the barrel down quickly and one said, "It's all yours now."

Taylor was sickened to the stomach. "Who or what do you think is in there?"

"No idea! But I'm sure all will be revealed after this search."

"Come on Marcus, let's get back to the office and try and get one step ahead of him before he starts his nonsense elsewhere."

They drove quickly to Fettes. Both sat quietly, not wanting to assume anything until the facts presented themselves. Marcus knew how Taylor thought although she held her cards close to her chest. He knew that she felt helpless to stop this man, this monster that was still free and out there waiting. One step behind him was not enough for Taylor. Marcus knew she would blame herself for not doing things quicker, even though there was no way she could have known that lead would be the one that would reveal the killer's identity. Had they gone the day before, the woman in the car would still be alive. It wouldn't matter to her that there were thousands of calls and leads to follow up and any one of them could have been the one and every one of them as important as the other until proven otherwise.

Marcus drove through the security gate; he waved at couple of cops driving out, Taylor just nodded. "Come on Nicksy. We'll get him. It's not our fault. We've been close twice, third time lucky."

Taylor got out the car, shook her hair out, pulled her shoulders up and took a deep breath. She looked into Marcus's eyes, her eyes wide open and angry. "You're right, we'll work every hour we can get and we will get him. We have to."

They walked together through the corridors, nodding to anyone who passed. When they entered the main office they could see through to the inspector's office. He was on the phone and was clearly angry about something. Taylor sat at the desk. Files were waiting for her and numerous post-its from people wanting things.

She asked one of the other investigators what Findlay's problem was. He replied, "What, you've not heard?"

"Obviously not! Come on, spit it out, what's made him that mad?"

"Two cops stopped John Brennan on a routine stop this morning. He had bloodied knuckles and they let him go because they hadn't seen his picture. They didn't go to the brief in the morning."

"You're kidding me?"

"Nope, not a word of a lie, the older cop was a bit suspicious but there was an assistance shout and they had to let him go."

"Shit, no wonder he's mad. Poor buggers, that was a fucking big missed opportunity, but it's not their fault they weren't at the briefing and couldn't detain him."

The door from the office swung open and slammed against the wall. Findlay stormed past Taylor's desk. She winced and watched him disappear out of the office, face red and flustered.

"Serves him right, it's about time he took some of the flack, the lazy git. If he'd get off his fat ass and do his bit then maybe he'd get more support."

Taylor logged on to her computer, and started to input some of what had happened to date, her mind flashing back to Lucy's eyes, desperate and lost, the stench from the barrel, the fact he was still out there and even more dangerous than before because he was on the run and being hunted. She felt vulnerable, a little broken and disturbed at this enquiry; Edinburgh had never had to deal with anything like this before. Murder, yes! A serial killer, no! They were something that you read about, not had to face on your doorstep. She stopped for a moment, her heart starting to race as Kay came into the main office at the far side. Taylor's eyes fixed on Kay's face. She hoped that she would look over, glance up, anything that would let Taylor back in to her heart. Kay talked with several of the officers and other people and carried on through the office, her eyes never close to where Taylor sat. Taylor knew that Kay had seen her, but had not let on, and she felt deflated, the pain inside ached through to her finger tips, a feeling she had never felt before; it was sore, her heart actually felt sore and she was sick to the stomach.

The door closed slowly behind Kay as she left the office, her hair lying on her shoulders, her figure sleek and alluring. It wasn't just Taylor who watched her; Findlay was back in the office and he too watched but with no affection only sleazy depravity.

Taylor's phone vibrated; her heart flat with the disappointment of Kay's lack of attention, she wasn't going to look but curiosity got the better of her. She lifted the phone. It was an unknown caller. "Hello, Taylor Nicks."

"I know who you are. Meet me in the interview suite."

Taylor's heart raced, her face flushed and she stood up and moved quickly through the office, hoping her exit wouldn't be noticed.

She leapt up the stairs in threes to the top floor and rushed to the third door on the left. Taylor pushed the door open and stepped inside. As the door closed behind her, she felt a hand on her shoulder, then it stroked down her back slowly. She felt warm breath on the back of her neck and Kay's hands came round her waist, pulling Taylor close. Kay's hands swept up onto Taylor's breasts and back down to her waist. She turned Taylor round by her hips and their faces met. Kay's kiss was so deep, so intense, that Taylor could not catch her breath; their tongues touched and the power of the kiss sent ripples of arousal coursing through both of their bodies. Taylor's thigh pushed sharply up between Kay's thighs. She moaned and pushed back hard against it.

Taylor rubbed against her firmly. Kay spoke softly into her ear, "I missed you so much, so much my body aches for you." Taylor moved Kay in front of her, and from behind she pushed her hands down the front of Kay's trousers, stroking over her. Kay moaned softly as Taylor's strong hands moved over her again and again. Kay wanted her so bad it ached. She gripped hold of Taylor's wrists and stopped her. Taylor asked, "Do you want me to stop?"

Kay gasped back, "God no!" and took Taylor's hand and pushed it down inside her trousers, and inside her panties.

Taylor's fingers slipped over her and into her. Kay was so wet, so turned on that she came almost instantly as Taylor's hand freed her orgasm, which was gripping, powerful and hungry.

Kay wanted more. She pushed Taylor's fingers deep inside her, whispering, "Fuck me, Taylor, please! just fuck me."

Taylor undid Kay's trousers and pulled them over her hips. She pushed her on to the chair, opened her legs and pushed up inside her, over and over again. Her mouth caressed and licked her as she thrust into her, Kay gripped Taylor's back and moved with her, their bodies working together to feel the release. Moaning and wanting, Kay's hips bucked up as the orgasm took hold of her. Her knees gripped Taylor's arm and stopped her hand for a second letting Kay gain some control of the overwhelming power of her desire. She let go and Taylor's fingers slipped deeper into the milky heaven as waves of pleasure took Kay to the point of no return and Taylor's tongue continued to push Kay further into her frenzy of passion, until she couldn't keep going. Taylor came up on top of Kay and kissed her open mouth, her mouth wet from being down on her, this turned Kay on all the more. Their kisses were so in tune with each other, hot, wet and desperate, but perfect.

Kay looked into Taylor's eyes, held her face and said, "I love you." Taylor stopped, and just looked back, her heart open and alive and her ears not believing what she had just heard.

She did not reply; I love you was not something Taylor would say. She took hold of Kay's head and pulled her into a swirling kiss. They both felt it from their heads to their toes, a kiss of passion and of love. Taylor felt it; she felt love for this woman. The feelings were so powerful they consumed them both, their breathing fast and heavy, their eyes fixed on each other's; love was definitely there with them.

Footsteps fell heavy on the corridor outside, both Kay and Taylor jumped up. Taylor helped Kay pick up her clothes and they pushed their way into the cupboard at the back of the room like a couple of naughty school kids, although they would be in real trouble if they were caught.

"Taylor, Taylor! Where are you? The boss is mad for you," Marcus called. Taylor and Kay kept silent as the office door opened.

"Marcus, you ever hopeful voyeur. Thank god it's you. What's up with wobble butt anyway?" Marcus scanned the room looking for someone else but Taylor took hold of his arm and guided him out and down the stairs. She said, "Let's see what he wants, shall we?"

Chapter 22: Watching

Smartly dressed with a well groomed beard and wearing glasses, he moved casually through the hospital, carrying a large colourful bouquet of flowers. He knew where he was going and what he wanted. He needed just a glimpse, a little information or maybe even a chance of discovering where he could find her. A week or so had passed. There was no longer a police officer present 24/7 so he could walk the corridors during visiting hours relatively unchallenged, although he was easily able to deflect attention with a very convincing résumé of reasons and excuses for being there. He did not look like himself anymore, almost coming across as charming; totally the opposite of the truth. His heart started pounding when he looked up at the admission boards; beside Susan's name was a release date - less than a week. The smile that came over his face was wide and demonic and if anyone had been watching him they would have felt instantly uncomfortable. His heart started to race with the anticipation of the hunt that now awaited Susan.

He didn't need to stay any longer; he didn't have to take the risk of ambushing her in the hospital any more. He could now have her where he had failed once before, where she should feel safe. Not anymore though, he would make sure of that. He turned on his heels with an inner sense of victory. He would win in the end.

He walked towards the entrance of the hospital and stopped to look up and stare at the CCTV camera, his eyes wide and focussed in a gesture that showed no fear, just utter defiance and arrogance. He turned to walk out but stopped dead in his tracks; just past the entrance door, Susan stood outside. She seemed relaxed and was talking to a young man wearing sports clothes. John almost growled in rage and disgust at how well she looked and he could see in the way the two of them were together that there was some sort of affection there. He wanted her to be swallowed up with fear, totally consumed in terror and unable to move on. He wanted her to fail to regain her confidence, to be trapped within his web of terror until he ended it permanently. He strode towards them, confident that she wouldn't recognise him. He walked almost through them, only allowing a couple of metres' distance as he passed, his stride heavy and full of purpose. Susan and Andrew barely looked up and their conversation didn't stop. He walked across the busy car park and stopped 50 metres away from where they stood. He faced them and stared, his eyes fixed on Susan's back, his mind focused on his next meeting with her and what he wanted to do, his hatred consuming him to the point that he began to rock back and forth. Susan's mouth went dry; an eerie sensation crawled slowly up her spine, her eyes narrowed and Andrew asked what was wrong?

She said, "I feel sick."

"You were fine a minute ago," exclaimed Andrew.

She could feel an unsavoury poison flowing through her veins. Her body felt chilled to the bone. She turned slowly and saw a tall well-built figure staring right at her, his head tilted to the left. She thought she could see a smile, a hideous but very familiar one. She quickly turned to tell Andrew and he looked into the car park but John had already dropped to his knees and was crawling towards his hire car three rows to the right.

Andrew said, "Are you sure? There's no-one there now."

"He, he was right there I saw him," she stuttered. "He was watching me. He was right there, I swear it. He was grinning at me."

Andrew put his arm around her, stopping her from going into

the car park. She was shaking like a leaf and very pale, her eyes wide with terror. Her mind flashed back to the evening of the brutal assault. She dropped to her knees and vomited violently on the ground. Andrew crouched behind her and stroked her back, trying to offer comfort but he could see how traumatised she was. There was no doubt in his mind that it had been John Brennan in the car park; even Andrew felt a wave of unexplained fear. He was well aware of what that beast had done to Susan as he had been there for her as she relived the horrors of the attack throughout her rehabilitation. He had also read the newspapers and knew that this man was capable of truly brutal savagery, even including men in his repertoire of victims. Andrew got out his phone and called the police.

Taylor was in the office when the call was received and it was redirected to her. She spoke with Andrew, getting a quick run-down of what had happened before setting the city road blocks in place in an attempt to prevent John getting away. There was a ten minute time delay, which in theory, dependent on his speed and the route he had taken, meant he could be on his way to the Borders by now. With no registration number, colour or make of vehicle, it would be like trying to find a needle in a haystack, but there was still a chance to stop him.

Officers attended at the hospital to seize the CCTV and take statements from Andrew and Susan. They tried to offer Susan reassurance but she was a quivering wreck. She kept repeating that she wanted to leave the hospital; she didn't feel safe there anymore. She had made the decision to pack her things and leave that very day. At least she would be reunited with her cat Baxter, another survivor. She just wanted to get as far away from John Brennan as she physically could.

Marcus had the CCTV tape playing in the office. Other officers stopped and watched over his shoulder, curious to see if he had been ballsy enough to walk straight into the hospital and whether Susan had seen him or had been mistaken. There was even the possibility that everything that had happened to her that night was playing with her mind as the time to go home got closer. Hundreds of people came and went. Marcus was amazed at just how busy the hospital was. *Good cover for our boy*, he thought. DC Fran Andrews walked past and Marcus put on his sweetest smile to ask her to get him a coffee; his reason for not getting it himself was that he didn't want to lose his concentration. She was going to tell him where to go but Marcus was such a charming man and genuinely did not want to leave his task, not even for a couple of minutes. He had also made his fair share of coffee for everyone in the past.

For this reason only, she took his cup and said, "Just for you."

Taylor picked up her cup and wiggled it at Fran. She was smiling too and also put on her sad puppy eyes. Fran took the offered cup, laughing at the two of them and shaking her head. Both Taylor and Marcus liked Fran. She was a good detective and a valued member of the team; good looking too, Taylor had already noted. Marcus and Taylor looked at each other with knowing smiles of mutual appreciation. They giggled like a couple of kids. Marcus kept on watching his screen while Taylor watched Fran's bottom as she walked over to the coffee machine. *Nice,* she thought to herself.

Marcus reached over to the pause button, not that he needed to. Brennan stood there under that camera motionless, his stare so hideous that even Marcus felt uncomfortable looking at him and he was only watching a screen.

"That's him, that's him! Fuck me, he's a clever boy. Look at this Taylor, he's totally changed."

Taylor came up behind Marcus, hand on his shoulder and leant into the screen, her eyes fixed on Brennan's.

"He's so fucking arrogant. He wanted us to see him; he wants us to know he hasn't given up on her yet, poor Susan. We need to see if we can get her some protection. He knows we know who he is and that's all down to her surviving."

"I can't believe she did survive what she went through. He did some job on her," Marcus exclaimed to Taylor.

"They'll do the usual and put a cop car outside her house with some wet-nosed inexperienced cops in it that couldn't do much to save her if he appeared anyway," Taylor sighed.

"She's not safe until we get our hands on him but we will. He's going to slip up soon. His little hospital stunt has proved he's prepared to be a bit careless to get nearer to her."

Chapter 23: Leaving

Susan's hands were shaking as she packed her things up from her hospital locker. The nurses popped in and out to say their goodbyes; Emily and Ann were still recovering from their own night of violence but still made the effort to come in and bid her farewell. The two nurses gave Susan huge hugs and words of strength and resilience, telling her not to let him win and to be strong.

Emily said, "You've beaten him once, you can do it again, but hopefully the police will do that for you though, eh."

Susan's eyes were welling up with tears of sadness and fear. She still had her life to live but she was terrified to have to do it.

Ann asked, "Will you be going home to your house? And how will you manage on your own?"

Just as she had asked the question, Andrew popped his head round the door and said, "She won't be alone. Are you ready to go? The car's just at the rear of the building."

Emily and Ann both looked at each other. They hadn't heard the gossip of how close Susan and Andrew had become and they nudged each other and gave Susan a knowing smile.

"Well done you, you've got yourself a good one there. Andrew's lovely."

□□□

He pulled the door shut behind him, checking it for marks where he had pushed the tool in but the rubber seal had moved back and disguised the tell-tale marks of his forced entry. He stood at the back door, leant his head back and inhaled the scent of the house once again, the familiar aroma of the place making his eyes narrow and his lips turn up at the edges. His teeth ground slowly together as the ferocity of his anger surged through him, saliva glistening on his mouth. His breathing sped up and his heart pounded. He took the steps three at a time and turned towards the bedroom; he stood and looked at his art work on the walls and carpets and the staining on some of the furniture. Although it was faint, it was still there despite much cleaning. He thought of the screams of terror and the pain that had filled the room on that night, the night he should have taken Susan's life. He breathed in her perfume, her alluring scent, and imagined doing it all over again, something he fully intended; of course this time, there would be a different ending, he'd make sure of that. He moved slowly towards the bed, and his huge hands reached down and picked up her pillow. He pushed his face into it and breathed in hard. She was there, faint and delicate, but still there. His penis was rock hard once more and obvious under his jeans; he had to stop himself from relieving himself there and then. He couldn't leave any evidence that he had been here again. That would spoil her homecoming surprise. He moved slowly and deliberately out of the room and stood below the hatch in the hallway. He was tall enough to open it and it slowly came down revealing the attic; he had remembered this from his first date with Susan, although he hadn't expected to have to come back. *How the fuck did she live, how? She's spoilt everything. I was just getting started. There are so many smug, cock teasing sluts out there that need me to teach them a lesson.* He pulled down the attic ladder and his feet clunked on the rungs as he made his way up. He had brought bag with food and beer in it, just in case she didn't come back straight away. He had no issue with relieving himself somewhere in the attic if time went on; he would never have to clean it up anyway. He pulled the attic steps up from below, leaving no evidence he was back.

ￜￜￜ

"Thank you so much for looking after him," Susan smiled.

"It was my pleasure. He's very cute and loves his cuddles."

A loud contented meow came from the cat box and Susan pushed her finger through the bars and tickled Baxter's chin. He purred loudly, delighted that his mummy would be spoiling him once again. Andrew put his arm round Susan's shoulder and guided her back to his car, taking the basket from her. She allowed him to hold her close and enjoyed the strength he gave her with his comfort and loyalty. He popped Baxter on the rear seat and opened the door to let Susan into the front. They put on their seat belts and Susan winced as she turned, the pain of her healing injuries still too fresh to forget, each stabbing pain a reminder that he still stalked her from within. Andrew asked if she was alright, knowing that this nightmare would never stop for her unless John Brennan was stopped, either by arrest or some other way. Andrew was uneasy about him still being out there too, but not enough to abandon Susan; he loved her deeply although they hadn't known each other long. His time with her in recovery had shown him just how strong she was and her determination to get through this; she was a real fighter. He had also seen her heart, her insecurities and her inner beauty untainted by Brennan's violence. *Why would anyone ever have wanted to hurt her, to do what he did to her? She's beautiful and has never harmed anyone in her life.*

"Come on, let's get to your house and pack up what we need. You don't have to stay there a single night longer. The for sale sign will go up tomorrow and even with what has happened some ghoulish person will want to live there but who cares as long as you get the money."

Susan smiled at him, happy that they were heading up north for a luxury get away. They would rent somewhere meantime until they were able to sell the house that was now tainted with evil. They needed to get away from everything and everyone, for a while anyway.

ⁿⁿⁿ

He shook his penis as he had just finished his second piss of the day, the vessel he used was a vase, obviously of value and cared for with the way in which it had been packaged. It was nearly full and he'd need to find another, as the last thing he wanted to do was just take a piss anywhere and have it leak through the ceiling and give him away; that would spoil their little reunion party.

They turned into the street, unaware of what lurked behind the four walls. Susan's heart pounded and she was breathing so fast that she started to get light headed. She gripped Andrew's hand to try to calm herself and his fingers curled round hers, giving her comfort and support.

"It will be okay, you know! It shouldn't take too long to get what we need to get out of here. We'll arrange to get the rest later."

Susan took a deep breath and pulled herself together.

A police car pulled up just in front of them with two officers inside. PC Lomond stepped out of the car and headed up to Susan's window.

"Do you want us to check the house for you?"

"No, no, it's all right. We'll manage. We just need to get a couple of things and we're out of here for good. Thanks though. I take it that you'll be outside until we leave?"

"Yes, we will and we will follow you until you are out with the city boundary."

"Thanks."

Susan stood staring at her house, one that used to be her safe haven, her den, but not now. She walked slowly up to the front door, her whole body tense and shaking almost uncontrollably. Andrew took her hand and put the key in the lock; the door opened as Andrew pushed it inwards. The hair on Susan's neck stood up on end as if someone had just walked over her grave. Her eyes were wide and transfixed straight ahead. Every painful memory came racing back, stabbing her skin like a million sharp burning needles. It was like the essence of him was still here, all over the house; little did she know that he was still in it. The hair on her neck knew he was, but she had forgotten her sixth sense, the one that can feel danger; she ignored it once again, putting the feeling down to the horror of that night and the memories that were flooding back to her, unaware that he was there to finish what he had started. Her first steps were tentative and cautious. She looked round her home; what used to be her sanctuary was now a house of horrors.

"Come on," Andrew said softly, "Let's get this over with. Let's get what we need and go." Susan lay down her handbag and other belongings on the hall table and carried on through the house. She was saying goodbye forever to what she used to know and love; all the good memories from living there were being scraped away with a wire brush, every bristle cutting her deeply. There was nothing warm there for her anymore, just a wintry coldness that crept into her bones, a probing sense of hate and evil scarred into every corner; there was nowhere to hide from what had happened to her that night. She stopped at the bottom of the stairs, her eyes watering and her knees buckling with fear as she looked towards her bedroom. The pain of that night was searing through her scars, her mouth was dry and her face wet with tears. Andrew watched as the woman he loved was overcome by fear. She dropped to her knees, her legs wet with the urine that trickled onto the floor; she was more broken inside that Andrew had ever realised.

"I, I can't do this Andrew, I can't go up there. I thought I could but I can't. He's everywhere. He's still chasing me in my thoughts. He's there, black eyes staring at me, his teeth gritted together with hate. I'm going back to the car, I can't stay."

Susan got up and scampered out of the door, not remotely embarrassed that she was wet, asking Andrew to get her things while she waited in the car.

"Don't come with me, just get the things and we're leaving, I can't be here. He's still there, he's everywhere and I just can't do it," she screamed out.

She couldn't get to the car quickly enough, the house looming over her like a shadow of terror, haunting her every thought, completely unaware that the devil was inside, lying in wait for her, and not prepared to rest until he had her life.

He heard every word they said, her fear filling the air and fuelling his pleasure, his stiff penis in his hand. He couldn't contain himself, excitement at hearing her words, the sound of her terrified voice and the sheer terror that he had created within her aroused him like never before. He muffled his pleasure as he came hard, his grimace now a sneer of desire and twisted relief.

He wanted her so badly that it was hurting him and his patience was wearing thin. He wanted to hurt her, torture her like never before and kill her slowly and painfully for daring to ruin his life, and this time he would kill her making no mistakes. He pushed his penis back in his jeans and was careful not to make any noise. He heard Andrew clattering around in her bedroom below, cupboards opening and closing, drawers opening and the sounds of a person in a hurry to leave. He was raging that Andrew was in her room, almost like she was being unfaithful to him. *Where are they going? I need to know. That fucked up little slut will not get away from me, not now, not ever, she's mine, she's fucked up my life for good and I'm gonna make sure she doesn't have a life at all, because I am going to take it.*

Andrew heaved the case off of the bed, and stopped dead in his tracks, his heart heavy as he took some time to look around the room. He had never been in this house before but as he looked around he could see his beautiful girlfriend's attack clearly on every wall and surface; it was like vandalism in blood. *How had she survived this nightmare, how?* What did he not do to her was the question he asked himself, his imagination running wild, anger welling up inside him. He was not going to let anything happen to her, not as long as he was alive to stop it. Andrew lifted the two cases and the jewellery box, something Susan had asked him to take for sentimental reasons. He made his way down the stairs and almost forgot to take Susan's bag with him. His hands were full as he manoeuvred out of the front door, slamming it shut behind him without a second glance; a glance he would later regret.

The booking form for the log cabin was in amongst what looked like a pile of old papers that Susan had brought in with her. They went unnoticed by Andrew and were not remembered by Susan as they pulled away in their car, the police following on closely behind. The house stood there behind them like a tomb of forgotten happiness; all that was left was a reminder of that night of pain, terror and the destruction of her old self, leaving her with a lifetime of fear, as long as he lived.

His arms held on to the ledge above as he stepped slowly down the steps from the attic, his face red with anger and from his efforts a few minutes before. He looked in the bedroom and licked his rough lips, tongue rasping over them as he imagined himself kissing Susan all over as she writhed beneath him, but not with pleasure. His footsteps were heavy on the stairs as he stomped his way to the bottom. *How the fuck am I gonna find that scared little cow now? I'll really fuck her up. She won't get away from me that easily and as for that wimpy little fucker she calls a boyfriend, I'll cut his balls off and choke the life out of him with them. She's fucking mine and I'll make sure he sees that before I kill the little rat fuck.* John's thoughts were running away with him, he could almost taste her, and he could picture the end scene as he raped her over and over as Andrew was made to watch. He chuckled deeply to himself as he walked through the hall and into the kitchen. He opened up one of the cupboards, then another and another until he eventually found something to eat.

"Biscuits, great! fucking nice ones too, the posh little bitch." He ate half the packet before walking back into the hall and seeing the papers on the floor.

They weren't here before, he thought. He bent down and picked them up. They had been under Susan's arms and touching her skin and he could smell her scent on them. His arousal once again obvious to see as he took a deep breath in. The smell of her was driving him wild. He came back to his senses and started to finger his way through the pile of papers, huge fingers clumsily flicking each page.

"Shit, pish, crap, useless fucking shit," and then he stopped and his heart skipped a beat as he could not believe what he was reading. The venue, the dates, the cost, the map to their dream escape, everything that he needed to hunt his prey down, once and for all, was there, almost gift wrapped for him to find.

"What a stupid fucking bitch. She deserves to fucking die for being that fucking dumb, unless she wants me to find her." He roared with laughter. It was as if he had just won the lottery; he was so amused by her monumental error, he felt like jumping up and down like a child at Christmas. He was going to get her and she had helped him find her. For a few moments he had wondered how he was going to go about this but, like in Hansel and Gretel's fairytale, crumbs had been left to guide him to the ultimate prize - Susan.

He pulled the curtains over very slightly to look outside to see if the coast was clear. Connie Anderson was also looking out of her window directly across the road, eyes fixed on her poor unfortunate neighbour's house; she had heard the car leaving a while before and was looking out to see if Susan was back again. She was sad about what had happened to Susan, thinking to herself, *if only I had looked out on the night that poor girl had been attacked I could have done something, phoned to help her, anything to stop it.* She had seen Susan and Andrew leaving half an hour before, but still wanted to look out for the house, just in case something was to happen to it when Susan wasn't there. *That's funny, I thought I saw the curtain moving. No, don't be silly, there's nobody there.* Connie doubted herself and made a point of focussing on the curtain where she thought she had imagined the movement, her ageing eyes struggling to focus. *See, it was nothing, silly old me,* she convinced herself. Just then she saw it: a hand, a huge hand at the bottom of the curtain leaning on the windowsill. Then a face, a face that stopped her heart and her breathing for that moment. Her heart started to thump through her chest almost painfully. Her blood ran cold as she watched him look up the street and terror flushed through her. His head was facing down the street, but it was slowly moving to scan the rest of the area including Connie's house. Her curtain was just slightly open and she did not want it to move and have it catch his eye. So when his face started to look straight at her window, she stood motionless. *Will he be able to see me? Could my curtain just be lying this way? What if he sees me? What will I do?* John stared at the house opposite him. He was checking to see when he could leave. He didn't know whether to go via the front or back door and what was the best option in daylight, as there were houses to the rear where he assumed there would be people, since this place was full of pensioners. Connie's eyes were going dry as she hadn't blinked, because she was too scared to stop watching him for even a second. At least if she could see him, he wasn't coming to get her. There was a net curtain on Connie's window. She could see out quite well but anyone outside would struggle to see her, she hoped. John picked his nose and wiped it on Susan's window sill; every little bit of his disrespectful behaviour pleased him, every degrading little action made him feel empowered. Connie moved her hand causing the net curtain to twitch and John turned his head like a jackal in the direction of the minute movement, his cold eyes focused and black. He stared right at her but could not see her; he sensed her as she watched him.

He pushed his face through the curtains, his facial expression like that of Jack Nicholson in The Shining when he pushed his head through the door to the terror of his wife. John no longer concealed himself, he wanted to frighten whoever was watching him. Connie's breathing was now so fast she felt light headed. She leaned her head down for only a moment and then resumed her position, only to see that he had gone - no hand, no face, nothing was left. She stood anchored to the spot, too terrified to move, her eyes fixed on the house in front of her. There was foliage both in her garden and in Susan's, enough to give someone cover if needed, as John knew all too well from his night with Susan. With her shaking hand Connie reached for the phone, still frightened to move, just in case she had not given herself away and it was just her silly imagination. She dialled 999 and it seemed like an eternity before she heard, "Hello, which emergency service do you require?"

That's not all she heard: heavy steps were coming from her kitchen. Her heart sank as she remembered that she had been out to feed the birds earlier and foolishly she hadn't locked the door behind her. *Oh what a fool,* she thought. *Ever since Susan was assaulted I've always locked up. Shoot! Have I got time to hide? I've got to try. Move!*

Her shaky voice quivered when she said, "Help me, quickly."

The footsteps inside got louder and were moving in her direction, Connie moved fast for an old lady. She went to the second door in the living room that led to a study and round into the rear of the house. John had not disguised his presence in any way but had underestimated his prey. Entering the living room, he fully expected to simply choke the life out of the interfering little busy body but to his surprise the room was empty and a phone lay on the table.

"Fuuuuccckk!" He lifted the phone and a voice spoke.

"Hello, hello! Are you still there?"

"I'm here. There is nothing happening. It was just my senile old mother imagining things and I couldn't stop her getting the phone in time. Sorry."

"Okay, are you sure you don't need any of the services?"

"No services needed - false alarm, sorry. Sorry to have wasted your time," John said convincingly.

"Sorry, I didn't catch your name Sir."

John hesitated, then replied, "Smith. Bye, then," he said quickly as he hung up.

The call taker put a call straight through to the police; there was no way she was going to let this one lie. She had to send a set to check everything was okay anyway. She read out the address to the police and that was when the street name sounded painfully familiar. Instead of a single set doing a quick check, she also sent out a call on the city wide frequency for any free set to make its way there as well, just in case there was something more sinister going on. John slammed the phone down and made his way to the other door; he knew the police would check things anyway, they were not that stupid.

Connie lay face down on the floor, her hand gently pulling the bed clothes down to hide her beneath the bed, her face pushed into the carpet. She began to sob, trying hard not to breathe loudly or make a sound. There were five bedrooms in her house and she'd gone into the third in the hallway. *Please come. Please, please, I don't want to die. That poor girl, that hideous man. Please help me, god, help me.* Her hands were clasped and praying for help. John rushed through the house. He saw all five doors and went to the fifth hoping that she would have hidden in the furthest room. He crashed through the door, door, slamming it against the wall. He yelled out a cry of rage, knowing he didn't have time to find her if he didn't want to get caught and he didn't want that. He was on a quest to finish what he had started with Susan.

He called out to Connie, "You're a fucking lucky little grass. If I had the time, I'd rip your loose mouthed jaw right off, you fucking old cow."

John crashed through the house like a wild bear. He had to be quick, some police weren't slouches. He sprinted up the street, turned the corner and jumped into his car. He heard the sirens when he ran; he heard them coming from town and he headed the opposite way. He drove at an average speed so as not to draw attention to himself, his hire car blending in with the other traffic causing no issues at all. He knew the drill, the road blocks would be coming out soon on the major routes and some of the smaller ones but he'd be well on his way up north by then.

Chapter 24:
Out of Touch

Susan laid her head back on the seat of the car, Andrew was looking forward when she looked at his face. She could see the worry etched there, although she knew he would try and hide it from her, to be strong for her. She knew even the strongest man would fear John Brennan. He was not normal; he was a very deranged and dangerous person, almost inhuman, capable of anything and she knew it.

Taylor could not believe what she was hearing on the radio.

"A male fitting the description of John Brennan has been seen within the home address of Susan Hamilton's house," and it appeared he would have killed the neighbour if he'd had the chance.

Taylor put her head in her hands and said to Marcus, "Pass me the phone, I need to at least try and tell Susan how far he's willing to go. *Get the Scenes Examination Branch down to Susan's house and see how he got in there and where he's been hiding all this time, as there have been cops there most of the day. Get in touch with the car that's been assigned to getting Susan out of the city. Get them to stop their motor.* "To PC Lomond, are you receiving," Taylor spoke into the radio, exasperation on her face, an almost painful expression had obliterated any warmth and feeling of pleasure that had been experienced earlier that day.

Kay looked over from the other side of the office She could see the tense body language in Taylor and the beaten dog look that hung over Marcus. She had heard the office whispers and knew that it wouldn't be long before Findlay would be on the warpath.

"PC Lomond, receiving."

"Constable Lomond, tell me you're still with them? Tell me they haven't gone yet and that they are still in sight."

"That's a negative, Serg. We made sure they got through the traffic quickly and they went onto the M9 over ten minutes ago. They've been out of visual contact since then."

"Received. You did well getting them away quickly in normal circumstances but we want them back. He's been in her house. Who knows what he knows."

"Did they say where they were heading before they left?"

"No Serg, sorry," PC Lomond stated.

"Marcus, get onto the other forces' Roads Policing branches and see if we can track down Susan's vehicle before he does."

"I'm on it," said Marcus as he turned to speak on the phone to the other Scottish Divisions. "Who the fuck has she told where she was going? Tell me someone knows what her plans are."

"Fuck, fuck, fuuuccckkkk! Please don't let him get her."

Andrew turned off the motorway quite soon after getting onto it and turned to Susan. "Scenic route, I think. Let's get away from all of it, even the speeding traffic. We're not in a hurry are we?"

"Nope," Susan said in a soft voice, as she put her hand gently on Andrew's thigh and squeezed it lovingly.

"Nobody will find us where we're going," Andrew smiled.

Where they were going was an isolated luxury log cabin in the middle of a wooded area, a large expanse of unpopulated beauty, as remote as it could possibly be. There was a loch beside the cabin with a couple of small rowing boats for the residents to make use of on lazy sunny days. There were hills on three sides and it was described as idyllic in the advert. A haven to escape from everything, a piece of paradise with a taste of Scotland's beauty. Without a map or previous knowledge it could prove a very hard place to find and that is why Susan and Andrew had chosen the location; they had been meticulous in their search criteria. The cabin was five star and had every modern convenience. It contained a sauna and a Jacuzzi, and a large cinema-screen television with a pre chosen selection of films. There was enough luxury food and provisions pre-paid for the weeks ahead with a couple of deliveries of fresh goods throughout the stay. It seemed to be the perfect getaway. It cost a bit, but the setting and what came in the package was exactly what they wanted. Susan had decided that life was for living and no longer something that she would take for granted. She was going to spend her money less wisely from now on.

Andrew's eyes were fixed on the road. Susan leant over to him and kissed him on the ear, whispering, "Thank you. Thank you for being here with me, thank you for everything you've done for me and thanks for believing in me."

Andrew's heart skipped a beat. He liked what he'd heard and he truly loved Susan, even though their time together had not been that long.

He put his hand onto her thigh and she met it with her hand. Glancing at her, he said, "I wouldn't want to spend my life without you now, every minute with you has been a gift. I've never met anyone like you before. You're beautiful inside and out."

He was about to say he loved her but decided to wait until they reached their destination. The setting there would be just perfect - a coal fire, nice wine and the perfect location.

The drive seemed to take forever; they got lost ten times on the winding roads and had to ask numerous people for directions, but they were finally on a single track pathway. Their car bounced from dip to dip, rock to rock and round numerous dodgy verges but they eventually found it. The cabin stood on the edge of the loch. There was a small jetty into the water and the views all around were breathtaking. Dark green fir trees merged with varying colours of other species of tree to cover the sides of the hills. There were small streams running down into the loch. The place seemed deserted, only a small herd of deer on the hill top, several does and a few fawns, and thirty metres or so away stood the most magnificent and beautiful beast they'd ever seen. The stag, with huge antlers and a thick wiry coat, watched over the females and their young and appeared to look in the direction of the approaching vehicle. Susan's smile was wide, her shoulders loosened and the tension she was not even aware of started to lift from her like a curtain going up in the theatre. Her heart came alive and she felt good. She felt happy and for that moment she felt free, a feeling she had not had for a long time.

"We've got to find her Marcus, what else can we do? There have been no sightings of their vehicle, nothing, absolutely diddly squat."

"That's what they probably wanted, an escape from everything, but the good thing is, if we can't find her then neither can he."

"We don't know that," Taylor said in a raised voice. "Forensics are back and that creepy bastard was up in the attic whilst Susan and Andrew were in the house. We don't know what they might have said to each other when they were getting Susan's things. They didn't want the cops to go in with them."

"Have you tried both their phones?"

"No answer on either one. They really must've wanted to disappear. Mind you, who wouldn't after what she's been through?"

Taylor looked up towards Kay but she had left her desk. However, Fran caught her eye and held her gaze; it was so quick Taylor could have imagined it but there was definitely a lingering look directed straight at her. In the past there would have been no hesitation, Taylor would have held the stare back and tested the water to ensure that there was actually some interest there. This time her thoughts went straight to Kay, the way she made her feel was very different to before and very powerful. Fran was a good looking girl and well worth a bit of flirtatious contact. Taylor would always struggle with women. She could not help herself when someone paid her that little bit of extra attention, especially if it was in a sexual way. She was about to look away as Fran was busy writing, but Fran must have felt Taylor's quizzical stare fixed in her direction. She looked up and their eyes met again. There was no doubt about Fran's intention; Taylor could feel her gaze in numerous places and was well aware of what that meant. Fran held her stare and then dropped her eyes in a seductive way before turning away with a slight but subtle and deliberate lick of her lips. Taylor cursed herself, cursed her beauty because if people didn't make a play for her, life would be so much less complicated, simpler and it would be far easier to remain faithful.

Marcus just sat staring at Taylor in disbelief; he shook his head in a comical manner and winked at her. "How come it's always you? I'm a decent looking guy, what about me?"

"You're fucking gorgeous Marcus, and you know it, they know it, we all know it. If I was straight, even I'd go there."

Marcus smiled as Taylor went on, "The only problem with you, which isn't really a problem, is that you're a good guy and no matter how much they flirted with you or how good looking they were, you wouldn't cross that line. You're married, so why try?"

"Hmmm, good point, so you're saying I am gorgeous then?"

Taylor took a huge sigh and threw a toy Bagpuss at Marcus's face. "Yessssss, you are but don't let it go to your head."

Marcus smiled and carried on with the search he was doing on the computer. Taylor lay back in her chair with her hands on her head. Just then Kay walked by and looked right at her, a slight smile crossed her lips, a knowing smile, one that oozed lust and desire, one that caused a flutter in Taylor's stomach. Taylor could still smell the scent of their frantic love making only a couple of hours before, subtle but a constant source of arousal, as her mind would flit back to their encounter. Unbeknown to the two secret lovers, Fran had also been looking at Taylor's lithe body stretch back over the chair, her blouse tight over her breasts, nipples visible, her neck showing with her blouse open down to her bra; she wore tasteful white gold jewellery, which complimented her olive skin. Fran was looking at Taylor's eyes when Kay had walked into the room and she had caught sight of the looks that had passed between the pair and was now well aware that this was far more than just a friendly relationship. *You must be kidding me. Kay? Never! I thought she was straighter than all of us, I thought she was a hot blooded heterosexual man eater. Hmmm, how wrong was I? I wonder how far they've got. That look was pretty heavy and it was most certainly mutual on both sides.* Fran was not a bad person in any way but couldn't help the way she was starting to feel for Taylor, and the glance she had just shared with her also had motive. Funnily enough this did not seem to put Fran off; she wasn't looking for more than just a bit of flirtatious fun. She knew Taylor was a player; she'd just never thought that she'd be one of the ones playing now.

Findlay put his head out of the office, "Nicks, come into my office, we need to sort this shit out!"

She got up from her seat and went straight to his den. She did not look around the office as she went but her rising up from her chair had caused at least two sets of attractive feminine eyes to look at her walk confidently into his office. Taylor was well aware of the unpleasant rants she was about to receive, the unrealistic demands on the team and the push for results to save his fat lazy ass. The blame was always directed as far away from him as possible, usually lumped onto Taylor and her team, even though they regularly got good results. In this case, however, they always appeared to have been one step behind and the suspect most definitely had the upper hand.

"We need to have a travelling squad, we'll need to liaise with the other forces and create a small task force. This serial killing mother fucker could be in any of their areas. We'll need someone that has seen him and at least another five cops and detectives, over and above you and Marcus. Pull out all of the stops, use everybody and anybody. We have the clearance to do this and there is a no holds barred budget. He's obviously still focused on Susan and I personally don't think he's going to stop!"

For once Taylor was in full agreement with her boss and she too wanted to get this beast. She was surprised that a full squad would be funded to travel the country in search of John Brennan.

"You pick the team and make sure you don't take any lazy bastards with you. This isn't a fucking holiday!"

Taylor had several officers that sprang to mind, the two from the hospital the night he assaulted the nurses, Lomond and his partner, Fran and the other senior troops in the team. As always there would be those that would be disappointed and question why they were not coming, answers that were always hard to give and receive.

ɒɒɒ

John cursed as loud as he could, his teeth grinding heavily against each other. He had the directions and this was the fifth time he'd got lost. He was in the middle of nowhere. He just put his head down on the steering wheel and calmed down as his thoughts wandered off to what he would do when he finally found them. There was no rush. She didn't know he was coming to surprise her and take the ultimate prize from her once and for all. His hand fell onto his crotch, his stiff penis welcomed his hand; he reached with his other hand for the beer that lay in the foot well of the car and cracked open a can. He was in the middle of nowhere and reckoned the police would not come here so he settled down for the night and put the seat back. He thought to himself with a smile, beer in one hand, cock in the other, *this should be quite a good night.* Anyone else in this place would be spooked out with the noise of the trees and whistling of the wind but not him, he just lay his head to the side once he had finished and slept like a baby, untroubled and looking forward to the time ahead.

Chapter 25: The Squad

The van was full of kit, the eight-strong squad and Taylor sitting up front. Marcus was driving and PC Lomond, PC Miller, DC Andrews, DC Brown, DC Noble and DC Blake were all in the back. There was a good humour within the van and a sense of expectation. All were committed individuals that believed that they would get John Brennan and deal with him accordingly. All of them had spent hours and hours of their time on this case, missed out on family life, friends and having very little down time, they weren't able to go out and see people, no time to relax or have the odd drink in or out. During a case like this, normality didn't come into it; you were lucky to have six hours in your house and that included eating, sleeping and washing, so there was constant fatigue. Four of the officers on the squad were firearms trained and had special authorisation to carry a sidearm and all could self-authorise if the situation required it as the assailant was such a violent man, capable of lethal harm. This type of unofficial posse had never been authorised before, but they hoped that it would prove effective for the unusual situation. Serial killers in Edinburgh were not the norm and this had not happened since Burke and Hare. The force was prepared to try out untested means to get this man stopped at any cost.

"Where are we going?" asked someone. "This is like a wild goose chase."

"Up north," replied Marcus. "There are lots of people on the case. They'll bottom out numerous lead so there is bound to be some sort of trace of their booking somewhere on someone's system and they'll give us the heads up on where to head."

"Let's go then," Taylor said.

Taylor never had a chance to meet up with Kay prior to their departure; there was no time for anything other than a quick bag pack and a shower. There was the usual crude banter en route, the men and women giving as good as they got. The humour was always filled with innuendo, smut and filth and none of them would have it any other way. There was always a line and it was very rarely crossed. Humour created its own boundaries as taking it too far was unfunny. Taylor pulled her sun visor down, opened the mirror and checked that her face was okay due to the rush to get ready. She looked into the rear of the van, scanning the troops, her eyes glancing at DC Andrews. She was reading something, so Taylor looked at her a little longer, checking her, not intending to be seen. Fran looked up at that moment as if she knew she was being watched and caught Taylor looking. She instantly fixed her gaze straight back at Taylor's eyes. Both were aware that this was more than just a casual glance; there was obviously some mutual attraction there, whether there was intent was yet to be tested.

Taylor closed the mirror over and sunk back into her seat, her stomach still fluttering lightly at the little encounter with the flirtatious glances, eyes being windows into the soul. Taylor didn't need more distraction and certainly not any more women with an interest in her. But she couldn't help thinking about Fran and what could happen and what it would be like. Taylor flicked up the visor to try and avoid appearing obvious and overly willing but she could feel a warm sensation on her back and she guessed that Fran may still be looking at her.

¤¤¤

He zipped up his flies, burped and got out of the car to take a piss in the trees. Getting back in his car, he started up the engine, put it in gear and moved off, more hopeful that he would find them today.

ㅁㅁㅁ

Susan opened her eyes. The sun shone through the gap in the curtains and for the first time in ages she smiled. She felt relaxed and happy. She rolled over to where Andrew lay, still asleep. She could feel the silk of the sheets glide over her skin as she slid over the bed. She put her arm over him and nestled her hand into his chest and gently stroked him. She fully intended to wake him up as she had something in mind. Andrew took hold of her hand and held it, his feelings transmitting through him like a beacon. She could feel his affection for her emanating from him like a warm glow.

He said quietly in a strong male tone, "Morning! How are you today? You look like you feel better already." He turned round to face her and he kissed her softly at first, until her desire became obvious. Her breathing told him that it wasn't a reassuring loving kiss she wanted, it was more than that. She pushed her tongue deep into his mouth in a way that sent him instantly into a frenzy of arousal, although he knew what ladies needed. He responded, his rugged unshaven face pushed against hers, their tongues met and their kiss was needy and excited. Both of them felt the release of their fear and felt blissfully free from their stalker.

Susan swung herself up on top of Andrew, his pleasure very obvious to see. She was careful not to please him too soon, but chose to tease him a little, rubbing herself over him, careful not to touch him where he wanted. Her pleasure glistened upon his skin, his hand came to her and caressed her, firm but sensual, her moan sending a tingling sensation to his toes. She was soaking and this turned him on even more. His experienced hand brought her to a climax very quickly as her arousal was already at fever pitch, his fingers entering her as she started going over the edge making her climax last longer. She deliberately pushed down on his fingers, strong and thick, her pussy taking them deep into her as she moved with him. She knew he was a considerate man and was aware that he was so excited that he would lose control soon if she didn't let him into her. She made her way down to meet the tip of his penis, rubbing over the tip of it with her slender hand and Andrew's moan was deep and grateful.

She paused where she was and worked herself on and around him, their kisses still desperate and lustful, until she pushed down onto him and he filled her welcoming haven to the point that she gasped, not in pain, but with the pleasure she felt; she had climaxed already and now wanted him to take her, to make love to her. Andrew's hand was still on her pussy as he entered her, heightening her pleasure as he was inside her. They made love in a frenzied response to the need of two people that had been frightened out of feeling anything for the last few months. Their passion was unbridled and very physical, both of them wanting more from each other. Sweat glistened on both of their bodies and their breathing was now noisy and unrestrained, but the more they made love the more they wanted. Andrew was a fit man and capable of a quick repeat of what Susan needed to take. When he was resting, his mouth became the next place for Susan to land her perfectly formed body. His hands held her bottom firmly above him, his mouth on her and his tongue exploring every inch of her, his hand and fingers also giving extra pleasure when her need became obvious. She then pleasured him with her mouth and hands as they rolled around the massive bed. The silk sheets were wrapped around their legs and clung to their sweaty bodies and were starting to restrict their love making.

They kissed each other deeply and as if they knew that they had no more to give, they flopped back onto the bed, panting and spent. They began to laugh; Susan's laughter was almost out of control and Andrew pulled her into him. "I won't let anything happen to you. We're smarter than him." He stared right at her and cupped her pretty face in his hands. "I love you so much, every little piece of you. You're so beautiful, inside and out, and you're also one horny lady when your thoughts are free."

"Is that a problem?" she teased him.

"Breakfast?"

"Oh yes please, I don't think anything we've had so far counts for any calories."

Andrew just looked at her and smiled, the fondest of looks from one to the other.

ᴏᴏᴏ

His smile was hideous as he pulled up over the ridge. The log cabin down at the shore of the loch looked idyllic. *A perfect place for no interruptions, for me that is. This place is like heaven for the task at hand. I bet they think I'm never going to find them. Wrong, so very wrong. I'm here and I'll make sure that they both know it, over and over until they die. I'll frighten them to death first and then torture him to within an inch of his life for temporarily taking her from me. Then I'll make him watch as I slowly take her sorry little life away from her and no mistakes this time.*

ᴏᴏᴏ

Taylor laughed loudly as DC Brown went into her usual rapport of humour, her tales filled with comical mirth, making those around her sore with laughter. Fran's laugh was by far the loudest, the females within the group far more vocal than the males, other than PC Lomond, who was also a bit of a joker. Everyone had their own single room, which secretly Taylor was happy with. She didn't know what she would do if she had had to share with DC Andrews; there was looking and then there was doing; the two were very different and she did not want to be put in that situation, not yet anyway.

Taylor spoke out once the laughter had subsided. "Work! Remember why we came," she said in a comical way.

"We've got two or three hopefuls, with names like Smith and Brown registering at various places in Aberdeenshire. They've obviously not used their real names and this really is a wild goose chase. Let's hope old Johnny boy doesn't know more than us."

"Meet at the van in an hour. That's enough time for everyone to get their stuff together, isn't it?"

Fran looked straight at her, her eyes bright and lively, full of mischief and Taylor enjoyed the feeling she got when their eyes met and she spent time in her company.

They smiled at each other and the intensity eased a little with the mutual appreciation of one another and an open acknowledgement that there was a warmth there.

John walked through the trees; they were thick evergreens and gave almost complete coverage as he moved slowly towards the cabin. The terrain was harsh under foot with a few hidden pot holes and foliage of the most hostile kind dressing the ground. John's footsteps were heavy and he was aware of the noise he was making as he walked towards the cabin. He wasn't close enough to worry yet but he would have to rethink his approach when the time came. He had left his car off road and out of sight, taking time to cover any tyre tracks he'd left as he drove off the main road, which itself was little more than a dirt track. He was about a hundred metres away when he stopped and just stared towards the cabin, his heart starting to beat faster as his mind floated back to the night he had spent with Susan. *Let the fun begin!*

Chapter 26:
Invisible Terror

The van arrived at one of the sites. Everyone jumped out quickly and made for individual chalets, checking all of them just in case Susan had been more inventive with her choice of name for the booking. It was quite an exclusive site with only eight cabins, well spread out and dotted round a very picturesque area with a forest and loch; an idyllic spot to escape from the world.

¤¤¤

Susan came out of the shower for the second time that day and stretched out on the sofa; Andrew brought a glass of red, in a glass that resembled a fish bowl, and a bottle of beer for himself. Night had fallen and it was almost pitch dark outside apart from the dim lights leading down to the jetty. There was a slight breeze which created an eerie sound that whispered its way through the tall trees. There were also the whines of foxes, the scurry of small animals and the haunting hoots of owls hidden within high branches. None of which was bothering the love birds tucked up in their warm, comfortable, safe and secluded cabin. The doors were bolted front and rear and everything appeared secure. *Perfect,* they thought. They settled down to watch one of the DVDs provided: Inception, a thriller starring Leonardo Dicaprio. Susan enjoyed the comfort and security Andrew gave her, and even though he could not eradicate the monster that persistently pursued her in every waking moment of every day she lived, he could at least make some of her time a whole lot better. With Andrew by her side, she wouldn't have to ever face John Brennan on her own, or so she thought.

"Negative on every cabin, Serg. They're not here."

"Shit! I knew it would be too good to be true if we found them on the first try. Next one, then," Taylor signed expectantly.

They packed up and headed further north to the next venue. They tried four more sites, with nothing, and this one would be the last that night. It was right beside a travel lodge and the troops were knackered; time to kick back a little and plan for the next day.

ㅁㅁㅁ

CRAAACK! The branch seemed to scream out a warning from beneath his foot. "Fuck," he rasped under his breath.

His fists tightened within his black leather gloves. He was wearing a balaclava and a camouflaged type of army jacket. To his delight someone could be standing 15 feet away from him in the pitch dark and he would be practically invisible; the moonlight was totally hidden by the cloud cover.

ㅁㅁㅁ

Susan's head flew off of the pillow with a start. "What was that, did you hear that? Andrew, Andrew, wake up! There was a noise outside, I heard a branch or something being stood on."

"You sure? I never heard anything?"

"That's because you could sleep through anything and you're totally worn out," Susan said with a semi smile, still unnerved by the noise she had heard outside. John stood still, didn't move a muscle; he knew it had been loud and very possibly heard within the cabin which was barely 20 metres away.

Andrew got up and said to Susan with reassuring eyes, "It was probably a fox or the wind, or something like that. I'll go and have a look. I won't be long."

"You don't need to. It was probably nothing."

"I'll just give it a look to put both our minds at ease. I'll take the baseball bat though, just in case, eh."

Andrew walked to the front door, smiling back at Susan. "It'll be alright, I'll make sure of that, or at least I'll die trying."

Andrew was a strong, fit, well-built man, who loved this woman. He meant what he said, and John had every intention of keeping him to his word.

Andrew opened the door slowly. He hid it well but he too was a little apprehensive about what could be outside. He brushed the feeling off as stupidity and stuck his head out the door, almost convincing himself that there was nothing there that could hurt him other than a falling tree or an act of god. He looked around quickly scanning the trees round about, trying to catch a glimpse of what might be out there, never considering it may be him. The trees concealed a terrifying darkness, like something you'd find in a horror movie, the trees whispering at him loudly as his imagination started to play games with him. He could feel a sense of unease but couldn't quite place it; there was nothing to suggest that there was anything wrong. He was really only taking a quick look to put Susan's mind at rest, but he felt it - strong and powerful, a searing sense of dread with nothing to back it up.

John's eyes remained fixed on Andrew like a lion with its prey, not flinching and barely breathing, not a movement, nothing. Andrew's breath could be seen in the light on the porch and John wondered if there would be any trace of his, although he was invisible between the trees in the pitch darkness. Andrew looked round one more time; John could see he was uncomfortable just by his posture. His head moved round and slowed as he faced towards John, and stopped. Andrew looked into the trees, straight at him, but was only able to see the first row of trees before him, the others were engulfed in darkness, a darkness hiding pure evil. His eyes seemed to be drawn into them, a pull from an unwanted chain, his head even visibly moved forward in John's direction. John actually began to worry that he'd been detected, as Andrew's eyes seemed to focus on him. He questioned what he'd do if he had been spotted. Would he be able to overcome them both without the element of surprise? Hairs felt like they were popping out of Andrew's skin as a shiver ran up his spine, and he couldn't help but make that shiver noise when it passed through him. He gave himself a shake and questioned why he was feeling like this; there was nothing there, nothing to see, nothing to hear. He turned back and pulled the door closed. John could hear the locks being engaged and sighed with relief that he had not given himself away. Andrew went back to his bed and held Susan tightly.

"There was nothing out there, no noise, nothing - bit creepy though, just how dark it is. I wouldn't like to be out in that on my own. Bbbrrruuuggh - spooky shit."

John's dark eyes narrowed as he heard a faint crack behind him in the woods. He shone a small light in the direction of the noise, showing no fear and oozing power; the badger that stared back into his face took a few steps backwards and moved off in the opposite direction, sensing danger from the man that stood before it. It didn't hesitate in taking heed of its instincts and retreating back into the darkness, away from the thing hiding in the woods.

¤¤¤

Taylor's lips sipped from her glass of Shiraz and she leaned back on the seat, her designer blouse silky and fitted. The team all sat round in the hotel bar chatting about the day and the disappointment at their lack of success. The voices all rolled into one another and everyone was relaxed as this was not their first drink of the evening. As the night went on the humour reached the suggestive lows, innuendo and smut to be expected at any gathering of police officers. They turned all of their war stories into something that could be dealt with and stored, to avoid the job damaging them. The laughter was a well needed release for everybody, taking their minds off the task at hand, humour the essential release from the reality needed to do their work. Taylor looked over towards Fran, who was deep in conversation with Marcus. Taylor allowed her eyes to linger longer than she should have. Sensing that she was being watched, Fran looked up towards Taylor, and they held each other's gaze. Each of their minds inquisitive, both looking for something more than a friendly glance. Taylor felt a slight flutter in her stomach as the corners of Fran's mouth turned slightly upwards into a flirtatious smile and her eyes sent a very clear message that she wanted more than just a smile back from her. Taylor was first to look away, her face a little flushed with the wine and now with the sense of arousal that was emanating through her body. Her mind was floating in and out of scenarios and how it would be to savour the pleasure of what was clearly on offer to her. Taylor kept thinking of Kay and how she had made her feel only three days ago and how this flirting could end something really good before it even got the chance to get properly started. Unfortunately for Taylor, she lacked willpower and this time she was not the one in pursuit and may not be in control of what could happen. With these thoughts in mind, she finished her glass of wine and excused herself from the group, in an attempt to set a good example to the team and try and prevent any awkward situations developing.

"Early start tomorrow and lots to do in the morning! Please don't get too drunk. I don't want to be a spoil sport but we need to keep our wits about us for when we do locate him."

They all said their goodnights and watched her as she left the bar area, her toned figure pleasing for most that watched.

"She is hot," PC Lomond commented and Marcus just looked at him with his eyebrows almost at his hairline.

"Really? You don't say."

"She's very attractive but I doubt you'll appear hot to her," Marcus said with a hint of mirth.

"What do you mean?" PC Lomond genuinely asked.

"What? You don't know?"

"Know what?"

"She bats for the other side you divvy."

"No way! She's fucking gorgeous!"

"There are lots of good looking lesbians, ya twat, and it's pretty obvious she's one anyway."

"I thought she was into me. She was looking right at me!"

"Through you, you mean, to the next female hotty that may walk in to her viewing arc," Marcus laughed wholeheartedly at him.

Fran was sitting beside PC Lomond and she knew those eyes were meant for her and not for him; she smiled inwardly that she was the one that had the attention of her highly attractive boss.

Taylor leant forward to press the button for the lift when another hand gently brushed over hers and pressed the button beneath. Taylor gasped a little as she had not been aware that there was anyone else in the corridor behind her. The touch was from a feminine hand that sent a rush of electric pulses to every sensitive place in her body. Fran came up very close to Taylor, a total invasion of her personal space, but she wasn't uncomfortable with it, although she should have been. There was a sense of nervous tension, an anticipation that excited her. Taylor was not used to this; she was always usually in control but not this time.

Fran stood beside her, looking straight at her boss with beautiful warm eyes, her scent luring Taylor to her. They both knew that this moment had been thought about; Fran's tongue passed over her lips lightly within her mouth, knowing that Taylor would be able to see it. Fran moved even closer, her face coming within an inch or two of Taylor's. Taylor instinctively moved back a bit, not knowing how this would end. As she did so, Fran took her slender hand and gently pulled her back towards her. Taylor's heart was pounding. *Do I want this to happen? Could I stop this happening? It feels so good, totally exciting and unexpected.*

Fran's eyes were fixed on Taylor, a hot passionate look, willing her to come to her, to give in to her desire. Fran leant forward and this time Taylor did not pull away from her; Fran was tentative, hoping not to be rejected, the softness of her mouth sending Taylor's insides flipping in circles, the power of that initial touch was so consuming. Fran's kiss was soft and not intrusive, mouths remaining closed. Another followed, this time a little more needy than the other. Taylor let out a small moan of pleasure as she put her arm round Fran's waist and pulled her into her. This time the kiss was full of lust, open mouthed, tongues meeting, but still gentle as any desire that had been felt was released all at that moment.

Ping! The lift arrived and Fran was pushed into it backwards, Taylor took control unable to resist the lustful feelings that surged through her with such ferocity. Fran's moan told its own story as Taylor's hand pushed down hard into her trousers and beneath her panties, fingers gliding over her already wet pussy.

Fran gripped Taylor's shoulders and bit down hard on her lip as she felt the power of what was happening to her, gripping her inside. Every movement of Taylor's hand sent waves of immense pleasure coursing through Fran's body.

"Oh god, oh god," she gasped, her moans arousing as she came so hard that her legs started to buckle beneath her. Taylor held her up, driving her fingers deeper inside, keeping the rhythm with the pulse of Fran's orgasm, keeping her where she wanted her to be, totally turned on. Taylor fucked Fran hard, making sure she didn't lose the heightened state of arousal, dropping to her knees to lick her intensely and intimately with such well-practised skill that Fran's next orgasm sent her head into a euphoric spin. She moaned as Taylor continued to pleasure her, bringing on another more desperate orgasm that continued sending tingles up and down her spine. The next one brought on by the intensity of Taylor's constant motion of her fingers was so powerful, Taylor could feel Fran's pleasure in her hand as she slowed down, allowing Fran to catch her breath. Taylor steadied her with her arm round her. Now standing, she kissed her open and very willing mouth. Their kisses were so intense that even Taylor was taken aback. They slowed down and looked at each other, both aware that this encounter was a little bit more than they had thought it would be.

Taylor spoke first. "My god! That was intense." They both smiled, shared another lingering kiss and began to make themselves look a little more respectable.

"Wow! I've got to go. You do understand that, don't you?"

"I do. I never thought we'd get this far anyway and I certainly didn't expect an invite to your room, because I know you're with Kay!"

Taylor stopped in her tracks and turned her head round really quickly to meet Fran's gaze, mouth open and a little speechless as she believed nobody knew about their affair or that Kay was even gay.

"How do you know that?"

"I have eyes. I watched you in the office the other week, for my own reasons, I watched the way you looked at her and the way she responded and I agree it was very subtle but, to a woman, it's obvious that there was affection there."

"So why me and why did we just do what we did?"

"It would be hard to put it into words but the last 20 minutes was something else. I didn't want it to happen, but I couldn't have stopped that."

Taylor leant into Fran and kissed her softly on the forehead, then on the mouth and they shared the warmth of each other one more time before Taylor pressed the button to free the lift and it carried on up to her floor. She exited and glanced back at Fran with fond affection, her mouth curled up with the thought of the exhilarating sex they had just shared.

Fran watched Taylor's lithe body walk confidently away from her and stop at the door to her room. She turned and smiled at her but guilt made her go into her room and shut the door without extending an invite to share her bed for the night. Fran sighed as she leant back in the lift but she could still feel the physical effects of what had just happened to her and she smiled into herself warmly. She went straight to her own room as she did not want any of her team to notice that her neck was significantly red and that she looked a little dishevelled. Knowing them, questions would be asked and the last thing she wanted was finger-pointing in the office where Kay also worked; that would be a little too awkward to face and she really didn't mean to harm Kay in any way; she was just drawn to Taylor and couldn't help herself.

Taylor sat down on the end of the bed, her head in her hands. She took several deep breaths before going to look at herself in the mirror. *What are you doing? Why can't you just leave things alone? I think I love Kay and I can still do that. What is wrong with me?* She took a deep breath and stood up, slipping out of her clothes and getting into bed, the scent of Fran still heavy on her skin. Her heart fluttered and she knew that the encounter was a little more than it should have been. Fran's scent still sent waves of excitement and pleasure through her body. Her eyes closed and she imagined hearing the soft moans that escaped Fran's lips as she made love to her, their kisses intense. Taylor sighed, rolled her eyes and turned over and went to sleep, her mind tormented at her ability to screw things up, because she was weak when it came to beautiful women and Fran was beautiful.

ꭓꭓꭓ

John sat down against a tree, his presence hidden from the

prying eyes of those he stalked, but he could see the log cabin from where he sat. His mind swirled with thoughts of Susan, thoughts that would send chills down the spine of any person. He was imagining their next encounter and how he would torture them both, Andrew first for soiling his bride and taking what was rightfully his. His mind was so twisted now that he actually believed that Susan was his property and she was his to do with as he pleased, for him to rule over. Normal thoughts were long gone from the mind of the psychotic killer, now so depraved and unfeeling he was a danger to anyone and anything that crossed his path.

Chapter 27:
Prowler's Encounter

The sun came up and there was a buzz in the hotel as the team gathered at 6.30 am for breakfast. All were eager to get on with the day and chatted amongst themselves about the next lead they had to follow up. Taylor was last to appear, not through lateness but because she had been in a conference call with the top table. Everyone that was anyone had an input in the investigation, and the team's progress or lack of it was hot on the agenda. On arrival at breakfast, Taylor apologised to her colleagues for being later than she had said they were to be there. Polite hellos and a little jibe or two followed but the mood of the team remained relaxed.

Taylor looked over at Fran. Their eyes met and only they felt the familiarity and fondness that their eyes passed to one another. There was no embarrassment or expectation, just a mutual attraction and the thoughts of their private rendezvous the night before in the lift. They all finished up their full English breakfast, with a bit of black pudding and haggis to add a little bit of Scots to it, retrieved their kit bags and moved off to their next area for investigation.

¤¤¤

John opened his eyes, blinking in the sun that shone brightly through the trees and onto his rugged unshaven face. He found it hard to focus on anything. The sun dazzled him and his vision was blurred. He was aware that he wasn't alone anymore and that there was something there in front of him but his eyes were still not working properly yet. He felt no reason to be afraid. He focused harder and there she was, two tiny little feet in front of him, a little girl was right there playing with twigs, talking away to herself, not at all bothered that he was just sitting there in the middle of nowhere against a tree. Unlike the wild animals that could sense the danger, she could not! John didn't move and discreetly looked around him for any parents that may be close by. It was still early and he was a bit uneasy that a child was out there alone, his human side re-emerging from within his twisted soul, worried about what might happen to such a young child on her own. His evil didn't and had never focused on children and he felt no feelings of ill will towards her; he almost cared about her welfare, instead of worrying that she had obviously seen him and where he was. She stopped muttering to herself and looked straight up at him and spoke.

"What you doing here? Are you playing with twigs like me too?"

John was taken aback at the child's lack or fear and her warmth towards him. He almost felt human, totally relaxed in her company, his murderous thoughts far from his mind as he leant forward to speak to the girl.

"I am. These are great twigs here, aren't they?" He picked up a handful, jiggling them in his huge hands. The little girl moved closer to him and John handed his twigs over to her. He was aware that he didn't want anyone to know he was there and that this little girl could turn out to be a problem for him. The little girl said, "Thank you," and started to move away.

John whispered to her, "Come here a minute," and the little girl stopped and paused.

John wondered if it was now he was going to have to take some kind of action to silence her. He thought, *this is when she'll remember the talk about strangers and the trouble she'll be in.*

He was wrong; she turned back and said, "Do you want your twigs back?"

He replied, "No, but I've got a secret that you've got to keep.

Come here so I can whisper."

John's eyes lost focus. They rolled back in his head, his thoughts twisting from right and wrong: his saviour or her young life. She walked closer, totally innocent and unaware of the monster she approached, her wavy blonde hair on her shoulders, her pretty clothes so neat and clean. She was now right beside him and she bent down to allow him to whisper in her ear.

John took a deep breath and knew he was making a huge mistake by letting her live, but he said, "You can't tell anyone I'm here. I'm a police man and I'm on a secret mission and you're now my little helper, but you can't tell anyone you've seen me because that will ruin my cover. Can you do that - pretend I'm not here - please?"

"Yeesss, I can do that. Can I go now? Mummy will be looking for me."

"Of course you can," he said, as the little girl moved away from him without a care in the world. She skipped as she left the cover of the trees and headed up the grassy area and out of sight.

John's heart was pounding. He didn't want to be caught and the last chance to stop her leaving was now gone, but killing a small child was not his thing and was very wrong in his twisted reasoning and logic. If he had killed her though, there would have been a major search of the area to find her. He would have been caught unless he left and then he would miss out on the opportunity to have his final party with Susan and Andrew. He'd just have to sit it out and hope that she did as he had asked her to do.

¤¤¤

Taylor sat in the front of the van aware of Fran's gaze that was aimed in her direction. Her face flushed in a subtle way, only noticed by Fran. A slight smile came over Taylor's face and Fran looked at her long enough to let Taylor feel her desire and be reminded a little of the previous night's tingling sensation. There were true feelings in Fran's eyes, and a little too in the look that was returned, which could only mean trouble for Taylor.

¤¤¤

Susan came out onto the veranda of the cabin, stretched her

arms and made noises of someone that had slept well and loved well, as she shook out all of her stiffness. John watched her as she winced at full stretch as if she felt a pain from one of her internal injuries. John smiled at this, taking the credit for all the pain he had caused and that still hurt her now, and possibly for the rest of her life, although that wouldn't be for long if he got his way. His smirk was short lived as Andrew came out and put his arms around her waist and kissed her neck. John could see his lips say I love you to her before she turned round to fully embrace Andrew face to face. The grinding of John's teeth was lucky not to be heard by them, it was so loud and forceful and only a short distance away.

The little girl got to her mummy's car and was helped up onto her booster seat. She hadn't been away long but had been out of sight long enough for her mum to tell her that she shouldn't go anywhere without her mummy or an adult because there were bad people out there and that mummies worried. The little girl sat back in her seat and looked at the floor, avoiding her mother's gaze. Her mum saw this but just put it down to her getting a telling off and feeling guilty for going away. She didn't think anything more of her daughter's furtive behaviour.

John's heart was pounding through his chest with rage, excitement and apprehension over what would happen next. He watched Susan as Andrew led her back into the cabin. John's blood was at boiling point. His head told him to wait and his heart told him to act now when he had the chance. He moved slowly round the side of the cabin watching where he placed his feet this time, careful not to make any noise. The seclusion of the cabin allowed the privacy that Susan and Andrew craved, and the privacy that John craved that little bit more. His mind floated back to the little girl. Why were they here? What had brought them to here of all places? *I haven't seen anyone else since I've been here and then out of nowhere a little girl is close enough to speak to. Do they have a cabin here? Where are they from? Shit!* He raised his head up enough to look through the window and watched Andrew as he lay gently on top of Susan, their kisses soft and tender, a loving union which sent glass through John's head. He felt heat rise within him and had to fight to contain his rage and deal with the situation logically, making sure he didn't mess up his plans through frustration and anger.

"There was a man in the woods this morning mummy," the little girl said under her breath.

"What's that you said, sweetheart?"

"Nothing mummy. I was just talking to my dolly"

"Okay, do you need a drink or anything?"

"No thanks mummy."

The little girl put her head forward, the guilt of not telling her mummy the truth weighing heavy on her tiny little shoulders but she didn't say another word as they got onto the motorway and headed back home to Edinburgh.

Susan moaned as Andrew's mouth released her nipple, his kisses lowering, his mouth and tongue loving Susan intimately, her gasps of pleasure encouraging Andrew to intensify his touch, his caress focused; focused on letting Susan release her desire. Her orgasm spiralled through her body, pulsing over and over, Andrew's desire purely for his lover's pleasure. Only when she gripped his hair and whispered I want you to fuck me did he allow himself any physical pleasure, although the excitement of pleasuring Susan had already left him in a euphoric state, almost climatic. He was still able to hold off long enough, however, until his rhythmical thrusts and carefully placed hands brought Susan to a deeper, longer and more satisfying climax than the last one. They held on to each other, their love making always charged with desperation, physical release and mental relaxation, although a hint of fear was always present and the pain, the pain from John Brennan's attack, was a constant reminder of his ownership of her, a sensation she felt would be with her for the rest of her living days.

John tried the handle of the back door; he couldn't believe his luck after all he'd put her through - it opened. There was a silent swish of the door as he entered the kitchen at the rear of the cabin. He heard Susan moaning in the bedroom, and it wasn't pain she was feeling; his heart pounded with uncontrollable rage as he passed through the hallway, his eyes narrowing as he strained to see through the space between the frame and the door as he stared into the bedroom. He watched. He was aroused and insanely jealous at the same time, his head spinning with what to do next and when to do it. He breathed out harder than he thought, a faint noise escaped into the air. Susan's body went completely rigid, she couldn't breathe with terror, a really familiar terror. Andrew felt her body change instantly but he had not heard John's sigh, a sound that Susan could never forget. John watched and realised his mistake as Andrew stopped making love to Susan. She pushed Andrew up and her voice shrieked in a hideous wail, "He's here! He's fucking in here!"

John moved swiftly round the door way, his teeth bared with his tongue gripped between them as he moved towards the bed. Andrew, naked and totally vulnerable launched himself off the bed and ran full force towards him with his shoulder down, straight at John. He screamed at Susan to get out and run. Susan hesitated but fear dominated her senses and she shoved open the small window, grabbing at some clothes and throwing herself out head first with no concern for where and how she would land, her only focus was to escape. She was crying loudly. She couldn't bear to be in the same room as him; her skin crawled with fear, as she got up, bruised, but unharmed, naked with bare feet.

Andrew's momentum had managed to knock John off his feet and onto the floor but he had not foreseen the power that was to follow as John gripped his neck and tightened his arm round it. His eyes felt like they were bulging out of his head as John's powerful forearm began to crush his windpipe. Andrew scrabbled at John's arms, tearing, gouging, gripping, all to no avail; John's strength was not a force to be reckoned with and he was not going to yield easily. He was slowly killing Andrew. Andrew fought as hard as he could but then, against all instinct to fight, he decided to change his tactic. Risking everything, he made himself go limp, allowing the full power of John to take over. Andrew's heart raced and his head spun with the lack of oxygen as he faked unconsciousness, which was now slowly becoming reality. Had he made a fatal mistake and helped John kill him?

Susan's bare feet crashed through the ferns and cruel cutting foliage, her legs running as fast as they could carry her. She could barely breathe as the pain of the undergrowth cut into her feet, legs, face and body and the fatigue of her sprint set in quickly, her body still pretty broken from John's last assault. She had to slow down before she expired. She paused for a second and pulled on Andrew's shirt, her pants and a sock, which was all she had been able to grab. She had no shoes and nothing for warmth or protection. Luckily the shirt was a nondescript, dull colour that would not be easily spotted in the woods and undergrowth if she had to hide later, which she knew she would have to do if she wanted to survive; she'd have to. Her heart sank as the realisation of her escape may well have cost Andrew his life, a life that he had put on the line to save the woman he loved. Blood seeped through the shirt's fabric from the many small cuts already covering her scarred body but she felt no pain as adrenaline pumped through her like a raging river, her desire to live overwhelming.

The area where they were was very remote with miles between lodges, roads and civilisation. Their choice of venue for their escape had become the worst they could have made, especially as they had brought what they were escaping from with them. Susan started to run again, with no idea of where to go. She only knew she had to get as far away from there as she could. Her eyes were wide like a scared animal but her will to survive was unparalleled. She would not be beaten by him; she would take her own life first if she had to.

ᴧᴧᴧ

Taylor lifted her phone to her ear, the Inspector was wanting an update. She leant back a little as she began to explain the next site they were going to check out, Findlay letting her know about further possible sightings and leads that had to be checked out. She turned sideways deliberately to look at Fran, who was already watching her, her eyes focused on Taylor's mouth. Her beautiful mouth was moving round the words with elegant finesse. She spoke with a majestic sensuality, effortlessly teasing anyone who wanted to watch. Her tongue would glide over her lips unintentionally and for anyone that liked her, this was a very seductive and alluring act. She looked at Fran, her eyes softly closing as she remembered the night before, the pleasure taken and given was still arousing them both. The swirl of desire was there for only these two to feel.

John shoved Andrew's limp body away from him, pushing down on Andrew as he pulled himself off the floor, his inner rage boiling over as this was not the way things were meant to happen. He wanted to be in complete control when he killed them both, instead he had not inflicted nearly enough pain on Andrew for interfering with his woman. Instead he'd had to kill him to save himself from a similar fate. He raised his foot above his chest and stamped down on Andrew's lifeless body, kicking him repeatedly, no groans, no movement, nothing. He spat on Andrew's bloodied face and headed out of the door. He walked over to the open window, looking at the long grass and seeing a noticeable trail disappearing into the wood where it had been disturbed by Susan's attempt to escape. He stood there motionless, listening, waiting, before letting out a satanic wail, which roared from deep within him. This marked the beginning of the hunt. He started to run with sheer focus in that direction like a blood hound on a scent. He tucked the hunting knife into his jacket, clicked on his torch and openly smiled his maniacal smile as he set off to catch his prey. He would not let her get away that easily.

Chapter 28: The Lead

The six o'clock news came on and the family sat in their Edinburgh home, the little girl brushing her doll's hair. She was humming a sweet tune, her affection for her dolly obvious. Her mummy leant over towards her, nuzzling her hair and asking if her dolly was okay. The headlines came on and there he was, his face filling the screen. The little girl sat bolt upright, her back rigid as she stared straight at the telly; her mum instantly asked her what was wrong. The little girl remembered what the policeman had said to her and looked at her lifeless companion, her dolly looking loyally back at her. She tried to focus on the toy, avoiding direct eye contact with her mummy, her gaze as far away from her mum's as possible, looking round the room now. Motherly instinct made her mum pursue the matter further and ask again, and again and again, telling her daughter that there should be no secrets from any mummy. Eventually the little girl confessed that she had met the man on the telly earlier on that day and that he had said he was in the police and she was to be his little helper on a secret mission. Her mum was taken aback; by now several stories had been shown on the news and she wasn't sure who her daughter was meaning that she had seen, but there was an uneasiness about who it might have been.

She flipped open her laptop and looked up news. The little girl was made to watch screen after screen until she tugged her mummy's sleeve and said "him", pointing at John Brennan .

Her mum felt instantly sick and got up and ran towards the bathroom where she threw up, tears clearly visible in her eyes and rolling down her cheeks from thinking of what might have happened to her daughter at his hands.

"What is it mummy? Are you not well?"

"Where? When? Are you sure you saw this man? You need to tell me, you're not in trouble, you can tell me!"

"I don't know where. It was in the trees."

"What trees? When was this. Where were we?"

"I'm not sure. It was earlier today, coming back from our holiday."

"When? What time? Did he touch you?"

"No, he didn't touch me! He just spoke to me and whispered in my ear. I can't remember where it was. We played with sticks together and he told me I couldn't tell anyone because it was a secret mission."

999 was dialled immediately, her hand trembling as she did so.

"What is your emergency? What service do you require?"

"Pppp, police please."

"Please hold when we connect you."

"Hello, Police Scotland, how can I help?"

"I need to speak to someone about the man being hunted for murder."

"What is the nature of your enquiry?"

"My daughter saw him today in the trees."

"What trees? Where was this? When? What time?"

"I can't be certain. It was my four year old daughter. She went still as a board when his face came on the telly and said she saw that man, and she said he'd told her he was a police man."

"How can you be sure this was the man seen?"

"By the way my daughter acted was enough for me to know, and she doesn't lie."

"Can I take your name and address and can I ask if it would be alright to send an officer round to get a statement from you straight away."

"Yes, I'm in right now. Come round now."

"Okay! There will be an officer round to speak to you right away."

Kay took the call, her heart pounding as she knew Taylor would have to respond to this. She missed her and had not heard from her for a couple of days, which wasn't normal for Taylor; recently she had been calling or texting every day unless there was a reason. Kay's stomach twisted. She knew that Taylor had a chequered past and was easily led when other women were involved and she hoped that this was not the case. She quickly relayed the information about the sighting of Brennan to Taylor, by phone, deliberately avoiding any unwanted attention from the fat lecherous prick that hovered around her like an unwanted insect. Her boss had made her make the call, just so as he could sit close to her.

Findlay slammed his hand down on the desk and shouted, "We'll get you this time, you fucking bastard," right behind Kay causing her to nearly jump out of her skin.

Taylor's hair stood on end as she listened to Kay's message. "There's been another possible sighting of him, 100 miles north of where you are."

There had already been numerous possible sightings and the tension rose and fell with each of them. This time though Taylor's heart was pounding more than for any of the others. "Are there any local sets going to go off at this one?"

"I think there is one car in that area and they'll be there as soon as they can!"

"Fucking police! That's not going to be enough. He's a dangerous man and armed as far as we know. What about the helicopter?"

"What about it? Nothing has been confirmed yet and there have been hundreds of sightings."

"And what if it is him? I bet you anything Susan and Andrew are there, and what chance do they have? That prick has the upper hand in every way. Just get there as soon as you can, 'cos if this is for real, I hope you're not too late. They just won't send everything on a four year old child's story!"

Taylor turned to her driver, "Lomond, head North, and put your foot down. He's got hours on us and we're late to his party already!" The van lurched forward and the obvious increase in speed made everyone bristle with tension, excitement and anticipation.

ㅁㅁㅁ

A squeal of pain pierced the air as Susan's foot landed hard on a sharp branch. She was already bleeding profusely where another upturned branch had pushed between the first and second metatarsals on her left foot, through flesh and bone. She felt even more sick than she had before. Her stomach churned with fear and fatigue from running since she'd left the cabin, which felt like hours ago. Her heart was punching through her rib cage, pain was pulsing through her head and foot, her head was swirling and she had to fight hard not to faint. She slumped back against a tall tree, long grass surrounding her; she had deliberately not followed any paths, not that there were many here, as the remoteness of this private development claimed to be second to none, and how right they were with their advert. Susan almost laughed at the desperate situation she had put herself in. She tried to stay sharp, focusing on her life, that special gift she so desperately wanted to keep now more than ever before; she'd beaten the odds once and she was sure as damn it not going to give in without a fight this time. She looked at her foot, blood seeping out of the wound and the stick poking through. She knew walking, far less running, was not an option now unless she could pull it out, and she was well aware of the dangers of doing that; it could make things much, much worse for her.

His head twisted like that of a jackal, senses primed to hone in on the weak and vulnerable struggling to escape. The sound had come from a fair distance away but at least it gave him a direction to choose whether it was her or not, the grass no longer guiding him and without that helping hand of fate, he would have gone the wrong way. He had wondered if it would ever be possible to find her in such dense woodland with such a vast sprawling acreage, designed for the most idyllic private luxury escape money could pay for. He moved quickly in the direction of the noise, teeth clenched, boots already covered in blood as he crashed through the undergrowth. An act he hadn't thought too much about but he didn't care about the noise he made now; the more frightened she was, the better it felt for him.

Susan's face needled with a deeper sense of fear as the noise of him crashing through the trees terrified her and her head snapped round to the movement in the trees up to her left. *It's now or never.* She gripped the small branch with two hands, closed her eyes and wrenched it right through her foot, the pain sickening her to the stomach. Her intention had been to run. Instead, nausea engulfed her and she listed uncontrollably to the side. Her eyes glazed over as the trees closed in on her like she was sinking beneath sand and her vision failed her. Her head thumped on to the ground, her muscles loose with no tension left because her faint had rendered her helpless and unconscious. The grass, ferns and nettles folded over her like a shield sent from above, her natural camouflage tucking her in tight without any effort. She had landed head first in the deepest foliage there was, hiding herself without even trying. Nettles stung her unprotected face as she lay in the grass, her breathing naturally calm as her desperate need for oxygen and fear had subsided along with her consciousness. Her breathing was soft and now almost soundless as his footsteps came thumping closer, branches cracking beneath him, his breath rasping as he had quickened his pace when he had heard her cry out in pain moments earlier. He slowed a little as he had judged that she should be near to this spot when she foolishly gave away her position. His head turned from side to side like a maniacal character from some horror film, his wicked glare and twisted face contorted with hate and revenge as he scanned the foliage around about him waiting for her to get up and run, or make a noise and give herself away, but that didn't happen. If anyone had been looking, they would have clearly seen the rage brewing within him.

¤¤¤

Blood dripped from his mouth, phlegm stretching from his lips to the ground. His breath gurgled as he slowly pushed up onto his arms. He pushed his tongue through the gap in his teeth, where a foot had smashed them to the floor as he lay there fully conscious as his neck was throttled, his body viciously beaten. He spat on the floor, wiping his mouth, and tried to push himself up. Pain sliced through his ribs.

"Susan, Susan! I'm coming," he whispered to himself as he staggered to his feet.

He teetered as his head was dizzy with pain. Picking up some clothes and shoes, he went through to the kitchen and collected the two biggest knives from the drawers and left the cabin. He too followed the fallen grass and tried to run in an attempt to find Susan, but his body was engulfed with pain from Brennan's brutal assault.

□□□

The wind was slight and northerly, blowing his hair as the trees whispered above him. The grass also whispered its secrets back and forth, hiding the soft breath of its visitor, protecting Susan's slight body as it nestled her in their care, almost instinctively hiding her from the monster that prowled carelessly within them. His feet were heavy on the ground, his senses twitching with the hunt, his ears honed in on his planned capture. He listened hard for the sounds of her footsteps moving away from him; he listened for her breathing close by, hoping the initial sounds he had heard before were that of pain and that Susan would be injured and his for the taking once again.

□□□

Head spinning, not really aware of where she was and what was happening, she raised her head from the ground slowly, unaware of the lurking presence 20 feet away, evil very close by. She could see that the back of his head began to turn in her direction almost in slow motion. Her breath stopped and she felt the warmth of liquid trickling down her legs, her involuntary motion flowing from her without control. She kept her body taut and controlled and slowly slipped back beneath the grass just as his eyes skimmed over where her head had been just a second before. The grass around her tried desperately to keep her hidden as the devil searched for his final dance, a dance he would make sure would go on and on until it was impossible for her to stay alive.

His thoughts kept him going, kept him pursuing her; she had made him weak, she had ruined his life. He could no longer live unnoticed in society and she would have to pay the ultimate price, one that she should have paid already.

"Fucking bitch," rasped from his mouth and Susan began to shake uncontrollably. She peeped through the grass at him, unwilling to take her eyes off him, her terror of being discovered almost making her take flight. Every instinct within her told her to run away but she remained as still as a statue.

The wind blew hauntingly loud around her and masked any slight movement she made. It rustled the trees eerily round about them. His movements were now openly angry, annoyed that this weak creature had once again evaded him. He looked straight at the place where she lay, her secret intact. Her eyes could just make out his silhouette through the long blades of grass and ferns. Terror ran deep into her veins as his stare seemed to meet hers but her nerve held as she lay there still once again. She stared straight ahead at him with glassy eyes as he started to move towards her; she wondered if he had seen her, but at the last moment he veered to the left and headed away from her, slowly but with motive, giving up on the thought she was there. He kept stopping and turning back, looking and listening as he went away, hoping his prey would give away its hiding place, if there at all.

ᴑᴑᴑ

"How long? How far to go?"

"About 20 miles, Serg. The roads here are really shit!"

"Have the other sets arrived yet?"

"Just one set has gone off so far and they've checked three lodges so far, with nothing of note, I hope this isn't another falsey"

"Fucking better not be, poor Susan!"

Chapter 29:
Cat and Mouse

She could no longer hear him but lay still for a while longer, terror gripping her like a vice, heart still racing unhealthily fast; she could feel every pulse of blood coursing through her, in her chest and neck, fear crippling her. *What if he's still here, watching, waiting for me? Do I just end it now, take away his control, his terror, his cruelty? I can't live like this anymore. One of us can't be here anymore and, either way, one of us has to die for me to be free, in life or in death. Right now, I don't care who. I need this to end.* Light had faded fast and her sense of direction was non-existent; she had no idea where the road was, no clothes, an injured foot and a hideous stalker that wanted to gut her like a pig.

Two officers pulled up at the lodge, both taking time to check their surroundings. Something wasn't right here; the door was ajar, a window also lay wide open.

"POLICE, hello, hello, anyone in there? It's the POLICE!"

There was no answer. Both of them racked their batons instinctively, in precaution against an attack and requested back up on the radio. Their suspicions were confirmed when they saw blood on the steps down from the front door of the lodge.

"We have a situation here - empty dwelling and blood on the outer steps. How close is the nearest dog? Should we go ahead and enter before back up arrives? Oh and where's the specialist unit. Have they found us yet? Is there an estimated time of arrival. We've been here a while," he said sarcastically with a hint of jealousy.

"Dog will be over an hour and the specialist unit can only be minutes away."

"How about air assistance?"

"I'll request it, and get back with accurate ETAs, but the top table requests that you go in with caution. There might be someone in there injured requiring assistance."

The officers moved into the lodge cautiously, careful to check all cupboards and rooms as they went. They moved into the bedroom and then they saw it there on the floor: a pool of blood and clear signs that there had been a violent disturbance. At least one person appeared to have been injured. Excitement rose deep from inside their bellies as the realisation of the enormity of the situation became clear; the serial killer was possibly close by and most likely armed and extremely dangerous.

"Do you have any further instructions for us or do we stand fast until there are other units here to back us up?"

There was a pause on the radio and, as there was no confirmation of a definite time scale for the others to join them, the decision was made for officers on the ground to begin a search of the area near to the lodge for any injured persons. Caution was to be taken when proceeding and no unnecessary risks were to be taken.

They looked at each other, "Fucking typical, cannon fodder once again, always the fucking front line officers."

"I know eh! Just pop your heed round there. There's a guy with a shooter but we've deemed it safe for you to continue."

"Too right, eh? Aye, on ye pop and die. Get your £2.50 out colleagues, if we don't make it."

Cop humour was the only comfort they shared. No amount of bravado could hide that both of them were apprehensive as the last hint of twilight ebbed away and gave everything a sinister edge. The noise of the wind was more than enough to creep out anyone who'd ever watched a horror movie. It was like a scene from a film just before another of the cast was picked off in the most hideous way.

They both laughed as they clicked on their torches. "You stay here, I'll check it out," one quipped to the other, pretending to play out the unrealistic choices they made in these films, queuing up the inevitable of one being left to be picked off.

"No fucking danger. I'll be so far up your arse it's gonna smart a bit".

"Fuck off, ya fanny. He might actually be in there and we better switch on or we might get fucking murdered. I mean it, switch on and shut the fuck up."

"I've got your back, Tony! Seriously I'm up for this."

They moved off together with a safe distance between them just in case they were attacked; at least one would be able to protect the other, dependent on who was assaulted first. They took in their surroundings and professionally relayed back all the information they could, allowing others to assess from the scene and terrain what they were describing. All banter and bravado was spent and the two focused cops did their jobs, their senses bristling with the task at hand and the potential danger at stake. They called up on the personal radio and checked their positioning on GPS and the strength of their signal prior to moving off into the wooded area, ensuring that they could find their way back to the locus, both still a little nervous.

Taylor's unit called up on the radio, aware that there was a set off at the scene already. They confirmed the exact location of where to start their search so at least they could offer an armed back up to the two officers who were clearly vulnerable and unarmed. Taylor may not have agreed with the initial decision to send in the local unarmed officers without back up but if someone was clinging to life nearby and they didn't act or search, that would be deemed even less favourable; the police were expected to risk their own lives for others.

Their van lumbered up the single track road, jostling Taylor's team back and forth, and causing a few of them to comment on PC Lomond's shit driving. They checked their kit and weapons. The fun had dwindled away and a sense of duty now took over; they couldn't fail tonight or someone else would suffer the ultimate fate.

ᴏᴏᴏ

He moved slowly, his direction unclear. "Susan, Susan," he muttered to himself. He looked at the blood on the ground, his heart racing at the sign of how close she might be. It proved she was carrying an injury that would slow her down and hinder her no doubt. Blood boiling, eyes pinpointed to movement he heard up ahead, he moved off slowly in that direction, his intent clear as he went stealthily forward.

Susan moaned softly as she forced herself to put pressure down on her foot; she had tried crawling, but her hands and knees were being cut to ribbons. She had put her only sock round her foot and padded it with leaves, breaking off a root and tying it round to stem the flow of blood, in an attempt to ease the pain, hide her trail and allow her to run or hobble, when the need came, which it would.

His breath rasped the air as he moved his head like an animal searching for its next meal, eyes squinting to focus as the light was virtually gone. He had turned his torch off, reluctant to give away his position. He wanted equal cover. In darkness like this a torch beam could be seen for miles and he wanted to remain the hunter, not the hunted. He knew it was only a matter of time before the police got there. *Hell, they might even be here already, but they're just police and this terrain is a match for anyone.* They were all only human and he was going to prove it the moment any one of them let their guard down. *Bring it on! She'll be mine before I become yours.* He believed that because he had escaped once, it wouldn't be impossible to do it again, but escape was a secondary thought. His mind was focused on avenging his pride. He couldn't believe that such a weak mortal bitch had brought him to where he was now, crawling around in the undergrowth like an animal, although that suited the way he was acting just now and the animalistic savagery he would show her when he caught up with her.

ᴏᴏᴏ

Taylor stepped out of the van, its headlights illuminating the lodge. She radioed up to control reporting their arrival, numbers and that they were armed. The control room responded and so did the unit already on the ground. This let them know exactly where they were to avoid being wrongly identified. Scenes Examination Branch officers were also on their way. Taylor entered the house slowly. She could feel for Susan wholeheartedly. That bastard quite literally was hunting her down to completely destroy her life mentally and physically. She looked through some of the paperwork, looked at the bed, the mess and the blood and her heart sank for Susan and Andrew. No-one should ever have to go through that kind of terror once, far less being haunted daily for as long as they both were alive. She saw the open window and hoped that they had both escaped. Looking at the blood on the floor, she could see that someone had suffered extensive injuries. Which one, was the only question?

"Marcus, we need to split the team and search for them. They don't stand a chance without us because someone left here in a hurry."

"No problem, twos or fours or what, what's best?"

"You'll cover more ground in twos but if he gets the upper hand, fours would be safer." Taylor googled the map of the area and looked at the vastness of what they were up against and just how secluded each lodge was. There was a Loch in the middle of it all with a couple of boat houses dotted along the shore. She put her hand on her head; the decision wouldn't be an easy one. She turned and looked at Marcus. His look said *I'd love to help but this one is your call.* Fran's eyes were fixed on her boss as well. She could see the problem; safety or the ground to be covered; the victim's rescue at the possible cost of the lowered safety of her team.

Marcus spoke up. "I'm easy with going in pairs, Serg. We're capable and there is always a risk, whatever job we're doing."

"Okay, let's do it. We owe it to Susan. Think of her and what she's been through or what could happen if he catches up with her."

There was a general buzz within the team as they collected their kit - maps, compasses, torches, and of course their side arms. It was unusual for a team to be armed like this but how often was there a serial killer on the loose in Scotland and in a position to hurt or kill more people? Taylor's phone vibrated. She turned from the group to look at the message: Kay. Her heart hit the floor, guilt twisting her already aching guts - nerves, lust and now guilt all wrapped in to one. Being away had made it easy not to think, not to feel any attachment. Without the contact, there wasn't the sense of reality but reality had just caught up with her with a punch to the stomach. Fran watched Taylor's turmoil inside and she guessed who the message had come from. Even she felt a pang of guilt because no one wants to be cheated on.

The message read, "Hey you, I hope everything is alright. I know you're really busy and I didn't expect much contact, but you know I worry about you and hope you're coping with everything okay as there is so much riding on this. How's the team? I hope everyone is gelling okay. You know what it's like when there are issues. Short one, just let me know if you're alright, love Kay x."

Taylor knew she had stepped over the line the night before although she had enjoyed every moment of the encounter, but she still wanted to be with Kay and have the dream relationship. She quite obviously had commitment issues, however, and big ones. Taylor acted on impulse and if she wanted something, she had it, usually over and over, satisfying any craving fully and openly if there was an attraction there. She couldn't help herself.

Taylor turned round to brief the team. Fran's eyes were gentle and filled with true affection, and a sense of what had just happened; she wasn't a pushy needy woman. She too had her head switched on and a grounded sense of reality. What had been was good and exciting but may never happen again, unless it was thought about or dreamt about. Their eyes locked, the truth hitting both hard. A fondness came into Taylor's eyes and she gave a virtually invisible flicker, which only Fran captured; it was a return of the true affection felt. Life was what it was and you could have true feelings for more than one person, though others may not like that or accept it. Both enjoyed their mutual appreciation. It gave them a sense of warmth and protection, when they knew there were no guarantees about events to come.

Susan limped through the darkness, the branches cruelly whipping her face and body. With every move she made, she felt that the sound was amplified to the monster in waiting. Her blood curdled at the path she was taking. What if she was walking straight into him? She fell to her knees, her sobs silent, her hands clasped as she prayed to be saved from him, be free from him, for the fear to lift from her shoulders and to give her strength and heart to face him and fight him. Above her she heard an owl calling, something she had rarely heard other than when watching nature programmes. It made her hair stand on end and she could physically feel the nerve endings in her scalp lift. An involuntary shiver rippled through her. She gave herself a shake, got back up and set off again. She didn't want to sit and wait for her fate to come to her. She wanted to be up and ready, or as ready as she could be, if he found her. Susan knew the strength of the man that was hunting her, his hatred and desire to inflict the most vile, torturous pain on those whom he thought deserved it. She wanted to find another lodge, a road, even the water, a person, the police - anyone or anything other than him. *Were the police here? Hmm, why would they be? We didn't call them, nobody knows we're here. God we've been such fools, coming to a place like this. It's a hunter's dream. How the fuck does that bastard know we're here now, how?* She felt sick to the core. She had just realised that she had left the paperwork in her house and that the only way he could have seen it was to have been inside her house to get it. *God he's sick. Why me you twisted bastard? Because I beat you? My miracle recovery has dented your twisted ego, my survival has ruined your reign of terror, you sick, sick fuck. You'll never leave me alone will you? I'm your prize, your trophy, the one that got away, the one who recognised you. My god, the one that stopped you. I'm to blame!*

ᴼᴼᴼ

They both sat silently, listening for sounds of Susan and Andrew. The wind was still preventing the night silence that would help everyone as they all tried to find or avoid one another.

ᴼᴼᴼ

Kay sat on her sofa, phone in hand. She pressed her teeth into her lips, and a little sadness inched into her heart. Her thoughts wandered to some of the passionate nights she had spent with Taylor but she was very aware of her lover's past and her self-confessed weakness for the finer sex. There was no answer from her text, no confirmation that she was safe, no comfort that everything was alright with them. Kay sipped from her glass of Merlot and wished that Taylor was there to share more than her glass of wine. She looked towards the ceiling and blew a kiss for Taylor and said, "Goodnight my love, be safe tonight."

¤¤¤

The teams moved off into the night, their torches lighting the way; they had no need to hide their arrival. They hoped that their presence would curtail the hunt and give Susan and Andrew a fighting chance to evade capture and heighten their chance of staying alive. It was quite clear John Brennan had no fear of anyone, even armed police, his mind so focused on avenging his failure that nothing else registered with him.

It took at least half an hour for him to catch a glimpse of the torch light. They were at least two miles back from him and not all were going the right way. *I wonder if she has seen them yet and is making her way back to meet them. If she does, I'll be waiting!*

Chapter 30: The Hunter and the Hunted

Taylor and Marcus pushed forward, trying to keep within the tree cover, no idea whether anyone was even in the trees or not. Who knew what had happened since the little girl had seen Brennan that morning. When were Susan and Andrew attacked by him? How long had they had to escape, or be captured?

"Taylor!"

"Yeh!"

"Are you alright?"

"I'm fine." She didn't turn to answer because she knew Marcus was astute and could read her like a book, and she certainly didn't want to tell him the truth about what she'd done with Fran and how she now felt about it. Work was bothering her as well. They couldn't fail today or someone would die unless they were dead already.

"It's just you seem a little preoccupied. Do you want to talk? You know I won't judge you, I'll just listen!"

"I know you won't. Thanks Marcus, I'm glad you've got my back. I think I'll need it tonight! Hey, did you phone your wife tonight Marcus?"

"Of course. Did you phone Kay?"

"No, I didn't have time!"

"What? Of course you had time. Why wouldn't you let her know you're alright, especially on a night like tonight? Who knows what'll happen here?"

They were both silent as they pushed through the under-growth noisily.

Andrew stopped to take a breath, to listen, adrenaline still pumping hard through his injured body, which thankfully was still staving off most of the pain. He crouched down and listened hard. The tall trees whispered above him, leaves creating an eerie noise above, a sinister cover for the predator hunting Susan. As he thought this, he realised that Brennan would assume that he was dead; he had certainly suffered more than he thought he'd have to, to look like he did. He pushed his tongue through the gap where his front teeth used to be, but his thoughts were not about his looks. He was glad to be alive and his only mission now was to keep his partner alive. He looked around him. The grounds seemed to go on for miles but a distance away to the north he caught sight of a faint light cutting through the trees, faint but definite. *A torch! Whose torch is that? Would he be that bold and not even hide his position, or is it him tricking us into thinking someone is here to help us and we'll just run straight to him, and game over? I need to find Susan. Together we might have a chance to last a little longer. What do I do? Shout out and let her know I'm alive, give her hope? She must be terrified out there on her own, cold too. No, no, then he'll know I'm alive. I have the upper hand at the moment.*

¤¤¤

Fran and Stevie headed westward. They were young and able to move quite quickly, their locations being checked and plotted by the control room. They also gave the location and coordinates of the others out in the field, allowing them all to try and cover a wider area in a semi-organised manner. The dog handler would be arriving in approximately ten minutes and would cover more ground faster.

"Shit! The land sharks will be here soon and we'll be on the menu as well as him. Police dogs don't discriminate do they?"

"I certainly don't want to be on the wrong end of one of them in the dark woods."

"Don't be such a shiter, I'd be a bit more afraid of that guy out there than anything else. Did you read the intelligence they have on him. He's a fucking monster and strong as an ox."

"Let's face it, I'm glad we've got guns. I wouldn't stand a chance one on one with him."

"Neither would I."

They both laughed nervously because they knew it was true; everyone out there tonight was in mortal danger.

John's eyes narrowed like that of a snake as he stood still as stone beside a large tree, listening to every word Fran and Steve flippantly made as they joked about the situation; he was only yards away from them. He studied their physiques, height and build and instantly had their ability measured. He was more confident in his own ability. He wanted Susan but he knew he could do more if he had a little time to spare. This could be his last day alive and he wanted to live it to the full, and he had someone else on his mind for now. His eyes pierced into Fran's back. He looked up her frame and then back down and licked his lips. He was already hard, wanting her and prepared to take a risk to have her. Fran stopped dead and turned on a dime, her eyes staring straight at the tree where he had been. Her blood ran cold, and she rubbed the back of her neck. The night air crept into her spine and fear buried itself deep inside her as she tried to shake it off, a chill that clung to her like death.

"What's up? Did you hear something, Fran?"

"No, not really. Have you ever had the feeling that you're being watched. You know, when you turn round and there is someone staring at you and it felt like you could feel it, if you know what I mean?"

"Yeah, I know what you mean. What are you saying? Do you think he's hunting us?"

"It's not impossible. He's a crazy fucker you know and he gives me the heebie jeebies."

Steve laughed but there was hint of apprehension in his tone too because they were out of their comfort zone by a mile and Brennan most definitely had the upper hand.

He watched the torchlight move off in front of him as he planned how he could get the better of two armed cops without dying himself, although he just needed to take out one as he wanted the other one very much alive for a while, or at least until she had given into him and he had her at his mercy, begging for her life. It was hard not to be heard so close to someone else but their steps masked his and the wind was his friend, not theirs. The moon came out from behind the clouds, not full but enough to light up the clearings a little. He hoped it wouldn't give away his cover but it also allowed him to keep an eye on them.

ⵣⵣⵣ

Andrew moved out into the clearing, still heading towards the torchlight, remaining cautious in case it wasn't the police and something far more sinister but it was a clearing he had to cross and he had to move as fast as he could.

ⵣⵣⵣ

Susan was shivering, the sweat from her exertion cooling her down and she couldn't warm herself up again. Her adrenaline had subsided and the pain in her foot was now throbbing, aching and making her limp heavily. The pain was excruciating and her cold clammy skin was making her shiver to the point that she couldn't stop. Her heart still pounded with terror at every turn. He could be watching her now, teasing her as he waited for her to weaken even more, just to take her life when he thought the time was right; he enjoyed the terror he commanded in others. She sat down on a grassy verge and put her head between her knees, cuddling her arms round them in a desperate attempt to warm herself a little. She felt sick, terrified and totally alone. Tears ran down her face, audible sobs emanating from her, uncontrollable shoulder movements started to rock her body, her bodily functions working overtime. She retched and then vomited, wetting herself at the same time. She was losing it. Her mind was flashing back to the night he attacked her, every injury and every scar started to ache as she remembered every punch, kick and stab, every act of oppression he had inflicted on her. He was winning; he had beaten her. She was in so much pain now, new and old injuries violating her over and over again. She rolled to the side, weeping and shaking in terror of what was hunting her, her thoughts now turning to death as a form of escape, one that she could control, unless she met him beforehand.

ᴅᴅᴅ

Stevie had dropped back a little from Fran, nothing significant, fifteen feet or so. He was looking up at an owl that they had scared with their torchlight, its big brown eyes peering down at him, making him stand and stare and lose concentration for just that moment. It was really big and Steve had never seen anything like it in the city. He was smiling at it as he kept talking to Fran who had kept on walking unaware that he had actually stopped at all. She was still talking to him quietly thinking he was just behind her, there on her shoulder. The owl suddenly took flight, startled by a sudden movement behind him. Steve's smile left him as a massive hand grabbed his mouth with great force and a sharp deep cut from a knife sliced his voice box wide open, rendering him unable to make a sound, the hand over his mouth holding him in a vice like grip powerful enough to crush the bones in his face. Steve was a strong lad, 25 years old, young and witty and a very popular man in the team. He was a naive man, interested in the world around him, like the owl that had made him take his eye off the ball. A fatal mistake, to underestimate the man they were hunting. Police officers sometimes had a wrongly placed sense of invincibility and it was very rarely that there was ever a creature they had to face that was as cruel and able as this man. Brennan held onto Steve's body with all his might to avoid letting him fall noisily to the ground. Steve's eyes bulged in terror, aware that it was his own blood spraying up and over him, blinding him in the process. Brennan held him almost in a state of levitation to prevent Fran hearing what had just happened. Steve's body was convulsing now, death taking hold as the last throes of conscious life left his young frame. Fran turned round but her eyes went first to the branches above and the owl, which had let out a horrendous screech. She said, "What have you done, Steve, farted or something? because Hooty there has certainly left in a hurry."

She laughed and her eyes dropped only long enough to see a demon slowly laying down her colleague's body in the long grass. She saw blood still spurting from the deep wound in his neck. Steve was quite clearly dying. She heard the gurgling as the blood flowed down his wind pipe. Her torchlight shone on Brennan's face, his wolf-like eyes lifted and stared right at her, his face haunting; an image she would never forget, if she was to live. His face was spattered with blood spray, which made him look even more terrifying. Her whole body bristled with terror and anticipation. She reached for her gun as he vanished into the darkness, his footsteps heavy but quick as he rushed away through the undergrowth. Fran shouted for him to stop as loudly as she could muster. No matter how much training she had received her mind raced with terror and revulsion at what she had just seen and at her clear vulnerability. This man was obviously an evil monster and a very capable one. She was now on her own and he wasn't that far away. She moved closer to Steve's body and tried to put pressure on the wound that had nearly taken his head off. The cut was deep and had been brutally inflicted and Steve's lifeless eyes confirmed that it had been fatal.

Fran checked Steve's body and felt for his holster, her guts twisting as she discovered it was empty. She gave a hysterical involuntary little laugh, thinking to herself *why take the gun? You're so mad and strong, you don't need a fucking gun.* She crouched motionless, listening to the sounds moving away from her, only to hear them stop dead. Her heart skipped as his escape had actually been a comfort. *Why has that fucking bastard stopped? What the fuck is he doing now?* Silence, nothing other than her heart pounding, terror bristling through her.

Taylor's heart lurched when she heard Fran's terrified voice on the radio,

"Officer down, I need assistance immediately. Steve's dead and John now has a gun."

"Confirm, you have seen the suspect John Brennan and he now has a gun?"

"Yes, yes, he now has Steve's gun and I think I'm next on the list."

"Say again. Repeat your last", Taylor quizzed, with genuine fear for Fran's safety.

"I drew my gun and pointed it straight at him but he was too quick and made off into the undergrowth. I didn't give chase and went to see if I could save Steve but obviously I couldn't."

Fran broke down and cut off her transmission, overtly aware of being alone and with an overwhelming feeling of being watched. *Why doesn't he just shoot me? You can quite obviously see me and I haven't a clue where the fuck you are, you monster.*

"You fucking heartless monster," echoed through the night as she yelled out in a manic display of lost control, fear taking hold. Taylor's voice broke her spiral into a gibbering wreck to an instant halt with her calm and supportive tone.

"Calm down Fran. We have your GPS positioning, and Steve's. How far is the body away from you?" she asked.

"Why ?" Fran asked, her fear increasing.

Fran's blood ran cold as it dawned on her; they knew where she was and where Brennan was.

"He's right beside me," she calmly replied, realising as she patted down his pockets, all of which were empty, that as well as the gun, Brennan had Steve's radio. Brennan realised too what a fool he'd been and angrily threw the radio as far as he could into the woods away from his current position. He wanted to hear what was going on but not at the risk of them being able to pinpoint his position. Fran heard something in the trees quite far away.

Taylor's message was quick and frank, "Twenty five metres north east. Run!"

Fran didn't need to be told twice. She was fit and very fast, and she turned in the opposite direction from the lair where he lay and bolted through the ferns and tall grass. She ran with intent and direction, an animal in full flight from the predator behind. She must have ran 100 metres in less than 12 seconds, fully clothed with obstacles in her way, her terror giving her super human ability. A gun at her side and she was still running with everything she had to put some distance between her and him, not feeling protected by the side arm at all; it hadn't helped Stevie one little bit, god rest his soul.

He smiled as he heard her futile attempt to escape as she crashed through the undergrowth. "My, my, she is quick," he muttered to himself. He was in two minds over what to do: take the time to hunt her down or give his full attention to Susan? He listened longer and harder and heard her stop, not far enough to be out of earshot or safe. The trees had stopped rustling and an eerie quietness smothered the woods. He heard her speak on the radio.

"Taylor, we need to get more officers here. This guy is fucking mad. He's hunting me, I think, fucking frightening the life out of me. Shit! I'm shaking here! Come and find me, help me, please come and help me."

She was a little embarrassed by her radio message but she couldn't help it; she was scared stiff and was losing a little self control. She'd watched her stronger and more physical colleague get snuffed out with relative ease; he hadn't stood a chance.

Susan had spotted two sets of torch lights up ahead. They were still far away but she decided to try and make her way towards them; she had decided that they were allies and not foes and was going to take a chance. Her foot ached more than ever and her skin was weeping with blood from hundreds of cuts and scrapes, none of which she could feel, as there were so many other, more damaged things taking up her pain receptors.

John flicked on his torch and sniggered to himself. "Come and find me, if you dare." He wanted Fran to try and get him.

Taylor kept checking Fran's GPS; she was a mile away. Marcus moved in Fran's direction, slightly quicker than Taylor and she told him to wait up, fearing that any distance apart could be a fatal mistake after what had happened.

The police dog moved through the undergrowth, barking loudly through the night. It was tethered to the handler by a long lead and was practically dragging him forward with it. The dog had been round the lodge and could smell three of the occupants so it was tracking Susan, Andrew and John. The chopper was on its way up from Glasgow, thirty minutes ETA.

John moved forward. He was brimming with confidence due to the ease of his last kill and the terror he had placed within the female cop in doing so. He had heard her on the radio and was feeding off her fear, having so much more fun than he thought he would and not even remotely concerned about his welfare.

He stopped and listened again; he heard her up ahead. Fran had changed direction a little to try and trace the torchlight of the others, unaware he now had his torch on. He sped up in her direction, decision made: Susan could wait. He listened for a few moments and went in a direction that would cut her off. She would run right into him. Excitement fuelled his speed as he manoeuvred through the undergrowth, thinking of the prize at the other end.

Fran could barely breathe as she battled her way through the thick foliage, her eyes focused on the sporadic flashes of torchlight a fair distance away. She could hear a faint bark a couple of miles away too. Her heart raced, her clothes soaked with sweat and fear. She felt she was really losing it. She had lost her self-control and was more scared now than she ever imagined she could be. "Fuck you, fuck you! Leave me alone, you hideous fucking bastard. You're not going to beat me," she said aloud over and over but she also whispered, "Save me Taylor, please save me! Don't let him kill me. Please don't let him touch me. Please, please let me find you."

Chapter 31:
Friend or Foe

Fran could see torch lights over to her left, right and straight ahead, all a distance away although the light to the left seemed to be travelling parallel to her and moving with her. Her throat was aching with the effort of running. She wanted to call out but also didn't want to give her position away.

Taylor watched Fran's progress on GPS. It was very staggered, both in speed and direction. She was worried for her as she too could see torch light ahead to the left and to the right. She didn't want to call over the radio and let him hear their progress but she didn't want Fran running headlong into danger either. Taylor decided to transmit, text only: "GPS, what's your position? I think we have an extra firefly out there and I think Fran's the target. Sorry Fran, but I think that prick has a torch on and you're his target. Stop moving and turn your light on and the radio. Make sure your volume is right down and ear piece in. He's flanking you, 800 metres to your right. We'll head towards him. Drop in the long grass, get your breathing sorted and hide. NOW!"

Fran kept on running, totally unaware that her radio had received a text. The torch to her right had slowed down and looked more sedate and that put her mind more at ease. She decided to head that way, believing that this was one of them, one of her team. There was another light a bit further back too, and if that was him he was blowing too close to the wind if he thought he was safe that close to the cops, arrogant bastard.

◻◻◻

Andrew groaned as the pain in his body let him know things were not as good as he'd hoped; he needed to get to Susan and she needed him, he had to keep moving. He too could see the lights ahead like warm havens in the darkness. He hadn't even thought that Brennan would be so dumb as to put a torch on and give away his position, or was he?

Taylor was worried. Fran's GPS was still moving towards the extra torch to the right. "Read your text, god damn it Fran," she whispered under her breath. Marcus kept going in front, barely out of breath. His hair was no longer perfect and slick but he cared more about others than his appearance. He too wanted to find Fran. She was a nice woman, very popular and witty, small and vulnerable and lost out there, traumatised after the murder of her colleague.

Fran's heart nearly stopped when she heard Taylor on the radio,

"Read your fucking text."

"Oh god!"

Fran grappled at her inside pocket for her radio, terrified that it had been heard. She read the words and knew she had to hide and quickly. She had been running like a moth to the flame and it was him she was running to. *God, how could I be that naive?* She knelt down in the longest grass she could find and held her breath. She focused hard but felt a warm stream between her legs and realised that she had wet herself, terror ripping through her as she could see him just metres away, his torch lighting the trees and long grass around him. *Please don't find me,* she wished. Please let me live. *Save me Taylor, let me feel the warmth of your safe embrace one more time. I'm here! Find me Taylor, help me beat him.*

He stopped dead. He knew she was very close. He had heard her up until a moment ago. How did she know to stop? She looked through the grass, silent and gulping down her needy breaths, as she focused on the light in front of her. She could see him, a large man, strong build, chiselled features. She looked at his eyes and nearly let out a terrified whimper. She had never seen anything like it in her twelve years in the police; the darkness in his eyes was so sinister, so evil, so lifeless and unaffected by normal emotion. This was all so clear to see with just one look into those shark-like dead eyes. She could see the devil in them, every horror film she'd ever watched rolled into one was standing there right in front of her, hunting her, frightening her. She knew she'd lost it and she truly believed he'd be able to smell her fear from where he was. She wanted to crawl backwards, a natural reaction to recoil to get away from him.

He knew she was there so he laughed his sinister laugh, knowing she could hear him, a blood curdling soul crushing laugh, one that sent shivers down her spine. Fran wept silently. She lowered her head into her hands as his head turned her direction.

He growled loudly, "I can smell you, bitch. I can smell your fear. I know you're here and when I get you I'm going to hurt you so bad that you will beg me to take your life, beg me to stop hurting you, and I will hurt you and you will want to die when I've finished with you!"

Marcus and Taylor saw the torch go off. They picked up their pace but both were feeling it a little. They were both cut and bruised with the constant whipping and scraping of the foliage tearing at them as they ran desperately to try and save Fran. They only had her GPS to go on, which was never the easiest thing to follow.

Darkness fell around her, the comfort of light drifting away; the only comfort now was that she didn't have to look at his hideous face anymore. But unfortunately now she would not know for definite where he was. She was a little confident that he didn't know where she was either or he surely would have been there by now.

The other two police teams, along with the dog, were homing in on Fran's GPS as well. Nobody wanted another cop to be hurt in any way, and certainly not in the way that that beast would hurt her.

He'd been here before with Layla and he was brimming with confidence; her fear would lead him right to her, she had already cracked.

Fran could hear him moving around, searching, flattening

grass all around her. She felt like a rabbit, remaining still as a statue, hoping not to be discovered and waiting for her chance to bolt when there was enough distance to escape, fearing that to stay still could also mean certain death. The grass crumpled too close for comfort and she couldn't bear it a moment longer. Shots rang out in the night as he lifted her into the air by her hair. She screamed out as loud as she could before his forearm stifled any further sounds Fran tried to make. He lifted her up and threw her down onto the ground winding her badly. She had never felt pain like it, she could barely breathe. She had dropped her weapon and lay there, weak and helpless. He bent over her and punched her so hard that her head whipped back, rendering her unconscious instantly. He ripped her radio from her belt and threw it as far as he could towards the approaching torchlight, which was still several minutes away. He knew he'd have to be quick so he cut through her belt at the back of her jeans, ripped her panties like a savage, his penis rock hard in his jeans. He stroked over her firm buttocks, bent over and licked her sweet and frightened skin. Gripping his penis, he stroked forcefully until he came over her. He didn't want to come too quickly when she woke up.

He flopped Fran over onto her back, tugging her jeans down over her knees to her ankles, her perfect pussy exposed in an undignified way. He stared at her. *Weak,* he thought, as he lowered his mouth down onto her. He wanted to taste her, his hand pushed up between her legs as he saw her eyes open.

"Welcome back."

The pain of his four fingers forced inside her burned as they penetrated her, tearing and stretching her.

"No," rang out through the night.

Andrew stood up and ran as fast as his pain filled body could manage. He raced straight up behind wielding a thick branch above his head. John was about to rape Fran following his foreplay. Andrew swung the branch as hard as he could at John's head. The thud was sickening as his head dipped to one side, blood instantly spraying all over Fran. He lurched to the side and fell off Fran to one side, momentarily rendering him unable to hold onto Fran. She kicked out with her legs as best she could with all the strength she could muster, her legs still tethered with the lowered jeans restricting her movement. Andrew didn't care, he kicked out blindly at John with all his might, and grabbed Fran by the lapels and heaved her to her feet. Dragging her limping out of her jeans, he pulled her through the trees, both of them running for their lives, every ounce of their strength needed to get distance between them and him. Andrew thought to himself, *fuck, we should've stayed there and killed the fucking bastard. It's just like in the shit movies we watch and scream at them when the people running in terror don't take the chance to end the crazed killer when they get the chance, but could I kill a man?* Footsteps light like gazelles, or so it felt as they ran joined by their arms, a new strength consuming them, a new lease of life at the exhilaration of escape, the chance to live on Fran's part and a little redemption for Andrew.

John put his hands up to his bloodied face. He was raging. He could smell the scent of Fran that lingered on his fingers. *So close. Who the fuck was that? If it was a cop, he would have just killed me. Surely, they're not allowed to do that? Don't tell me that her fucking prick of a lover is still alive. What the fuck do I have to do to fucking kill these people?* He laughed out loud to himself as he thought of clinical checks he'd need to do in future to confirm the death of his victims, and actually make them full blown murders and not attempted murders. *I'm just going to have to put a bullet through their heads next time and stop these futile attempts to use primitive murder methods.*

He put his fingers in his mouth and sucked her from them, rock hard and full of vengeance he moved off quickly in the opposite direction of the torchlight, fully aware that the bitch would be able to pinpoint where he'd been. Plus, there was now a fucking trail for the dog and shit loads of blood thanks to whoever that was. "Prick!"

Fran felt the pain of his violation between her legs as they ran together; her jeans had had to be discarded and her pants nearly gone too. She didn't even know this man that had saved her from the raging demon, but she trusted him with every bit of her ravaged body. They ran and ran and she held onto him with a tight grip, the torchlight getting closer and closer. This time they both knew it wasn't Brennan and the torches looked like they were also speeding towards them. Fran shouted out into the night, all self-control out of the window, her will to survive superseding everything.

Taylor and Marcus heard Fran's voice. It wasn't too far away now. Their guns were drawn and pointed out in front of them as they sped as fast as the trees would let them. Their torches beamed ahead lighting up two figures. "POLICE!" Their words rang out loudly in the night. They pointed their guns straight at Andrew's central body mass and told him to get on his knees. His face was so bruised, swollen and covered in blood it was unrecognisable to them.

He dropped to the ground immediately, raising his arms, not wanting to be mistaken for Brennan and be shot dead in error, which was a real possibility right now. "Don't shoot, please! It's Andrew, Susan's partner." They lowered their guns, and moved quickly towards them.

Fran was naked from the waist down apart from a torn pair of pants grasped together by her hand. Her face was swollen and bleeding, tears rolling down her cheeks making clean rivers through her blood stained face. She ran like a child greeting a parent straight into Taylor's strong arms. Taylor gripped her tightly, the warmth unmistakeable as she held her close, her soft words instantly comforting Fran.

"Thank god you're okay, thank god. I thought he was going to kill you."

"He was. He was going to torture me first and then kill me."

Fran looked at Andrew, their eyes connecting; together they felt strong. Fran mouthed the words, "Thank you," to him, and then winced at the searing pain all over her body, pain where Brennan had thrown her, hit her and violated her. She broke down and sobbed loudly with her face in her hands. She was totally spent and just wanted to go home. but could they? Who was hunting who? It seemed a very level playing field out there but the darkness and the undergrowth were certainly on his side. He had the upper hand and he wasn't frightened.

Andrew introduced himself to Fran. She took a sharp intake of breath when she realised he was Susan's partner, the man from the photos they had in their briefing packs. His facial swelling was grotesquely disfiguring. He turned his head to Taylor, who was on the radio ordering a medical chopper.

She turned to Andrew and Fran and said, "Both of you have to get out of here. There's nothing more you can do!"

"I'm not leaving her behind. He's desperate now; there's nothing for him to lose and Susan is the reason he's here. I just hope she can keep away from him."

Marcus put his hand gently on Andrew's shoulder. "You have to get out of here. We have more resources coming and we can't let you get more hurt than you already are. Look at your face, your body, it's a mess."

Fran looked up at Marcus. "I'm so sorry, so, so, sorry." Fran kept on crying; she was broken inside. She could not believe a person could feel so weak and vulnerable, even with a weapon. "I need to leave," she said with no remorse at all. "I'm no good to anyone, now, no one," she wept.

Taylor came over and held her round her shoulders, careful not to hurt her but she gave a warm embrace and gently kissed her head. Marcus watched and wondered if this was because of the night's events or a little more than that. He let it go though. This was certainly not the time to question or challenge anyone. Fran needed her security, needed to feel safe. A cold shiver ran down her spine as she heard a shot ring out in the night. The barking of the dog turned into an ear piercing whine. Then another shot silenced the night.

The radio crackled and the dog handler's voice came over the airwaves. His tone was one of shock and filled with tension.

"To control, that's the perpetrator heading north towards the lake, and the bastard has just killed the dog. She was off the lead and she bolted away from me, obviously after something, which certainly wasn't a fucking rabbit."

Radio protocol had all gone to pot as fear ripped through everyone on the ground. The specialist units were all still on their way. The spot was so remote and so far north none had been close by and this played right into Brennan's hands. He had a gun, he had the element of surprise and he had fear on his side. Darkness was also his best friend.

Chapter 32:
Sink or Swim

Susan limped north. She wanted to get out of the woods, find the lake and maybe even a boat. The woods filled her with fear and dread. He could be within touching distance and she couldn't stand it anymore. The not knowing was killing her; her guts ached at the thought of his face coming out of every pitch black pocket.

John also moved swiftly north, pondering where the sly little bitch might go. His mind raced. For the first time he wondered if this would be his last day on earth. He shrugged. "Who gives a fuck!"

He could see a lodge near the water. Lights were on and a warm glow was emanating from it, an inviting haven to escape to, and other people to give you a false sense of security. He smiled, *that's where I would go - into the safety of the arms of others. The more the merrier,* he said to himself.

Susan also saw the lodge and her heart wanted to go there and be in the light, be with people, but she knew that if she went to it she would be putting the poor innocent people holiday-ing there in grave danger. She needed to find the police; they were the only ones that could help her now. Susan had heard the two shots earlier and the painful whine of the injured dog. Her heart had sunk at that moment as the realisation of her situation became clear. If he could shoot a police dog, then who was in control here? Susan turned west and continued towards the loch, steering well clear of the lodge. *What if he goes there anyway? Shit! Shit, those poor people. Fuck! I'd die if I tried to save them. Have a wee prayer from me - be safe.*

ￂￂￂ

The log fire gave the living room a warm glow. The children were tucked up in their beds and the couple sat having a glass of wine as they watched television. The luxury apartment was the best money could buy, in a tranquil setting and filled with all the mod cons needed and spotless luxury fittings. They sighed happily as they drank their wine, totally relaxed at the mellow surroundings. In front of them was a window the full length of the room with a view onto the jetty. Small boats were clinking together in the light wind, the metal on them chiming in the evening air. The moon shone brightly onto the loch, small squalls rippling across the water. The view was truly breathtaking; the setting worth every penny, they thought.

His hand gripped the handle tightly. He expected to just walk right in but to his surprise the door was locked. *City dwellers lack so much trust,* he thought to himself, amused. *Shit, maybe they've locked the door because she's already here and they know I'm coming, they think a little lock will stop me.*

He moved round the house slowly looking into each window. None of the curtains were drawn. His eyes searched for her in every little space. He moved to the room with the children lying in their beds, the heat from his breath steaming up the window. His eyes were cold and black as he peered into the room; he scanned around, but couldn't find her. His head gently bumped the window as he looked into the corner of the room. One of the children heard this and woke up. He sat bolt upright and stared at the window, eyes wide and terrified. John hadn't noticed the child. The wee boy couldn't move or speak. Terror engulfed him as he thought he was looking at the face of the boogeyman. Quickly, he slumped back down onto his bed and pretended to be asleep; just in time, as John's eyes stared straight at the children again. The boy felt tears roll down his face and tried with all his might to stop himself moving, or visibly shaking. He slanted his eyes to try and see if he'd only been dreaming but he could still see John's bared teeth and hideous face was still there staring right at him. John eventually dropped his gaze and went round towards the front of the lodge. He moved a little further away to enable him to look in the massive window without being noticed. He didn't want to kill these people unless they were hiding Susan but as he watched them, there were no signs of any distress or trying to hide something or get away. They were just sitting chilling. He was about to move off when one of the children came running through into the living room. He looked alarmed and was very animated as he explained something to his parents, pointing back through to the bedroom. The male that had been sitting down took the boys hand and led him back out of the living room, through to the bedroom John presumed. He watched the woman, who remained seated on the couch not looking overly bothered. He was about to leave as he didn't think Susan was in there.

"He was right there at the window, staring at us. He was horrible and mean looking. He was right there, see dad, right there dad, see." Trembling, the little boy pointed. He wet himself and started crying loudly. His dad put his arm round him.

"There's no such thing as the boogeyman. There was no one there. You must've had a dream little lad, come on, back to bed."

He went to lift his son up and realised he was wet. He thought that this was not like his little boy, and why was he shaking so much? Something must have really scared him. Letting go of the boy, he went to the window and put his face up against it to see out into the darkness. He saw marks on the outside of the window, marks that showed that someone had leant their face on it right where the boy had said he'd seen the man. The father's blood ran cold and a horrible shiver rolled slowly up his spine as he allowed his imagination to run wild, fuelled by his little boy's terror. He shook himself to regain a little control of his mind and put some logic into the situation. He looked one more time to reassure himself that there was nobody there, more for himself than the kids and again pressed his face right up against the pane to peer into the darkness. As he did so a figure loomed up from beneath the window. His face was almost touching the window, a blank and expressionless face stared right back at him.

The father stumbled backwards, grabbing his son in a desperate attempt to get some distance between him and this thing that was at the window. He saw the boogeyman put his finger up to his mouth and make a sign as if to warn him to keep quiet, his eyes silently threatening, his face twisted with hate and intimidation. The man grabbed for his other child who lay there still asleep, scooped him up like a rag doll and scampered backwards through to the living room, dragging the first boy off his feet in haste. He yelled to his wife to get out of the living room but it was too late, the boogeyman had moved quickly. He was light on his feet for a big man and was already outside the large picture window. John could see the terror in the face of the good looking woman frozen in front of him, eyes watery and fear oozing from them as her husband dragged the screaming children through to her, trying to escape the nightmare. Her motherly instinct kicked in and she dropped to her knees, grabbing the kids in her arms, surrounding them in an attempt to protect them. She faced up to John like a wild cat and screamed at him, "Leave them alone! What do you want? Please don't hurt my children, please don't hurt us." She didn't show any concern for herself as she stood facing the window shielding her precious boys from the eyes of the devil. John stood there staring at the bravery of this woman. He had a gun and was a very strong man but this woman was standing her ground, unfazed by the threat he posed to her.

John raised the gun towards the window and aimed it straight at her head, only glass separating them. Her defiance made him want to teach her to respect him but the children being there disturbed him; they plagued his conscience. He hated women and how they made him feel, but children were innocent and he wouldn't gain anything by slaying their mother. The situation he had created was now taunting him to decide. His eyes narrowed and his teeth clenched. His finger moved to the trigger.

The rumble of a boat's engine cut through the night. John snapped out of his trance-like state instantly. His head snapped round towards the loch. It was pitch dark and he tried to focus on where the noise had come from. He looked back to finish the job but the family had scurried out of the room and out of sight. He blasted through the window firing several shots as he moved away from the house, a gesture of dominance and show of what he could have done to them. The glass shattered into thousands of diamond-like pieces. Screams rang out from the lodge, all of them fearing for their lives, believing he was coming straight through the window to slay them. Susan's head snapped round at the shots and she looked to where they had come from; they were at the lodge. She sighed. Her instincts had been right and saved her own life but her heart sank for those who were in the lodge. She hoped that they had survived. The distance from where she was and from where he'd just revealed himself to be was not far enough for her, and she felt like a scared animal being hunted once again. He was too close for comfort now and she knew it.

The cops changed direction and headed towards the lodge, fearing the worst for whoever was at the wrong end of the shots. They also heard the gentle purr of the boat's engine as it moved towards the opposite side of the loch. Their focus was now the loch and lodge, all units now converging in that direction.

The control centre received a call from the lodge house. The woman on the line relayed the events of a moment ago, her voice clear and to the point; she sounded worried but very much in control. She relayed the facts to the controller at the end of the phone, stating exactly where they were, what the male looked like and that they weren't staying there for another second. The controller arranged for a rendezvous place to allow them to be met by armed officers, where statements and medical attention would be taken and given. The family made towards their car in haste, taking their chance that the man at the window had left them at that time for a reason and this was their moment to escape. The woman had truly believed he was going to kill her. There was fear in her voice, but a strength that could be heard over the phone, a mother's strength to protect her family.

The GPS position of the lodge was relayed to all the officers on the ground. The helicopter was now up above them, the dragon lights shining down into the trees and over the water. The whirring of the rotary blades displaced branches and leaves, the down draft powerful as the chopper dropped and raised back up in the sky, searching for him and her. Armed officers were on board and they decided to cover the family leaving the lodge to afford them some protection as they got to their car.

John sprinted down to the loch and ran along the edge of the water. There were several small motor boats moored at the jetty. He looked back at the lodge and watched the chopper hover above it. He had chosen well not to stay there any longer. *Stupid bitch! She's left me a boat or two for use, and she's taken herself away from the very people that would maybe be able to save her.*

He looked up into the sky and watched the chopper circle above the trees, the light beam shining across the water and onto Susan's boat and back to the trees. Torchlight shone up from the trees from several places, one after the other. He watched this as the positions of all the cop's locations were revealed.

He smiled and said, "Thank you for everything."

He pulled the cord of the engine with force and it instantly rumbled into action. Flipping the rope into the water, he headed straight to where her boat had been lit up in the water. He was totally focused on Susan now. Everyone was closing in on him, everything was a ticking time bomb, his life and hers both hanging in the balance. He had to beat them all to her; he couldn't let them find her first after all his effort to reunite them.

Taylor had also looked out on the water and seen the little boat cutting across it in the light beam. She knew Susan's position had been compromised by those searching to save her. Her radio crackled as she gave direction to everyone as to where Susan was now and where she was heading, trying to give rough coordinates. They had to get to her quickly because they weren't the only ones that would have seen and heard her. Marcus picked up the pace, as did all the others. "How are we going to get over there? I hope there are more boats for us, or it's a fucking long swim."

Taylor moaned at the cop half-humour, a slight panic in her voice because she realised just how vulnerable Susan was now.

The front of Susan's boat crunched into the pebbled shore, a deep groove scarred the beach where it had landed. The tree line lay close to the shore, the foliage again thick and intimidating but she couldn't remain where she was, totally exposed and out in the open. Every ounce of her heart feared the closeness of the trees and the terror of what they could hide. Nevertheless, she felt safer at this side of the loch, knowing that she'd left him behind back at the lodge; at least now there was some distance between them. She worried a little that all of the torchlight was also left far behind but her heart hoped that more officers would be joining the search from this side. She didn't realise that resources in the north of Scotland had to be sourced from elsewhere and travel far to get to where they were needed. Nothing was ever instantaneous in that part of the country.

She took a deep breath and moved into the trees. Instantly she felt claustrophobic and trapped; Susan couldn't get her breath as terror took hold of her once again. Her mind raced back to the night she'd been attacked and how much Brennan had already taken from her. *Is this the end of me, my life? Is he going to win, once and for all? Would it be easier to just give in and wait for him to kill me, take the enjoyment away from him, make a stand and take back control of my life again?*

ㅁㅁㅁ

His fist gripped the throttle and twisted every knot out of the small boat; it cut through the water with relative ease, the nose lifting at the front, his weight and the speed pushing the boat upwards and forwards.

ㅁㅁㅁ

Tyres screeched as the family left the lodge, the kids screaming and crying in the back, the couple looking ahead in concentration, escape being their only thought. The road ahead of them was single tracked with blind corners and every turn could potentially reveal him standing there. Their fear was obvious, eyes wide, apprehension raw and mind altering. Turn after turn they made, all of them unwilling to relax and believe that they were free from the boogeyman. They reached the main junction and only then, with a couple of miles behind them, did they look at one another with a little relief that the nightmare was really over.

ㅁㅁㅁ

Taylor shone her torch on the lodge; the whole front window was in a thousand pieces. Her heart raced at what she might see within these walls. She had spotted toys outside the chalet and hoped that everybody had escaped with their lives. Marcus searched the bedrooms, his guts churning at the thought of a dead child within, his thoughts with his own beautiful little boy having to endure this beast that they all hunted. His heart skipped into happiness as the rooms revealed no horror, just empty beds and the signs of a hasty retreat, all belongings abandoned where they lay - toys, clothes, full glasses of wine, nibbles and signs of the normal enjoyment of their holiday, up until the unexpected visit from Brennan. Marcus returned to Taylor with a smile, the first of the night. "There's nobody here boss. Something changed his mind. It's not like him not to maim and torture people."

"He's seen her from here - Susan! We saw her and so did he. Fuck! We've got to get over there now. We have to get to her and help her."

"There must be other boats around here, Marcus. You could hot wire the best one, none of these shitty little fishing boats."

"I'll see what I can do but we need to move on this one. He's got nothing to lose."

Taylor relayed on the radio the possible movement of Susan and John and her team's next objective. The control room also confirmed that Fran and Andrew had been successfully airlifted from the area and that they were heading for the nearest hospital.

Fran broke down as the paramedics knelt in front of her, her face swollen beyond recognition, her body aching all over and her pride shattered beyond recognition. Her weakness she perceived had been opened up in front of everyone - her colleagues, Taylor and worst of all, him!

Andrew's warm face gazed at her, his eyes offering her a knowing comfort, his face the double of hers. Their eyes met full on and there at that moment they understood exactly what the other felt and what they had been forced to endure. He moved over to her side, the noise of the helicopter deafening them. They sat in silence and Andrew put his arm round her shoulder, not a bit intrusively, just that of someone who genuinely cared and understood, offering purely comfort. They shared a moment together, both of them worried for those they cared for. Fran had watched one of the strongest cops she'd ever known being brutally slain with relative ease. How safe was Taylor, and poor Susan? Both Fran and Andrew hurt in every way as they flew over the woods and only then did they realise how remote this place was. The irony of Susan and Andrew's choice for their remote escape now very clear. It was the worst place on earth they could have ever gone. Andrew put his head in his hands. He hoped with all his heart that Susan would make it and that the police would deal with this vile creature, permanently.

Chapter 33: Deception

Susan made her way through the trees as fast as she could, her head throbbing with exhaustion, her legs aching with the effort of running for so long. Her already damaged body was cut all over, blood oozing from the wounds and her heart hadn't stopped pounding for hours. She was starting to think it was going to just stop altogether some time soon.

Officers arriving were sent to the opposite side of the loch in an attempt to intercept Susan. They were armed and well-trained. All had specialist knowledge and equipment. The chopper floated above them but would be unable to set down anywhere close by due to the extensive tree coverage. The heat seeking equipment was lighting up all over the place on both sides of the loch. GPS alerts for all the cops lit the screen like fireflies, with only one obvious extra but who was it?

John's boat thundered into the shore, cutting deep into the pebbles. He stood up and stared at Susan's much less powerful boat, smiling at the realisation he would have gained some time on her. *Poor choice, stupid cow! Do you want me to fucking gut you like a pig, because you're going the right way about it? You've just left all of your friends behind you.* He was totally unaware of the new

224

arrivals on his side of the loch and that time was running out for him too. Officers in decent numbers were heading to where the boats had landed on the shore.

Taylor and Marcus took another boat from the jetty and it rumbled into life, heading straight towards where they thought Susan should have landed. She had at least 20 minutes on them. They had just left the lodge as it was, no cordon, as everyone was needed for the hunt to save Susan; the evidence there could wait and the family that were in the lodge were now in safe hands.

John yelled out like a wild animal, almost goading them to find him, but he also wanted to frighten Susan into giving her position away. He hoped the terror within her would finally give way and he would have her once more.

Susan listened to him bellow out through the night, the cold silence causing his voice to reverberate off every tree; it clung to the air like hideous rotting flesh and echoed through the night. She ran faster and faster, unaware of every branch that ripped her already torn skin. Every new cut on her feet failed to burn anymore, she wanted to live, to survive, to get away from him. His cold voice gave her the motivation to try even harder to escape, even more than before. She never wanted to set eyes on him ever again.

Four police cars were parked in a small clearing in the trees, their spot inconspicuous, all of the officers who had just arrived now making their way through the woods towards the position recently given by Taylor, whose boat was only just landing near to the other two. One officer was left to watch over the police vehicles. He was armed and well warned of the danger presented by John Brennan. He was alert and twitchy at the possibility of coming face to face with him. The cop didn't even consider he might come off second best, he was just running through how he would kill Brennan if he came anywhere near him. He wasn't frightened, just itching to get a bit of action.

John knew how the heat seeking equipment worked. The trees were perfect for him. Every time the bird went over, he had already sought the most crooked, large trunked and well branched tree to cling to in the hope that all of him would be covered by it, *'cause once they get a glimpse of you, old son, they'll cling to you like shit on your shoe and lead the others right to you.*

Blood spattered the windshield like water spraying up from

a puddle with force. A shot rang out in the night and the uniformed muscled body slumped to the floor, a bullet hole clean through his head, brain matter scattering all over the bonnet of the cop car. His skip cap flipped through the air with the force of the bullet. He had only looked down at his perfectly polished boot for a second. His eyes had been focused on his surroundings all of the time before that. A moment off the ball and his life had ended with heartless ferocity.

Susan scampered through the trees and clambered up a hill covered in fern and thistle. A clearing revealed a small single track road, the first she'd seen since she'd escaped from their tranquil, luxury lodge. Tears flooded her eyes, sadness for poor Andrew filling her heart. *Did he die saving me? Did he die because I wanted to get so far away from everyone? I played right into his hands; stupid, stupid, stupid.* Her mind allowed her to feel that she might just have made it. She heard a crack in the trees 40 to 50 metres back. She panicked and scurried silently up the road. Southwards, as she thought that would lead towards where she believed there was a slightly bigger road and a heightened chance of escape. There might be someone there to help her, more police. *There have to be more police,* she thought. She knew there were cops everywhere, but he was also out there. *Why can they not just find me, now?*

Her eyes raised up as she heard the vehicle coming towards her. Eyes blurred with tears she felt total exasperation. Focusing hard, she saw the light box on top of the car, the driver had a marked cap on his head and a radio on his lapel was lit up in receipt of a call. A slight smile curled at the side of her mouth and she felt her body weaken with the anticipation of being rescued.

Susan raised her arms over head and stepped out into the road, waving for attention, and the car slowed down. The passenger door swung open and a soft voice said, "Quick! Get in - he's close by." Susan did what was asked of her without hesitation and a large muscular arm reached across her and closed the door. The feeling of relief welling within her was short lived though, when the voice in the car changed to a very familiar one, one that sent terror straight through her heart.

She barely dared to look up, her stupidity at falling so easily into his hands after what she had just been through burnt her deeply; she should have noticed there was only one officer there. Why would that be? Because he wasn't an officer, that's why.

Her eyes clouded over as his hand gripped her mouth and nose so tightly that she felt her head was going to explode. "Welcome back Susan. We've got some unfinished business to attend to."

She slumped onto the seat unconscious and he viciously shoved her further down towards the floor and out of sight for those who may have looked in on them. The car moved slowly off, lights on and driving carefully round the winding road. He thought the chopper would have followed but they obviously hadn't found the body of the cop yet so he moved away in plain sight, totally unchallenged. Several miles passed and he came to a junction and turned slowly right onto a two way carriageway. He moved off and saw his first car, then another and another. He flicked on the blues and pulled over the next car, smiling when he realised it was a woman at the wheel. She looked up and asked, how can I help you, officer?"

Her face whipped round as his fist slammed against her cheek. She fell out cold straight away, jaw clearly broken and blood pouring from her mouth. He dragged her to the police car and threw her into the back seat before dragging Susan's limp body over to his new wheels - a nice four by four with plenty of space for both of them. He lifted Susan up like a bag of potatoes and shoved her on the floor of the passenger side. He turned the ignition and started to drive, happy that he had survived and that he had got what he came for, a great twist of fate after he'd thought it was all over for him. He turned onto the nearest field, cutting across as many drivable fields as he could without the lights on, this enabling him to miss the arterial and minor route road blocks that the police had set up.

Where now? He thought as he headed back to Edinburgh. He had stripped the woman of all of her personal belongings to slow down the police in finding out, who she was and what car she may have owned, that's if she didn't come round too soon. He'd dump this car soon too and steal the next one he came across as that wouldn't be discovered till morning and he'd be long gone by then.

"Officer down," rang out on the radio. "A police vehicle is unaccounted for, I think Brennan has fled the scene. Get the helicopter to trace 79's GPS. Track that fucking car. NOW!!" The cop's voice was shaky and quite obviously angry; he had found his friend lying there with his head blown out. The sight had quite clearly got to him and his words revealed an emotion that he rarely showed at work. He also requested an ambulance even though he knew that there was no chance to save his partner, but how he wished the opposite.

Taylor could not believe what she was hearing on the radio. "How the fuck did that happen? How did he get a set of wheels? I bet he's not just escaping. He's probably got Susan as well. Marcus! He's got her, he's fucking got her."

"Calm down! How do you know that for sure?"

"I know that bastard wouldn't leave here alone just to save himself. He's fucking got her and wants time and privacy to do it right this time. He's going to make a show of it."

"Really? Do you think he's that bright and thought this through?"

"I do, Marcus, and we've got to save her. We can't let her down, not after what he's put her through and for Fran, Steve and the other armed response officer"

"We'll have to confirm it though, boss. We can't just leave on a hunch!"

Taylor called over the radio. "To all sets, rendezvous point the following coordinates. Then could the chopper do a sweep of this portion of the woods with the heat seeker and confirm or not whether there is anyone else here with us? Susan wouldn't hide. She should be clearly visible."

Everyone gathered together. The time delay frustrated Taylor as she just wanted to go. All of them had to make their way back to the vehicles first, and that would be no easy feat. A crackled message came over the radio, "Negative for the first sweep. There appear to be no extra bodies other than those that have been plotted."

That was enough for Taylor. She rounded up her group, two less than she'd come with, and left those from the local area to deal with the evidence gathering at all of the multiple crime scenes throughout the once peaceful woods.

Chapter 34: Reunited

The car rumbled away, his newly stolen vehicle perfect for the task at hand. This time it was a Land Rover, one big enough to hide his victim with ease. John thought hard about where he could go, what would be the best ending for his prized possession and tonight's events. He'd read about a lot of successful and powerful women in his time but was now a bit lost as to where he could go. The last thing he wanted was to be captured without having his party first. He grinned as he thought up a suitable and sinister ending for those that had cost him so much, all of them.

¤¤¤

Inspector Findlay came over the radio with his brash and intrusive manner, "Phone me, Sergeant Nicks, at your earliest opportunity."

"Fuck! How did that prick get hold of this so soon? I thought he'd be in his bed."

"Good news travels fast," Marcus sighed.

Taylor dialled the inspector's number and Marcus could tell instantly that she was getting a roasting at the end of the phone, being blamed for others that she did not have control over back there at the scene. They had been a totally separate unit that had only just joined them and probably hadn't grasped just how cunning Brennan was and how ruthless he could be when trapped.

Her face got redder and redder, anger etched across it as she was ordered to return to Edinburgh and stand down from the enquiry. Others would be taking over the lead from now on as the bosses were on his case and he couldn't allow for any more failures. "How the fuck did you let that bastard get away, and where the fuck has he gone? He couldn't just have disa-fucking-peared," Findlay yelled down the line. Everyone in the van heard it and felt for Taylor; it wasn't through her lack of trying or the commitment of everyone present that they'd failed.

Findlay didn't seem to care a damn about those who wouldn't be coming back tonight. There was silence after the phone clicked off, mouths agape with his decision to stand their boss down.

Taylor threw her radio on the dash board. "Fucking fat bastard," the silence now broken as she shouted, "We're off the fucking case as from now. What the fuck does he know? Nothing! Stupid twat! He knows fuck all about how it works out in the field, the useless fat desk jockey."

Marcus kept quiet along with the rest of the team.

"Oh, and all operational statements regarding your involvement in the whole case have to be completed and forwarded to the replacement team by the end of your duty tonight. Arsehole! That will take bloody hours. Who needs sleep!"

The drive back was silent and very uncomfortable. It was tinged with sadness for the two dead cops and for poor Fran - for her ordeal and the humiliation and degradation she had endured for all to see - and for Andrew and poor Susan. To even contemplate a repeat of anything she had suffered before was incomprehensible.

John pulled into an unfamiliar road but he knew the number of the house where he intended going. The road had cars parked on both sides and was lit by orange lamps, leaving a sinister glow on the silent street; there was no movement anywhere and no lights on as John parked the stolen car.

He left Susan inside and went to the door of the house, a modest dwelling in a decent part of Edinburgh. The house looked pretty secure as he made his way round the back. One hopper window on the second floor was open. He knew he would be able to get in.

"Thank you once again for your help," he muttered.

As everyone arrived back at Fettes HQ, there was a little more chat but, not the usual banter, just general chat about families and partners who had not been seen for days. Everyone was oppressively tired from the events of the night and the journey home. They were all dirty and stank of stale sweat. Many headed for the showers before they sat down at their desks to begin their marathon typing sessions to complete their operational statements.

Taylor leant back on her seat, tired and despondent at the way that she and her team had been treated after what they'd been through. *We have worked our asses off for this enquiry and risked our bloody lives and just because there was a little heat from the top, instead of standing up for us, that weak minded fool felt he had to take some sort of action. The wrong action, of course,* she thought to herself.

Some civilian staff were still working late in the building. She looked over anxiously, guiltily, at Kay's seat, which was empty. *Why's she not here today? God if I'd only phoned her, been civil and respectful and given her her place, I would know what's going on with her now. Fool! What a fool I've been.* Taylor put her face in her hands and shut her eyes. She could feel the sadness welling up inside her again, everything overwhelming her tired senses.

Taylor jumped as two hands gently clasped round her eyes, a scent of pure beauty surrounding her. The familiarity and the instant affection she felt left her in no doubt who this was. The touch of the hands was tender and caring, not that of someone who no longer cared; Taylor could feel a familiar stir within. She swung round on her seat and her flushed face melted into a smile. She stood up and gave Kay a warm and loving hug, one that would be given to any friend but that had a hidden portion of affection only they were aware of. Marcus looked up at them. It was different for him; he knew the score and he smiled a knowing smile at the genuine warmth in their shared embrace.

Kay just stood and looked at Taylor before saying in a seductively loving voice, "You stink, lady." She flicked her hair back over her shoulders and laughed aloud. "You all stink." Her tone was jovial and kind. The rest of the team smiled and acknowledged her. She wasn't wrong; they did stink.

Everyone went back to typing their statements and Kay continued to gaze at Taylor. "I was really worried about ... about us, about everything."

Her eyes were a little hurt and fragile, although she still held eye contact in a loving way.

"You could've called me, though. I do realise it's difficult being in a squad but all I needed was a one liner to let me know you were still okay and we were still okay."

Taylor's eyes dropped only a little as she replied, "Why wouldn't we be alright?" Her response was calm and said as innocently as she could, trying not to arouse any suspicion.

Kay put her hand up to Taylor's cheek and stroked it downwards in a warm and loving manner, not caring who was watching, before going to her desk. Taylor questioned herself. Why had she had done what she did with Fran? Had Kay noticed the guilt in her eyes because Taylor certainly felt it!

Kay sat back at her desk. She knew that Taylor was hiding something, her forced response obvious to another woman. She didn't know quite what it was but there was something amiss.

She picked up her phone and messaged: "Yours or mine? We need to catch up on everything, and I need what you have to offer me - all of it!"

Taylor lifted her phone, and read the text. Guilty or not, she still loved Kay and wanted her more than ever. She smiled and raised her eyebrow and then her eyes and looked over at Kay, lust now filling her body and her heart still full of love for Kay. Just the thought of going home for a shower would be classed as a tempting invite.

She texted back, "Mine! I want you so much, x"

Kay smiled over and replied, "Not without a week in that bath first, stinky, x"

Taylor lowered her head and began to type furiously. Her mind was all over the place. Her anger had now gone and being off the case until someone saw sense wasn't the worst thing that could have happened. Everyone was totally worn out and showing the strain of two murders and a serious assault on a colleague. Taylor squirmed as she remembered her illicit rendezvous in the hotel lift with Fran. *Poor Fran, I hope she's okay. I hope someone is there for her. Does she have a partner? Hmmm, I don't really know her that well.*

Chapter 35:
Home Sweet Home

Taylor followed Kay into the ladies' and walked up really close behind her, pulling her round by her waist, their faces so close they were nearly touching. Their hearts raced and they were about to kiss when the door behind them swung open. Instantly, the space between them widened and their conversation became forced. The woman went into a cubicle and Taylor pushed her key into Kay's hand, smiling.

"I'll not be in until later. I hope you'll wait up for me," she whispered in her ear. Both went back to the office a little warmer than when they left and the gentle hum of conversation was comforting after what she'd been through in the wood earlier. Fingers tapped on computer keys, and war stories of the previous night being regurgitated with animation and excitement, and for once no one had to exaggerate; no one could have dreamt of being involved in something so horrific and each and every one of them could have died at the hands of this psychotic killer tonight.

◻◻◻

He looked around the quiet dark street before coming out of the front door and back to the car. He heaved Susan out, her body floppy and awkward to lift but his strength made light work of it and he launched her roughly over his shoulder and moved swiftly into the house, closing the door and locking it again behind them. He went into the living room and threw her down on the couch, tiny dots of blood spraying lightly onto the sofa, virtually invisible to the naked eye. He looked around the house at all the nice furnishings. *A touch of class; a bit of a pad going on here,* he thought to himself. There were personal photos in the hallway along with some nice colourful artwork above them, nothing tacky. He stroked a picture with his large thick fingers, and licked his chapped lips. *You're stunning. I'll enjoy you tonight to and I bet it's been a while since you've had what I'm going to give you.*

He went back through to the living room and pulled Susan up again; this time he just carried her, mindlessly bumping her off the doors as he went, almost deliberately hurting her to wake her up a bit. He looked around for something to tie her hands and found a silk sheet in a cupboard. Taking out his blood stained knife, he ripped through the soft material, the sound pleasing to his ears; luxury sheets for her restraint amused him. He was ruthless as he pulled the material cruelly tight on her wrists, so tight she felt it burn her skin but instinct halted the noise that stopped dead in her throat. Her heart raced into action, every sense skipping into survival mode. She could feel him so close to her that she wanted to recoil away from him but she just lay there limp and still looking believably unconscious. The last thing she wanted was for him to know she was awake, his attention was something she had to avoid for as long as possible. She knew him a little, enough to know he wanted her awake for his finale. He wanted to look into her eyes as he ended her life and he wouldn't make a mistake this time.

Kay smiled over at Taylor as she left to head off to Taylor's house. Taylor mouthed, "See you later," and she watched Kay's lithe body glide out of the room. Taylor was now more motivated to type faster. She was looking forward to a bath and some wine and the comfort of another close beside her, her motivation not necessarily sexual but a need to feel close to someone and to feel safe in her own home after the long night.

Kay drove through the quiet streets, her thumb gently tapping on the steering wheel to the sound of the stereo. She was glad Taylor was back and looked forward to her touch and love. She pulled into Taylor's street and parked as close to the house as she could. Her slender leg stretched out from the car, her ankle smooth above her designer high heeled shoes that were not quite stilettos. Out into the cool night air she went, taking time to take a deep breath, smiling at how good life could feel. Her heels gently clacked up the street in a seductively feminine way, classy and not a hint of anything else.

He stood still behind the door of the living room and heard the key turn in the lock. His heart quickened to an almost uncontrollable pace, his body tense like a coiled spring, his erection almost a hindrance. He heard her walk straight through to the kitchen, instead of where he thought and hoped she would go. This made him really angry. He was about to go after her when he heard her turn on her heels and come back through, her steps letting him know her direction and pace. She returned with a large glass of wine and threw herself casually down on the sofa, leaning her head back and stroking the sofa to feel the soft texture on her fingertips. Her eyes opened wide as her hand stroked over a sticky substance on the fabric. Fear crawled through her as she looked down at the redness on her hand. Suddenly, her head was yanked back with formidable force, every strand of her hair pulled painfully backwards. She thought her neck was going to break. His face was bristly and rough against hers, his scent vile and unwashed, and his breath putrid and offensive.

He licked the side of her face and said, "You taste very nice, whore. Good enough to eat, and I will eat you, literally." He then bit down hard on her shoulder and she screamed out in pain. He ground his teeth into her and blood oozed out into his mouth as he moved his head back and forth like a dog ragging a small animal. Tears rolled down her cheeks as her pain-filled cries filled Susan's ears, anger, terrorising her to the core. *Leave her alone you evil bastard.* He pulled Kay's hair hard once again, dragging her onto her front on the floor, her skirt askew with the struggle and movement. John gripped her inner thighs and stroked up to her panties and back down again. Kay felt sick as his hands rasped at her skin violating her beautiful body with his unwanted touch. He bent over her and rubbed himself hard up against her, biting down on her firmly clenched buttocks, scarring her with his hideous tooth print, branding her as his property. He owned her. Again she screamed out in pain, struggling so violently that even John was taken aback. Pushing up with her knees, she thrust her backside firmly upwards slamming hard into his nose. She'd drawn blood and he winced as his eyes began to water. His rage intensified and he punched the back of her head full force, sending her face slamming into the floor, the deep pile rug the only cushion stopping her head from hitting the hard wood flooring full on. The blow was enough to break Kay's nose and send her teeth through her lip. She moaned with a little less spirit, now badly injured and shocked at the unbelievable situation she was in. It was at that moment she realised who her assailant. As she rolled onto her side to get her breath back she looked up at his face. It was the face that covered every wall of the briefing room - John Brennan. *Oh my god! Oh shit, oh shit! Taylor come home, please come home. Hear me, please hear me.* As she went to drop her gaze, he was ready with his hands raised to strike her again.

"Who do you think you are looking at? I'll tell you when you can fucking look, breathe, scream or die. I'm in charge, you fucking dyke bitch." The sting of his hand burnt her face as the back of it struck her with the speed of a whip and the force of an anvil. This time she didn't raise her head back up. She deliberately kept quiet and dared not move. Her stomach churned with fear and her head felt like it was going to explode with the ferocity of his assault.

Susan struggled so violently the silk cut deep into her, rubbing her skin away and leaving weeping burns beneath. The material only gave a little and not quite enough to get a hand free. Susan's face was still badly swollen and bruised from his previous assault when he'd captured her. *Where am I? Whose house is this I'm in?* Susan looked around her. The only light was from the hall; he'd left the light off to subdue her senses. Susan looked at the photos in the room and had to do a double take as she looked straight at Taylor's face. She was in uniform and was receiving an award. She looked strong and courageous, her uniform enhancing her physique and presence. *When are you coming home? You won't take any of his shit, will you? Well you look like you won't. Don't let us down. Where are you? Hurry up?*

Taylor was still typing away on her keyboard. Marcus had just finished, and Taylor wasn't too far behind him. Marcus couldn't wait to hold his son, cuddle his wife and tell them how much he loved them. He had really believed his life was in danger tonight. They had all lost a close friend and seen another humiliated by a madman, who was now on the run with his prize captive. Taylor stood up and gestured for Marcus to come over. Open armed and with a warm smile, Taylor held him tight and whispered, "You take care, you, and look after yours. You know we can't stop hunting him. It's our duty. Oh, and I love you - in a sisterly way of course."

Their bodies parted and she gently shoved his shoulder and told him to get back to his family, where he belonged. Taylor loved Marcus and his perfect life. She even wished she could experience the love of a child. Their warmth for each other was apparent and the years they had worked and socialised together had created an unbreakable bond; the many traumatic situations they had shared would bring anyone closer together. He looked back at her and said, "I love you back, you big womanising goddess." Taylor faked a shocked look at his comment and waved as he moved to the door. She also sent her statement off and went through to Findlay's office. Her face was not a happy one as she had to ask if there was anything else he wanted her to do prior to finishing up. He deliberately made her wait asserting his power over her. He knew she was raging and disappointed at being stood down from the operation but he wasn't bothered. He was just covering his own back without a care for anyone else, even though they'd all put in a load of work and lost friends and colleagues tonight.

"I suppose you're good to go then. Oh, and I'm sorry you're off the case. We just needed a fresh team, new eyes so to speak, no hard feelings eh?" She could feel his insincerity. *You condescending fat prick. We worked our fucking fingers to the bone and this is what we get. I fucking hope you get demoted you useless twat,* Taylor thought to herself before he dismissed her like a school child from a head master's office. Taylor turned quickly on her heels to exit the office as quickly as she could.

"Anything nice planned for the evening?" he called after her.

Not that I'm going to tell you about, you slimy creep. "No sir, just a quiet night in." *With the sexiest woman in the office, that you can't keep your piggy little eyes off and probably have wet dreams over.*

237

"Nothing to write home about, just a well needed rest, boss". And she left, refusing to be drawn into more probing chat about her life.

Taylor practically marched out of the office as fast as her feet could carry her. She went to the locker room and quickly stripped off her clothes and had a much needed shower, the spray strong and hot massaging her head. She moaned in relief as she pushed her fingers through her hair, then stood motionless as the real-isation of the night finally hit home. Tears filled her eyes as she thought of Steve and the other officer who had fallen in the line of duty, slain like animals, no chance to defend themselves. Her mind then floated onto Fran. How she had been assaulted cut deeply into her heart. Taylor knew that Fran meant something to her and she had crossed a very dangerous line. She put her head right back and soaked her face, shook herself back to the present and got out of the shower and hurried to get dressed.

Faded jeans, trainers and a cotton top, fitted of course, and a unisex fragrance sprayed all over her to please Kay, rather than the aroma she had shared with her earlier in the office. Her heart also longed for Kay. She was puzzled over the possibility of having true feelings for two women, not just the urge to sleep with them. She actually cared for them both. Taylor bounced down the stairs and almost ran out of the building. The car park was still dark and there was no-one about, an eerie silence hang-ing over the night. Tingles crawled up the back of her neck that made her hurry to her car. The events of the night had affected her more than she had thought. She wasn't as confident as she had been the other night; he had taken that from everyone who had been in the forest. Once in the car, she looked in the rear seats immediately just to make sure she was alone. *Get a grip woman! He's really got under your skin tonight, hasn't he?*

ⅱⅱⅱ

Susan continued to struggle in the dark to no avail, fear and sad-ness taking over her senses. She felt desperate and about to lose control. She wanted to take back some sort of control of her life, or at least how and when she would die. She took several deep breaths and clenched her fists and gritted her teeth as the pain made her head go fuzzy.

Kay lay still on the rug. There was no movement from her at all, John was furious and stamped down on her ankle. The snap was deafening and Kay couldn't keep up the pretence up any longer. She screamed out in agony as he broke her bone.

He slapped her face and said, "I knew you were faking it. Do you think I'm fucking stupid, you slut? Fucking bitch, bitch, bitch." He hit her and punched her with every word. He was losing it too, full of rage and apprehension of being detected. He was a man on the edge with nothing to lose apart from his life.

Taylor sped through the night, a trained driver well aware of her surroundings. She was excited about the evening ahead but also fearful of the gut wrenching infidelity she hoped wouldn't be too obvious to Kay, whom she knew she didn't want to lose. She arrived in her familiar street, a fond homecoming, unaware of the danger within her precious haven, and drove a little more carefully up to the house. She pulled into her driveway, totally unaware of the extra guests that awaited her inside.

Kay's ears were ringing from the sustained and brutal assault but still pricked up as she heard the familiar sound of tyres on the gravel outside and the hum of Taylor's engine purring before the ignition was switched off.

Susan also sat bolt upright, her heart pounding with expectation and hope. *Help us, Taylor.*

The key was pushed into the lock and the sound of the door opening sent three people into action.

Chapter 36:
Two's Company,
Three's a Crowd

Taylor floated into the house, Kay's scent instantly filling the air. She called out for her, announcing her arrival. She could see the dim lighting from the living room but couldn't hear anything so she called again in case she was upstairs. Taylor smiled at the warm glow that invited her into the living room. *I bet she's fallen asleep, poor thing. Who cares! I just can't wait to hold her.* She moved excitedly towards the room, looking forward to seeing Kay's beautiful face, to kissing her and just being with her with no-one else to get in their way.

Taylor put her head round the door and her jovial mood was deleted in an instant. Terror ripped through her insides. She saw Kay's body lying on the floor covered in blood. She moved as quickly as she could to be at her side and knelt down, trying to pull Kay's hair off her face. It clung to her with thick congealed blood, sticking to her like a vile glue. Her only thought at that moment was Kay's welfare; it looked like she was dead. Taylor's heart was screaming *no*. When she moved Kay round, she flopped over and to Taylor's surprise, her lips whispered softly. Taylor jumped and her heart skipped a beat, "Taylor, he's here. He's in here. He's in the room somewhere. Run!" She floated back out of consciousness and her weight lay heavy on Taylor's legs, a dead weight.

Her eyes suddenly caught a movement from the corner of the room. Despite her training, she had just waltzed straight in to the room and headed for her wounded lover without checking why she was injured, who had done it and with no thought of any danger that could still be there in the room beside her. John's eyes were fixed on Taylor like a snake ready to strike, its prey in focus; he had watched her come into his place of work on several occasions and he'd had unnatural thoughts about her then, never thinking he was ever going to get to live them out. His desire heightened, which fuelled his venom to hurt her, to have her; he had the upper hand and the strength to beat her. He moved quickly and powerfully from the void behind the door. Totally focused on Taylor, he sped towards her with the strength and speed of a silverback gorilla. Taylor saw the figure careering in her direction out of the corner of her eye. She leapt to her feet and skipped backwards, trying to put some distance between them. She looked at John, right in his eyes, and her heart jumped as she realised that she actually knew him; not from the photos but from the CCTV unit. She had worked alongside him on occasion and she'd even spoken to him more than once. She just hadn't been able to make the connection until now, as she stared full on into the cold and unfeeling eyes of the devil. They were filled with hate and rage and frighteningly focused on her. She recalled the discomfort she had felt back then at being in the same office as him, sometime last year, and could not believe she hadn't made the connection when hunting him from the photos until this fateful moment. It was totally unlike her, her mind refusing to contemplate that a work colleague could be the killer. He lunged forcefully towards her, stumbling slightly forward as his foot clumsily landed full weight on Kay's thigh. This enraged Taylor into making her move with the agility of a gazelle. She crossed over into his fighting arc and swung a vicious kick towards his head. High, skilled and powerful, it struck him forcefully, right on the temple. He grunted as the pain rocked him backwards and, stunned, he stumbled and fell on top of Kay, landing heavily on his backside right on her back. Kay just lay there completely motionless, there was no noise, no cries of pain, nothing at all. She was lifeless. Taylor's eyes dropped to look at her, faltering at the thought she may be dead or dying, but she quickly focused again. Taylor reached into her pocket for her phone as she headed for the doorway in an effort to escape the room, hoping that he had finished with Kay for now because, if she was still alive, any more pain would certainly kill her. He was like a cat with a bird; it was only fun when there was a response from the prey, and now there was nothing, so Kay's chances were higher.

Taylor had underestimated his ability to move quickly; he pushed down hard on Kay to get himself back up and reached out his hand, grabbing Taylor's trailing wrist so ferociously that she thought it was going to break. He twisted it round so hard that she had to tumble to the floor and manoeuvre round to stop him breaking her forearm. The phone was gone, ripped right out of her grip, strong that it may be for a woman, his was much, much stronger. This was the least of her worries, however, as she was now like a snared animal, with a monster moving in to feast upon her. He still had her arm in a vice-like grip and she could feel his strength as his finger dug deep into her muscle, pain searing through her; she could feel the fibres tearing. This kept her animal instincts on fire; she was not about to be raped and brutalised by this beast without putting up the fight of her life to prevent it.

He hauled her up close to him, forcing her arm up her back, their faces almost touching. Taylor curled her face away from him, her mind racing. She was totally frazzled with everything she'd been through in this very long day, disbelieving the predicament she was now in. *What do I do? How can I beat him? Marcus, Marcus, I wish you were here.* Brennan gritted his teeth and almost snarled at her, a savage beast, his breath rancid and his eyes filling her with dread. She was starting to believe she might actually die tonight.

"John, what the fuck do you think you're doing? What the fuck is wrong with you? Get a fucking grip of yourself!" she yelled straight into his face. Spit flew as she shouted at him, terror coursing through every single vein within her. She was trying to find the human inside him, trying to dominate him verbally. She hoped there was a little normality left to reason with, trying to shock him back to reality. He just smiled back at her like a demon in a horror movie, a real life one for her. Nothing stirred in the deep black pools of his dark and lifeless eyes. Taylor swallowed hard and tried to hide her fear; she had to try not to show him any weakness, although she knew she was in some serious shit here. No gun; it was locked up in a box back at the office. Her only other weapon was lying up in the bedroom, a weighty metal baton; it was kept close to her bed for protection, too far away to help right now though.

Marcus kissed his wife as if the world was ending, almost like there was no tomorrow. He had held his son earlier with tears in his eyes, knowing that two people had not returned to their loved ones that day. He felt blessed as he tried to express the horror of the night they'd all faced without going into too much graphic detail. His wife held him tightly, hugging him like a mother holding her child. He could feel the moistness around his eyes as the realisation of still being alive hit home hard.

He looked at her and said, "You know, he's not been caught yet. He's got Susan and nobody knows where he is."

She felt cold, ice cold, instantly, as she watched her strong, steady almost invincible husband weep before her eyes. This news met her with dread; the thought that such a monster was still on the loose made her sick to the stomach. No-one was safe.

"Well, it's up to you to work out where he would go, officer." Her strength and support flowed into him. He was aware that she could see the love of her life almost broken from the cruel reality of defeat.

"He's just a man, Marcus, a demented, deranged and very damaged man, but a beatable man. You're stronger than him. You're good and good always beats evil in my world. All you need to do is believe it, then prove it!"

"I'm off the case. They took the whole squad off the case and changed all the personnel because we were at risk of being affected by the death of our colleagues today."

"Really? That just sounds like a crock of shit to me. You know more about that man than anyone else does. That's not the real reason and you know it. What's your boss saying about it?"

"Who? Taylor or Findlay?"

"Taylor of course, boss is a very loose term for Findlay. Weak slime ball is more apt," she said with annoyance in her eyes.

They both laughed out loud. She knew them both so well from how Marcus had described them to her on many occasions.

"What's Taylor doing tonight anyway?"

Marcus looked down, almost guiltily. "Having a quiet night in I presume," he replied very furtively.

"Alone?" she probed.

"Probably not, knowing her."

"She's surely not going to take it lying down, so to speak." She laughed as Marcus got the double entendre. "You know what I mean. She won't be beaten by him or the politics at work. You'll need to speak to her to see what she's going to do about everything."

"You're right. I'll go and see her later and have a wee chat with her. There's no way I'll sleep anyway. I don't want to spoil her night though. I'll give her an hour or so, then go round. Longer, I reckon, if I know her and what she'll be up to."

"I didn't mean go round. I meant just phone her to talk about it and let her know how you feel."

"Oh, right! Good thinking, I will," Marcus said as he reached for his phone and keyed in her name.

The phone ring tone continued over and over again but there was no reply. He retried the number several times to no avail, gave it a couple of minutes and rang her again, just in case she was right in the middle of something; she usually picked up eventually.

The phone sounded and vibrated in the corner of the room, the noise ringing out sadly in Taylor's ears as she looked down at Kay, still motionless and most definitely seriously injured, if alive at all. He cackled loudly as he saw and felt Taylor's desperate desire to answer the phone. *Please miss me. Please check we're alright here, whoever you are. If you know me, you know I always answer my phone. Marcus, if it's you - think where he'd go and why. He has nowhere else to go. He craves maximum harm, total depravity and vengeance. Think, think, think !!!*

Marcus put the phone down and smiled. "Typical! She'll be having the night of her life with Kay."

"Kay! Kay? the gorgeous straight woman from your office? The one you've talked about before? Her! She's turned to the dark side, has she? Mind you, Taylor is drop dead gorgeous too."

"She is, isn't she? Really stunning, inside and out," Marcus agreed.

His wife said, "If I was ever to turn to that side, she'd be the sort I'd go for."

Marcus laughed heartily and pulled her towards him, reassuring her she was straight, because he loved her, wanted her and needed her. Passionate kisses were shared as Marcus guided her to the sofa. Neither of them held back any of their feelings as passion absorbed them totally. They couldn't get their clothes off quick enough. Their arousal was instantaneous, their sex mind blowing, physical, desperate, passionate and needy, desire absorbing them, all consuming, their love for each other so strong, never to be taken for granted, especially after tonight.

John tangled his thick fingers around Taylor's beautiful hair and started dragging her round the room like a pit bull with a rabbit. She occasionally let out a yelp of pain when she could gulp a breath. He threw her against the wall, hitting her off the units, smashing the glass, which cut her forearms deeply as she tried to protect herself. His voice rasped viciously at her, "I'll show you, I'll fucking show you, you dyke bitch. I've watched you strutting yourself around as if you're something fucking special. Well you're not, you're just a dirty dyke slut, and I'll treat you how a slut should be treated. I'll fuck you so hard, you'll wish you were dead like your dirty whore bride here." He gestured towards Kay's lifeless body.

He threw her down cruelly on top of Kay, quickly following her to the floor, grabbing at her jeans and groping her like the deviant he was. He was salivating as Taylor tried to get up on all fours to get away from him, dazed and winded from being smashed off every wall; the view excited him even more. Taylor's head spun, the situation surreal and hideous, an unbelievable position to be in for someone of her strength and stature. *Fight him, fucking fight him, or play dead and he'll either kill you or rape a corpse. You've got to do something though.* His knife cut into her back as he carelessly cut through her jeans to expose her perfectly formed buttocks. She winced and pulled forward with as much strength as she could muster but his muscular grip tightened and he pulled himself up towards her, his groin moving closer to meet her bare flesh.

¤¤¤

Marcus lay there smiling as his wife trotted off to the bathroom, full of satisfaction from their amazing toe curling sex. She loved him more than life itself and knew full well she could have been a widow tonight. He thumbed in Taylor's number again as he gently stroked his stomach, inhaling the scent of his luxurious lover that was all over him. He tried again and again, knowing the phone was ringing out and not switched off. *Come on Taylor, answer your phone. Even you need to take a breather from whatever you're up to. Answer the phone or I'm coming round.*

ㅁㅁㅁ

Taylor kicked back at Brennan like a wild horse trying to escape from a stable, the force rocking him backwards. His grip loosened momentarily and she took her chance to wriggle free from him and crawled away as fast as she could, adrenaline pumping inside her. He stood up and started to move towards her but stopped as his feet pushed against Kay's body on the floor again. This gave him an idea and he stared very deliberately into Taylor's eyes as he slowly knelt down beside Kay's body and took hold of her head by her matted hair. He pulled it back exposing her carotid artery, where for the first time Taylor could see that Kay was still alive as there was blood visibly pulsing through it. "Leave her alone you fucking vile beast. Fucking leave her or I'll kill you!"

Marcus grabbed his keys, instinct driving him to check on Taylor and Kay. He knew Taylor was horny, but not that horny, and he had to see if she was okay before he could get any sleep. He got into his car, driving casually at first before ending up racing through town. His mind had turned to John. *Where would he go? Where would I go?* He was still reluctant to call it in as he pushed on through the traffic, unsure it there was something up. As he got closer to Taylor's house, his gut told him that there was something really wrong now and he keyed in 999. He raced up The Mound and through Chambers Street and down Minto Street, setting off more than one speed camera on the way whilst relaying his fear and intended destination. He was shaking and started to sweat, his heart racing as he pulled into the street where he saw the stolen motor vehicle from up north parked close to Taylor's house; he had memorised it as Taylor always made him do, one of her little foibles. Realisation hit him like a sledge hammer to the face. *Fucking hell, he's got them! Hold on, I'm coming. Please don't be dead in there!* Armed units were mobilised instantly. Marcus was instructed by the dispatcher to stand fast on his arrival and not to enter the premises until back up arrived. The top table didn't have to think twice about the arming of the response units, it was a no-brainer for them; Edinburgh hadn't had too many serial killers in the past, Burke and Hare probably being the last. Sirens could be heard as they rang out echoing through the city streets.

His knife cut into Kay's throat just as Taylor leapt off her feet to stop him. Blood oozed from the wound as the knife started to cut. She hit him full on in the face with her shoulder, stopping the incision in its tracks. She punched his face over and over but all he did was laugh at her, although swellings and welts appeared where the blows landed. Taylor was no slouch when it came to self-defence and could convey power in her punches but she was up against a soulless unfeeling monster and her sustained attack had no affect on him. He slashed out towards Taylor, stabbing into her shoulder and stopping the assault instantly as her arm went limp, the blade going deep into her muscle, preventing her from using her arm at all. He turned her round and forced himself on top of her, grabbing her throat with his massive hand and squeezing hard in order to control her. His mind was now focused on raping Taylor as viciously as he could. His other hand tugged violently at her jeans, which were already sliced at the back. Her eyes were staring right at him but she was unable to speak as she started to float in and out of consciousness, thankfully, as she was aware of what his intention was and didn't want to be awake when he raped her and much more.

Marcus moved quickly round the house, peering in under the blinds of the living room. He could only just see certain areas of the floor. He caught a glimpse of a pool of blood   and Kay's bloodied and badly swollen face. He was in two minds over what to do as he could make things worse for them if he tried to get in and failed, which would alert John to his presence.

Taylor's neck was released a little. Barely conscious, she kept up the struggle with every ounce of energy she had left within her, bumping her hips up from the floor to try and stop him entering her but she was becoming resigned to the fact that her attempts to escape were now futile. He licked the beautiful skin on her stomach, his hands roughly pulling her legs apart, jeans now at her ankles, cruelly trapping her feet, his four thick fingers poised to enter her.

A blood curdling thud sounded loudly in the room as a ferocious blow struck right in the centre of the head, causing blood to spray across the walls like harsh rain on a windscreen, skin splitting with the force, and the sound of it echoing round the room. Again and again, over and over the sickening blows rained down on the exposed head, causing more and more damage, bone now splintering and brain matter starting to show as the strikes came in quick succession, the perpetrator relentless in their quest to kill.

Marcus squeezed though the bathroom hopper window, as armed response vehicles arrived further down the street outside. He could hear the violent blows reigning down in the other room and his heart sank deep into his chest. He thought Taylor must definitely be dead.

A loud hailer echoed through the night from the police gathered outside. It sent out clear instructions for Brennan to show himself and to come out through the front door unarmed with his hands up. The shuffle of stiff boots scuffed across the pavements outside as protected firearms officers moved quickly and efficiently into position and stopped. The sound of the sickening, frenzied and brutal assault could be heard from outside. There was no clear line of sight to take any sort of shot or even have a glimpse at who or what to shoot at, and they could only guess what was going on inside the house and where the target might be situated.

Eyes transfixed like that of a lifeless mannequin, Susan raised the baton above her head again and again, inflicting blow after blow on what remained of John's head. She was intent on killing him; she would not give him any chance to survive. She did not want to wound him; she wanted to kill him, to stop him haunting her forever. Taylor couldn't move with the dead weight of John on top of her, his frame had changed from rigid control to a lifeless weight lying full-weight over her. She could feel the vibration of every blow emanating though his body into her body, blood now flooding down on top of her, the weight restricting her breathing, the blood blinding her as it flowed onto her face. Marcus rushed through to the living room, expecting to see Brennan murdering his best friend but he stopped dead in his tracks, mouth wide open. He couldn't believe what he was seeing. Surprised, but relieved, he watched as Susan pummelled John's head beyond recognition. She was quite clearly making sure he couldn't hurt her ever again and her intention was definitely to kill him, not just stop him. He stalled, maybe deliberately, as he didn't want the monster to live either, and shits like him had a cockroach-like ability to survive, no matter how severe their injuries.

Ambulances appeared in the street as the door was crashed open by armed officers. The blood bath they were met with was one none of them had ever experienced before and would ever forget.

Marcus took hold of Susan with a certain level of control, with no intent to harm. She screamed, frantically turning in a threatening way towards him. She was so overwhelmed with emotion and fear that she thought she was being attacked by someone else. His strong arms engulfed her and held her in a non-aggressive manner, stopping her assault and controlling her with minimum force. He calmed her down with his warm friendly voice, his caring face, one she recognised from the investigation. All of a sudden she crumpled and Marcus nearly dropped her onto the floor as her legs could no longer hold her weight. Her wrists were weeping as there was no skin left on them; she had had to tear her own flesh off to escape from her bindings. She had listened to every blood curdling assault going on downstairs until she couldn't take it anymore. She knew if he killed them, she would be next, the grand finale, and he wouldn't get it wrong this time. She knew it and she had to act to have a chance to live. She finally lost it and used every ounce of strength and will she could muster to break out of her sadistic binds. Once free she found Taylor's baton at the side of the bed. Swinging it in the bedroom, she practised her first blow; she couldn't afford to get it wrong by not hitting him hard enough to count. Her faint into Marcus's arms took away the horror of her living hell, giving her instant solace and peace. He lay her down gently on the sofa and went to help the others. Kay was clearly in a bad way and Taylor looked badly injured too. Three women lay in the room, brutally violated. It was sickening to see. Marcus heaved Brennan's body unceremoniously off Taylor, revealing his blood-soaked and wounded friend. Her eyes were open but blood was seeping into them, Brennan's blood, making her look frightening. He pulled her to him and held her tightly, letting her know everything was alright. She clung to him too, like a child to its mother.

"Keep your eyes closed, Taylor, it's mostly his blood on your face. Who knows what that twisted fuck might have done to you? The paramedics will rinse them out for you, 'cause you look hideous." She managed a laugh, her arms wrapped tightly round his waist. She needed him right now; she didn't want to let him go.

"Help Kay, please help Kay. I don't know if she's still with us, Marcus. I've not seen her move for a while."

"Medic, medic, we need a medic!" Marcus shouted at the top of his voice, although they were already on their way into the room.

Chapter 37: Finally

Marcus walked into the ward, four bouquets of flowers almost covering the whole upper body of his muscular frame. He asked the nearest nurse if she could help him with them, which she did and then he asked where to go. He stopped off at the first ward and asked the nurse to give the first two bunches of flowers to his colleague Fran, and to Susan. He then walked further up the corridor to the first of the high dependency single rooms where Kay lay; she was in an induced coma so he left the flowers with the ward sister, squeezed Kay's hand and whispered positive words into her ear. Finally, he moved on with more enthusiasm, up to the last single room on the right of the corridor. 'Taylor Nicks' was written in thick black felt pen on the white board outside. He smiled as he read her name and said it out loud to himself, just to ensure he believed that she was still alive. He had visualised what he thought was going on in that house, when he heard the blood-curdling blows crunching into their target the night before: Taylor being the victim. He swung round the door and his smile beamed from ear to ear when he saw her sitting up in bed. Bruises covered her face but she still had that old twinkle in her eyes, sincere, alluring and very much alive. She beamed back at Marcus, her giant smile hurt her face as she made it, but she was truly pleased to see him. She beckoned him forward for a warm embrace. He could feel her emotion, her need for his strength and security right now. She had been beaten yesterday and Brennan would have killed her. It unnerved her to know how close she had come to dying.

"Where were you last night, you little shit? You took your bloody time."

Marcus made a face of someone affected by the comment. His face was one of humour and warmth, but he knew if he'd gone there sooner, things might have been very different. He also knew Taylor was joking.

"I was taking a leaf out of your book and giving you your space to savour your night. How was I to know? I'm so sorry, Taylor."

"Don't worry about it. It wasn't your fault. It took a woman to save me though, eh?" She poked him in the ribs with her elbow and gave him a relieved smiled. "I couldn't give two hoots who saved me, I'm just so lucky she did. Where is Susan? How is she?"

Marcus just smiled at her and said, "Thank goodness she did save you. Thank goodness she had the strength and will to do it. Many would have just given up or been too frightened to!"

"I know, bless her," Taylor smiled again.

"She's just up the corridor, near to where Fran is," Marcus said innocently.

Taylor's face flushed a little with mixed feelings of guilt and sadness, and a momentary vision of the encounter they had shared.

"How is Fran doing? I hope she's going to be okay. This is going to screw her up a bit." She paused and then said, "A lot, and for a long time."

Tears welled up in Taylor's eyes. She asked, "How's Kay? How is she? She looked in a really bad way yesterday, I thought he'd killed her."

"She's still in a coma and has only just come out of intensive care, so that must be a good sign, although she's not out of the woods yet!"

"I don't deserve her you know, Marcus. I've let her down, really, really badly and she doesn't need someone like me in her life."

"Whatever you've done, whatever it is, she'll forgive you. She knows you. She knew what you were like before she chose to be with you and, believe me, she will definitely need you after this."

"I love her, and the old me just couldn't let a situation like that go by without savouring it," she said referring to her encounter with Fran. "I wouldn't do it again you know. Not now, not ever. I would never have forgiven myself if he'd killed her!"

¤¤¤

Andrew sat by Susan's bedside holding her bruised hand. For the first time in months she smiled with peace in her heart. Her eyes gazed at him, free from the terror that had stalked her to the brink of death, eyes now calm and not those of a scared little girl.

"I love you so much, Andrew," Susan whispered.

Andrew smiled at her, stood up and kissed her bruised forehead with great tenderness and said, "I love you back with all my heart but I hope things will get slightly easier for us in the future."

Both laughed a bit, both scarred and seriously injured by the same demon, he who had only made them stronger, and they laughed at that even more, because he had failed in what he had set out to do.

Fran sat up and stared at the flowers. Marcus had signed the card from Taylor and himself. Her mind floated back to their night at the hotel. She knew she had feelings for Taylor and they weren't just lustful. She sighed and touched the card gently, rubbing her thumb over Taylor's name, almost caressing it. She wished the kisses on the card were real and she could feel her lips against hers once again and relive those wonderful feelings they had shared. She smiled as her mum came into the room. She put the flowers to one side, just as she thought she should do with Taylor, but could she?

Findlay took the call from the Super. He had been summoned to his office first thing that morning, and these invites tended not to be for praise. Findlay banged his desk with force, cursing loudly at everyone apart from himself; he never saw any fault in any of his actions or lack of them, although they were clear for everyone else to see. He had failed as a leader and made several wrong decisions in the way he had handled the case from start to finish.

John's body was zipped back into the bag after autopsy, the cause of death quite apparent to even the untrained eye. There was very little skull left to speak of and parts of his brain were exposed. Susan had made sure she had killed him and that he couldn't hurt another person ever again. The marks unfortunately proved a different scenario from that of self-defence; they clearly showed intent to kill. The wounds had not been intended merely to injure, they had been ferociously inflicted, a definite intent to take a life. John would have been rendered defenceless after the first few blows and there must have been close to twenty five strikes to his head that could be proven as individual injuries. The pathologist finished writing his report and submitted it to the fiscal.

A couple of days had passed and Susan was starting to feel a little better; her progress was good and she would be discharged soon. The nurses left the room after telling her the good news. As they were leaving, officers appeared outside the ward and asked where Susan's bed was. They had legal papers in their hands. Their heads were lowered with embarrassment at the system they had to follow to ensure justice was afforded to all parties, even those who didn't deserve it. Any reasonable person looking at the circumstances of the case would feel that there had been no crime committed and that Brennan deserved every single blow he got and more. Unfortunately for Susan, she would have to stand trial. She would have to fight once more - this time to prove her innocence. She would have to make her case for self defence and the preservation of the lives of others, giving her justification for the level of violence she had used on that night. Her sanity would be called into question and she would have to relive the ordeal all over again.

Chapter 38:
Justice or Not?

"All rise," echoed through the court.

Susan stood up, her legs trembling as she looked over at Andrew. Taylor, Marcus, Fran, Andrew and Kay had all given their evidence and it was now Susan's turn to take the stand.

"Can you please raise your right hand." Susan's hand quivered as she raised it. She took a deep breath.

The End.